ABOUT THE AUTHORS

USA TODAY bestselling author **Jacquie D'Alessandro** grew up on Long Island, New York, where she fell in love with romance at an early age. She dreamed of being swept away by a dashing rogue riding a spirited stallion. When her hero finally showed up, he was dressed in jeans and drove a Volkswagen, but she recognized him anyway. They now live their happily-ever-afters in Atlanta, Georgia, along with their son, who is a dashing rogue in the making. She loves to hear from readers and can be contacted through her Web site at www.JacquieD.com.

Despite a love of Southern Christmas decorating begun after a holiday visit to Natchitoches, Louisiana, **Joanne Rock** likes snow sprinkled liberally over her December festivities. She had fun bringing a Southern heroine to Lake Placid, which isn't far from the home Joanne shares with her three sons and husband in the Adirondacks. A three-time RITA® Award nominee and veteran of thirty romances, Joanne believes Christmas is the perfect time for a happy ending. Visit her at www.JoanneRock.com to enter monthly contests and learn more about her work.

Kathleen O'Reilly loves Operation Santa Claus—it's a New York City institution, first started at the Thirty-third Street post office in the 1920s by several softhearted postal workers. The tradition continues to this day and has expanded to handling over a hundred thousand Dear Santa letters at the New York post office alone. As for Kathleen, she is an award-winning author of twelve romances, two lady-lit novels and three novellas, with more books slotted for 2008. She lives in New York with her husband and two children, who outwit her daily.

A Blazing
Little Christmas

Jacquie D'Alessandro
Joanne Rock
Kathleen O'Reilly

A sizzling Christmas anthology

HARLEQUIN®

TORONTO • NEW YORK • LONDON
AMSTERDAM • PARIS • SYDNEY • HAMBURG
STOCKHOLM • ATHENS • TOKYO • MILAN • MADRID
PRAGUE • WARSAW • BUDAPEST • AUCKLAND

ISBN-13: 978-0-373-79367-9
ISBN-10:   0-373-79367-7

A BLAZING LITTLE CHRISTMAS

CONTENTS

HOLIDAY INN BED
Jacquie D'Alessandro

This book is dedicated with my love and gratitude to my wonderful book club buddies Susie Aspinwall, Sandy Izaguirre, Melanie Long and Melissa Winsor. Thank you so much for the brainstorming and all the laughs— but not so much for all those depressing books y'all like ☺. Thank goodness for romances! Hope you gals enjoy this one!

And to Brenda Chin, editor extraordinaire, whom I will someday manage to get to a mall— hopefully before she manages to get me into a kayak.

And, as always, to my fantastic husband, Joe, who makes every day a Holiday, and my terrific son, Christopher, aka Holiday Junior.

Prologue

"THERE'S MAGIC IN the air," Helen Krause said, leaning across the reception desk at the Timberline Lodge to smile at Roland as he entered the inn.

Her husband of forty years stomped snow from his boots onto one of the large red oval rugs that marked the entrance to the lodge's cozy lobby. Together they owned and operated the rustic lodge, which sat on the shores of Mirror Lake, in the quaint village of Lake Placid, New York, a location that drew both local visitors and vacationers from all over the country.

"That's not magic," Roland replied, gazing at her over the stack of freshly split hickory logs he carried. "That's a storm. And a bad one. Much worse than they'd predicted, and it's comin' sooner than they thought."

"Last night's weather report warned of only six to eight inches and that it wouldn't hit until late tomorrow night," Helen said, coming around the desk to relieve him of part of his bundle.

"Well, five minutes ago they predicted two to three *feet,* startin' now. Wind's picked up and the snow's comin' down hard." He shook his head. "Crazy weather people. What other job allows you to be wrong so often yet not get fired?"

"Mother Nature loves to throw curveballs," Helen murmured, walking with Roland toward the roaring fire crackling in the stone hearth. "So…looks like folks might be getting snowed in."

"Oh, boy. I recognize that tone." Roland deposited the fragrant cut wood into the curved polished brass log holder then held out his cold-reddened hands toward the dancing flame's heat. Shooting her a half-indulgent, half-exasperated look over the tops of his bifocals, he said, "Now, Helen, just because Christmas is less than a week away—"

"Don't go getting any ideas in my head," she finished, peering right back at him over the top of her own bifocals. "Have you noticed that we have this same conversation every year right around this time?"

"I suppose," Roland admitted, sounding grumpy. But the effect was ruined when his blue eyes twinkled at her.

"And do you know *why* we have this conversation every year?"

"I suppose. But just because folks have fallen in love here at Christmastime in the past, doesn't mean it's going to happen again this year."

"Which is what you say every year. But you can't deny that romance somehow always strikes our holiday guests. I'm not sure if it's the snow, or the scent of pine from all the Christmas decorations, or something in the lodge itself."

Roland turned toward her and drew her into his arms. Even after all these years, her heart still skipped a beat. His once thick dark hair was now mostly silver and mostly gone, and his ruddy skin bore the signs of his sixty-four years and hard work. But to her, he was still the handsomest man in the world. And the most wonderful. Not that there weren't times she'd been tempted to thunk him upside his head with a skillet—he was a *man* after all and therefore frequently exasperating—but after forty years and five children together, she still loved waking up next to him every morning.

"Uh-oh," Roland said, pulling her closer, until her reindeer-decorated red sweater bumped against his green flannel shirt. "You have that matchmaking gleam in your eye."

"Hmmm. You seem to have a gleam in *your* eye as well."

"Probably because I'm standing under the mistletoe with my best girl."

"There's no mistletoe right here…"

Her words trailed off when Roland pulled a twig of dark

green leaves accented with small white berries from his pocket and waggled it over their heads.

"You were saying?" he murmured with a grin, lowering his head toward hers.

After he'd treated her to a kiss that curled her toes inside her sheepskin-lined boots, she leaned back in the circle of his strong arms. "Goodness. I was saying you have a gleam in your eye," she managed to say, sounding as breathless as she felt. "Clearly I was right."

"Not bad for an old guy, huh?" A devilish grin creased his cheeks and he leaned down to nuzzle her neck. "You smell mighty good, Mrs. Krause. Like sugar cookies and pinecones. And…" He breathed deep and nibbled the sensitive bit of skin behind her ear. "Magic."

"As I said, it's in the air," she murmured, savoring the pleasurable tingles skittering down her spine.

"Every time I'm near you," Roland agreed, lifting his head to smile at her. Then his expression sobered. "But I don't want you gettin' your hopes up that romance will bloom here this week and then bein' disappointed."

"Nonsense. We have a number of single guests registered, you know. And all my 'Christmas Magic' senses are tingling."

"That's because I just kissed you."

She laughed. "True. But that special holiday magic is shimmering all around us, Roland. I can *feel* it. You mark my words. Before Christmas arrives, love will once again bloom at Timberline Lodge."

1

JESSICA HAYDEN gratefully absorbed the delicious warmth emitting from the snapping fire, which danced in the huge stone fireplace in the lobby of the Timberline Lodge. She wasn't certain how long it would take Eric to get them registered, but after braving the two-hour drive here—the last few miles at a crawl due to the sudden heavy snowfall—then the blustery wind that hit them on their walk across the parking lot, she didn't mind lingering near this heated coziness, at least for a few minutes. But more than thawing out by the fire, she was anxious for her and Eric to get to their cabin, where they'd generate their own heat.

Which couldn't happen soon enough for her.

God help her, she couldn't wait to get her hands on him. It had been so long…way too long, since they'd made love, and now that their much-needed weekend was upon them, she was about ready to burst. The stress and problems that had been wreaking havoc with every aspect of their lives—including their love life—didn't exist in this rustic lodge. Here they would have the time and privacy to get themselves and their relationship back on track.

She pulled off her gloves and her gaze rested on the sparkling round diamond adorning her left hand. When Eric Breslin had slipped the engagement ring on her finger four months ago, it had been the happiest, most magical moment of her life. She loved him deeply and she'd believed, they'd *both* believed, that everything was going to be perfect.

They'd both been dead wrong.

Everything was, in a word, a disaster.

Little had they known their engagement would spark a family feud that made the legendary Hatfields and McCoys look like rank amateurs. After much discussion, she and Eric had reached compromises regarding the *big* issue—her managing Hayden's, her family's upscale restaurant in her hometown of Marble Falls, and Eric's opening last year, less than a mile away, a Chop House, a national restaurant chain known for excellent food at reasonable prices. Even though Chop House was technically the competition—a fact that had caused them some difficulties at the onset of their relationship—Jessica had discovered that Eric was everything she'd ever wanted in a man.

She hadn't believed in love at first sight until she saw *him*. That first instant spark of attraction in the cheese aisle at her favorite gourmet food shop had all but fried her where she stood. The fact that he'd chosen her favorite Brie and knew the subtle differences between Gorgonzola and Stilton had piqued her interest. They struck up a conversation and by the time they made it to the wine aisle she knew, in her heart, he was The One. And the next six months had only proven her correct.

He was kind, loving, patient, honorable and generous. He made her laugh. Made her happy. Sure, he had his faults—but hey, what man *didn't* leave his socks on the floor and coffee cups all over the place? Growing up with four older brothers, she didn't let silly little "guy things" bother her. And best of all, Eric loved her as much as she loved him.

Unfortunately their families mixed about as well as oil and water. Jessica's mother and four overprotective brothers considered Eric not only business competition, but looked down on his franchise restaurant, considering it fast food compared to Hayden's. Marc, Andy, Robbie and Carl all glared at Eric at every opportunity, resenting both his opening the restaurant and him "stealing" their little sister, whom they ridiculously felt was way too good for him.

To make matters worse, Jessica's mother had dreamed about

her only daughter's wedding since the day she'd finally given birth to a girl after four sons. Maybe, just *maybe,* Carol Hayden could have gotten over the fact that Jessica was marrying "the competition," but she simply could not accept that Eric's sister, Kelley—who was more like his mother since she'd raised him and their two younger sisters after their parents' deaths when Eric was twelve—was a wedding planner. A very successful wedding planner whose recent clients included an Olympic gold medalist, a daytime television actress and a state senator's daughter.

Kelley had very definite ideas about her only brother's wedding. Ideas that did not in any way mesh with Jessica's mother's ideas for her only daughter's wedding. Indeed, Carol Hayden viewed Kelley's expertise as a threat to her own plans for Jessica's wedding. Toss into that volatile mix Eric's sisters' resentment toward Jessica's family for looking down their noses at their beloved brother, and the entire situation was as explosive as a powder keg piled next to an open flame.

Holy family feud.

The bickering had spilled over into Jessica and Eric's relationship, even in the bedroom where they hadn't even ventured during the last several weeks. These last four months, instead of being joyous, had brought them both to the breaking point. They desperately needed this long weekend away from the relentless arguing, needed this time *alone,* to put their relationship back on track. To reignite their currently nonexistent sex life. To recapture the magic that had surrounded them right from the beginning. And they would. They *had* to. Because the alternative—not being together, not sharing their lives—was a concept she simply couldn't wrap her mind around.

Yet there had been times since they'd announced their engagement when she wondered if they'd actually be able to rescue themselves from the quicksand they'd stumbled into and make that walk down the aisle together. She wanted to marry him, wanted to spend her life with him. But…how could she ignore all the shrapnel hitting them from the family fallout? And even though he'd never said so, she knew Eric wondered, too. And she couldn't help but worry that he'd grow so disgusted with the whole situation, he'd just walk away.

Well, she couldn't worry anymore. She needed to know. She loved Eric and knew he loved her. But, as she'd unfortunately learned over the past four months, the adage that sometimes love isn't enough was sadly true. She also knew, in her heart, that this weekend was going to either make them or break them. At the least, it would result in some drastic changes. Because they simply couldn't go on any longer the way they were. For the past four months she and Eric had tried to keep everyone happy and the result was that no one was happy. *Something* had to give.

Shoving aside all thoughts that even hinted at sadness, Jessica focused her attention on her surroundings. The rustic inn definitely lived up to the color brochure that had enticed them to choose the Timberline Lodge for their desperately needed getaway—that and an enthusiastic recommendation from Eric's best friend, Dave. Rustic, yet boasting every modern convenience, the lodge and its recently added cabins were the perfect winter wonderland-type location for a sexy, romantic holiday away from it all.

A huge, gaily decorated Christmas tree, its branches glittering with garland, soared upward in the far corner of the A-framed building. Knotted wood beams lined the ceiling from which antler chandeliers hung, casting the room in a warm, golden glow. Swags of fragrant pine boughs dipped along the wooden mantel accented with cheery red stockings and thick candles that resembled candy canes. Comfortable leather and Adirondack-style chairs dotted the room in intimate groupings, and colorful braided rugs—the sort she used to help Nana Sophie make—were strewn about the hardwood floors.

The deep, familiar rumble of Eric's laughter caught her attention and she turned toward the reception desk. The mere sight of Eric, his thick, dark hair gleaming with dampness from the snow, made her pulse jump and her throat go dry with longing. He was smiling at a man and woman standing behind the reception desk, a couple Jessica judged to be in their sixties. They must be the owners, Helen and Roland Krause, she decided. The brochure had given a history of Timberline Lodge, how the historic building had been in the Krause family for generations. They reputedly treated their guests like family and were continuously working to further upgrade and improve the facilities. Dave had told them the place was a labor of love and based on what she'd seen so far, she agreed.

Mrs. Krause glanced toward her and offered a grin and a friendly wave, both of which Jessica returned. Eric shook both their hands, then walked toward her while the Krauses gave their attention to the young woman who was next in line to check in.

Jessica watched Eric striding toward her and everything female inside her came to immediate attention. With his parka unzipped, sturdy snow boots, his favorite Levi's that hugged his long legs, and a thick, cable-knit sweater that stretched across his wide chest and exactly matched his dark blue eyes, he looked rugged and masculine and absolutely delicious. That same *whammo* of attraction that had all but knocked her unconscious the first time she'd seen him almost a year ago slammed into her now—as it did every time she looked at him. She'd dated some very attractive men over the years, but Eric was the first one who could knock the breath from her lungs with a mere look.

A look like the one he was giving her right now.

The one that curved up a corner of his gorgeous mouth and resulted in a totally sexy lopsided grin that dented a shallow dimple in his cheek and made her knees feel like freshly kneaded bread dough. The one that made his eyes glitter with that wicked gleam and sizzling sensuality she loved.

Heat that had nothing to do with the roaring fire poured through her. Looking at him now, it was impossible to believe their relationship could ever teeter on the brink of imploding. Or that their sex life was suffering. How was it possible that for weeks she hadn't found a way to wade through the morass of stress and make love to this man who could make her nipples hard by just *standing* there? Surely with this time alone, away from everything and everyone that had been conspiring to pull them apart for the past four months, she'd be able to relax. And together they'd find a way to solve their problems. All they needed was a break. And here, at the Timberline Lodge, that's exactly what they'd have.

Thank God.

When he reached her, he didn't say a word—he just pulled her into his arms and kissed her. A deep, lush kiss that tasted of pent-up frustration and anticipation. One that revved her pulse and ended way too soon. After he lifted his head, his eyes were smoldering. "We're all set. Our cabin is just a short walk and overlooks the lake. You ready?"

"Absolutely." She lightly bumped her pelvis against his. "Are *you* ready?"

A half laugh, half groan escaped him. "God, yes. Unfortunately there's nothing I can do about it until I get you alone. But once I do—" he yanked her tighter against him, making it very obvious that he was indeed ready "—you're in big trouble."

Good Lord, she hoped so. She wrapped her arms around his neck and lifted up on her toes to brush her lips over his. "Oh, yeah? Watch it, big guy. Maybe you're the one who'll be in trouble."

"Sweetheart, I've been in trouble since the first moment I saw you."

"You make it sound like that's a bad thing."

He shook his head, framed her face between his large hands that still bore a hint of chill from outside and looked at her through suddenly serious eyes. "Best damn thing that ever happened to me."

Jessica's heart flipped over and she swallowed around the sudden tightness in her throat. He leaned forward and rested his forehead against hers. "Everything is going to be okay, Jess. I promise. Have I ever broken a promise to you?"

She shook her head and their noses bumped. "No."

"And I'm not going to start now. We'll work this out. All of it."

She leaned back and looked at him. There was no doubt he believed what he said, and that confidence, along with the love shining in his eyes, bolstered her belief that he was right. And here, in this cozy setting, where it was just the two of them, free from all the outside pressures that constantly bombarded them, the way it had been for those first six glorious months they were together, before they'd announced their engagement and all hell broke loose, all seemed right with the world.

"You are, without a doubt, the sweetest, kindest, most patient—not to mention the sexiest—man I've ever met."

"Can't tell you how glad I am to hear you say that," he murmured, punctuating each word with a nibbling kiss along her jaw. "Now about that 'sexiest' bit…I'm dying to give you a personal demonstration."

"Hmmm…a tempting offer, but my fiancé will be arriving any minute now and he might object."

"Damn. I might have guessed you were taken." He slipped his hands inside her coat and ran his palms down her back, leaving a trail of heat in his wake. "Your fiancé is one lucky guy. I hope he tells you that every day. Right after he tells you that you're the most beautiful, sexy woman on earth." He nuzzled her neck. "And that no one smells better than you. And that he loves you so much he can barely think straight most of the time." He lifted his head. "Does he tell you that every day? Because if he doesn't, I'll have to hurt him. Bad."

The wave of love that washed over her nearly drowned her. "He tells me."

"Good. Then he can live to see another day."

She shot him an exaggerated leer. "Now, about that personal demonstration you mentioned—"

Her words were cut off when he grabbed her hand and started across the lobby with such a brisk, long-legged stride, she had to jog to keep up. Laughing, they half ran, half skidded across the parking lot to Eric's SUV, which was already covered in snow. After retrieving their overnight bags, they held hands and headed down the tree-lined path leading toward their cabin. Snow fell in a white silent blanket, coating the roofs of the cottages dotting the trail. Smoke puffed toward the slate-gray sky from the chimneys, indicating the occupants were enjoying the intimate warmth of a fire. Their progress was slowed by catching snowflakes on their tongues and exchanging lip-warming kisses, each one lengthier and deeper than the one before, notching up their arousal. She hadn't felt this carefree since they'd announced their engagement, and she offered up a silent thank-you that they'd decided to take this weekend for themselves. *Everything is going to be fine,* her inner voice whispered.

By the time they reached the cabin, they were both breathless from their last tongue-dancing kiss and the stunning cold. Eric unlocked the door and they practically tumbled into the warmth. Before she could even glance around the room, her back was pressed against the door, Eric's lips were on hers and his clever hands were unfastening her coat. Clearly he was as anxious to make up for lost time as she was. Thank God. He hadn't even touched her yet and already she felt like a bomb on the verge of exploding. Every thought fled except getting all of him on all of her.

"Are you trying to melt my knees?" she asked against his yummy mouth.

"Absolutely. Is it working?"

"Absolutely."

Their heavy parkas hit the floor at the same time and Jessica's hands immediately plunged beneath Eric's sweater to run up his smooth back, just as his palms cupped her breasts. They both groaned.

"Damn, it's been so long," he muttered.

"Too long," she murmured, nipping kisses along his jaw.

"Thirty-two days, seventeen hours and nine minutes—not that I'm counting. How the hell did we let that happen?"

"I don't know. Clearly we're insane. Eric...I love that you're so warm."

"I love that you're so soft."

She rubbed herself against his erection. "I love that you're so hard."

He flicked open the button on her jeans and eased down the zipper. Slipping his hand beneath her lacy underwear, he stroked a long finger over her already swollen folds. A moan escaped her. "I love that you're so wet."

"All your…ah…fault."

"God, I've missed you, Jess."

"I've missed you, too…" Her words evaporated when he slipped two fingers inside her and slowly pumped, his tongue matching the lazy rhythm as he kissed her. An edgy pressure quickly grew inside her, one that demanded relief. *This*…this magic was the way it was supposed to be between them. The way it *had* been before their families had gotten involved. She reached out, intending to unzip his jeans and show him two could play at this game, but he changed his rhythm, quickening and deepening his strokes, touching her in exactly the way he knew would drive her over the edge. Her climax was roaring down on her, the sweet, hot pulses of pleasure just a heartbeat away when a knock sounded on the door, right next to where her head lolled, startling her. And chasing away her orgasm, leaving her panting and frustrated.

"Ignore it," Eric whispered.

Before she could reply, another knock sounded, then a muffled voice came through the door. "Eric, open up. It's me, Kelley."

They both froze.

Kelley? His sister? Here? She squeezed her eyes shut and swallowed the scream that threatened to strangle her.

Looking as angry and thwarted as she felt, Eric muttered a curse then slipped his hand from her.

Fighting to regain her composure, Jessica quickly zipped her jeans, scooped up their parkas and walked toward the closet, while Eric opened the door. "Kelley?" she heard him say in a stunned, tight voice. "What are you doing here? Is something wrong? Are Lara and Chloe okay?"

"They're fine," came Kelley's familiar, clipped voice. "What's wrong is that your wedding is only two months away, Eric. There are a thousand details we need to discuss."

Several long seconds of silence passed and Jessica, still clutching the parkas and standing like a statue near the closet, looked at Eric. She could almost see the waves of tension rolling off him. "We can talk about them when Jess and I return to Marble Falls on Tuesday," he said with a hint of impatience.

"We need to talk about them *now*."

Jessica pressed her lips together. Good God, could this get any worse?

She walked to the door, intending to greet Kelley and stand firm with Eric that anything that required discussion could take place on Tuesday, but the words died in her throat when she saw that, good God, things could most definitely get worse.

Striding up the snowy path toward the cabin were Jessica's mother and her brother, Marc, both of whom looked extremely displeased.

Yes, this could definitely get worse.

2

"MAY I COME IN, Eric, or are you going to let me turn into a Popsicle out here?"

Standing in the doorway of the cabin where he and Jess were supposed to spend the next four days alone, where they'd just been on the brink of making love for the first time in weeks, Eric stared at Kelley and tried his damnedest to swallow his frustration and annoyance. But it proved extremely difficult, especially when he caught sight of Jessica's brother, Marc—or the incredible glaring hulk as he mentally called him—and his future mother-in-law—who in spite of being a good foot shorter than Eric still somehow managed to look down her nose at him—making their way along the snow-covered path toward the cabin.

Damn. In less than two minutes this situation would deteriorate from *worse* to *catastrophic*.

"C'mon in," he said, not seeing that he had much choice.

"Thank you." Kelley sailed into the room, and Eric closed the door to keep out the snow and cold air until the next batch of uninvited—and unwanted—guests arrived.

Jess, who clutched their parkas to her like a down-filled shield, came to stand beside him. "Hi, Kelley," she said. "This is a, um, surprise."

Eric wrapped an arm around Jess's shoulders, noting the stiff tension in her body. "A really big surprise," he agreed, failing at his attempt to not sound irritated. "Kell, I left the message telling you where I'd be this weekend in case of emergency only."

"This *is* an emergency, Eric," she said. "We need to discuss the menu, the invitations, the decorations…dozens of details you both have been putting off. I told you last week that these things *had* to be finalized by this week. Obviously you forgot because here it is this week and now they can't be put off any longer. Tomorrow is the drop-dead date to have everything ordered and since you decided to go away until Tuesday, you left me with no choice but to come here."

"You could have called."

"I did. I left half a dozen messages on your voice mail. Have you checked your cell phone at all today?"

"No. Because I'm on *vacation.*"

She cocked a single brow at him, in that I'm-not-gonna-take-any-crap-from-you-or-anybody-else way of hers. "Believe me, Eric, I'm not any happier about driving all the way here than you are to have your weekend escape interrupted. But if you'd bothered to check with me before taking off instead of just leaving a message on my machine, I could have saved us both a lot of trouble. This shouldn't take more than a couple of hours, so why don't we get started? That way you can get back to your *vacation* and I can get home."

Eric raked his free hand through his hair and bit back the terse *hell no* that rushed to his lips. God knows he hated fighting with his sisters, especially Kelley to whom he owed a debt of gratitude he could never hope to pay. At the age of nineteen she'd quit college to raise him, Lara and Chloe after their parents were killed in a car crash. Kelley's new fiancé had decided he didn't want to take on the responsibility of caring for three kids under the age of twelve and had dumped her. To the best of Eric's knowledge she hadn't had a serious relationship since. Dates, yes, but nothing serious. He'd often wondered if her career choice was in some way connected to her heartbreak over her own thwarted wedding plans.

Yet while he hated to fight with her, he couldn't take the pressure this wedding and both their families were putting on him and Jess any longer. Damn it, he didn't even care if they had a freakin' wedding. All he wanted was for Jess to be his wife. For him to be her husband. To share their lives. He didn't want or need any fancy-schmancy wedding. But knowing how girls dreamed about that sort of stuff, he was willing to do whatever Jess wanted.

But like him, Jess was caught in the cross fire of the missiles being lobbed between her mother and Kelley. Kelley, although she meant well, tended to come on very strong. She'd planned Chloe's and Lara's weddings with a military-like strategy and co-ordination—as she did for all her clients—plowing through any and all obstacles until the perfect results were achieved. Her efficiency simultaneously awed and scared the crap out of him. And occasionally annoyed the hell out of him, especially when it caused arguments. The tension between Kelley and Jess's mother—who had her own strong opinions about the wedding—hovered like a thick fog whenever they were in the same room together. It had gotten so bad, especially during the last month, Eric worried that Jess might cave to the pressure and just call the whole thing off.

A knock sounded on the door. "Jessica?" came Carol Hayden's muffled voice. "It's Mom and Marc."

Speak of the devil. Oh, boy. His gut churned with unease. He had a bad feeling about this. His future brothers-in-law, especially Marc, had all made their low opinion of him perfectly clear. He was the bad guy, Jess was a haloed saint and at any given moment they looked like they'd relish getting him alone in a dark alley and flinging him into a Dumpster—after they roughed him up and loosened a few of his teeth.

He could certainly understand a brother's protective instinct toward a sister. Hell, he had three sisters he felt that way about. But the fact that he was the business "competition" had pretty much sealed his fate from moment one with the Hayden brothers. And with Carol Hayden as well, although she also objected to Kelley being in any way involved in planning her only daughter's wedding.

Lord, what a mess.

For at least the hundredth time he wished he and Jess could just hop on a plane and go to Vegas and get married. He'd suggested as much to her, but she'd demurred, saying she just didn't have the heart to disappoint her mother that way. In truth, he didn't want to disappoint Kelley by running off to Vegas, either. But with each passing day, he grew closer to believing he could find a way to live with it.

But he wasn't sure Jess could. Even though she was twenty-five and her own woman, her family meant a lot to her and they were really putting on the hard-court press and doing their damnedest to interfere in her life. And even though he knew Jess loved him, he was afraid she might think the chasm forming between them might prove irreparable. Which meant they had to fix it. *Now.*

Reaching for the doorknob, he tried to remind himself that Jess's family loved her, that she wouldn't be the vibrant, wonderful woman she was without their support. But sometimes, like right now, it was damn difficult to remember that.

He opened the door and Carol and Marc marched in amid a swirl of fat snowflakes and icy air.

"Hello, Eric, Kelley," Carol murmured as she walked past him and his sister on her way to envelop Jess in a hug, blobs of snow plopping off her coat with each step. "Are you all right, dear?"

"Of course." Jess accepted a brotherly peck from Marc, who offered Eric a terse nod and his usual glare. Jeez, did the guy *ever* smile? Eric felt his own tension rise at the frosty hello and frowning scowl Marc bestowed on Kelley—as if she was Public Enemy Number One. Kelley's greeting to him was equally curt and her glower just as forbidding. He could almost see the sparks of animosity bouncing between them.

Great. Just another happy family reunion.

"What are you and Marc doing here, Mom?" An anxious look crossed Jess's features. "Is something wrong at home?"

"Everything's fine," Carol assured her. "I needed to speak to you but you didn't answer your cell. Marc offered to drive me to the lodge, so here we are."

Jess shook her head, clearly confused. "If nothing's wrong, what on earth did you need to talk about that couldn't wait until after the weekend?"

"Why, the wedding, of course. When I couldn't reach you, I called Kelley's office hoping she could give me Eric's cell phone number." Carol flicked a glance toward Kelley whose frown resembled a thundercloud. "That's when I learned that Kelley was on her way here." This last statement was said in an unmistakably accusatory tone. She then turned fully toward Kelley and hiked up her chin. "Since it was obvious you were coming here to discuss *my daughter's* wedding plans, I figured I'd best get here as quickly as possible."

Eric could almost hear Kelley bristle, like a porcupine extending its quills. "They're also *my brother's* wedding plans, and since I have all the contacts—"

"Listen," Eric broke in, knowing this was about to escalate into another nasty argument. Looking at Kelley, he said, "This is exactly why Jess and I came here this weekend—to get away from all the stress."

"There wouldn't be any stress if we could just nail down the details," Kelley said. As much as Eric wished that were true, he knew the wedding details were only part of the problem. "It needs to be done. *Now.* Then I'll happily go home. It's not as if I don't have a life besides this wedding, you know. I actually have a date tonight."

Eric raised his brows at her defensive tone, but saw that she wasn't even looking at him. She was glaring at Marc, who stood in tight-lipped silence, glaring right back at her. Good God, he needed a machete to cut a swath through the tense undercurrents clogging the room.

He glanced at Jess who looked like a teakettle about to spew steam. He knew exactly how she felt. He wanted nothing more than to tell all three of their uninvited guests to scram and leave them alone, that the only voice he wanted to hear between now and Christmas Eve was Jess's. Unfortunately he knew that would only lead to World War III, which would only upset Jess, which would only lead to more tension. Damn, it was like the freakin' Bermuda Triangle of ulcer-inducers.

So in an effort to keep peace, he swallowed his frustration and said in as pleasant a tone as he could manage, "As long as you're all here and this has to get done, why don't we go up to the lodge, order some hot chocolate and take care of this so we can all get back to our plans?"

Right. Because hopefully no one would cause a scene in the lodge. But instead of hot chocolate he might have to opt for a stiff drink. Or two. Or twelve. Not exactly the chilled champagne he'd planned to share with Jess in the cabin's jet tub, but the sooner he got rid of their uninvited guests, the sooner he and Jess could get back to their weekend.

Everyone agreed. After he and Jess had slipped on parkas, they all filed out of the cabin. The snow was falling in earnest and the wind had picked up considerably, jabbing icy needles of stinging cold in his face. Holding Jess's mittened hand, they trudged back to the lodge, with Kelley leading the way, followed by Carol and Marc who had their heads together, with Carol whispering to her son. With each step Eric tried to bury his growing resentment that both their families had not only thrust them into this untenable situation, but had now intruded on their private time together. Especially since their families were exactly what they were trying to get away from. He slowed their pace until he and Jess fell behind enough to not be overheard.

"You okay?" he asked in an undertone.

A humorless sound escaped her, causing a puff of frosty air. "Not really. I'm suffering from a major case of coitus interruptus."

He stifled a groan at how close they'd been. "I hear ya."

"Although I suppose it could be worse. *All* my brothers could have come with Mom."

Since agreeing with that statement might be tantamount to tossing gasoline on a fire, he did what generations of men with sharply honed survival instincts did—he kept his mouth shut.

"I'm not happy about this, Eric."

"Neither am I."

"This has disaster written all over it." She pulled her hand from his and pressed her mittens to her forehead. "This was supposed to be our time together. We *need* this time."

"I know. And we'll have it." He took her hand again, not liking the sensation of her pulling away from him one bit. "I could have insisted they all leave, but I figured it would save time in the long run and be easier all around to just hammer this out here and now and be done with it rather than to first spend two hours arguing about whether or not to hammer it out here and now."

"I suppose. Especially since I don't think insisting they leave would have worked."

"It would have required several tons of dynamite, and I'm fresh out."

She didn't so much as crack a smile. "The crazy thing is that all these nitpicky little decisions just don't matter to me, and they're making me crazy. I don't care if the napkins are 'dusty rose' or 'desert blush.' Maybe because I'm more tomboyish than girly-girl. Or maybe I'm just weird because my wedding dreams have never centered around a white poofy dress and a fancy party. They've always just revolved around the man I'd someday marry. Just me and him. A simple setting—a few flowers, lots of candles. Speaking our vows."

That sounded…perfect. "Have you told your mom that?"

"Of course, but she doesn't listen. This wedding she wants for me? It's really the wedding *she* always wanted but never had."

Eric nodded. She'd told him how her parents were married by a justice of the peace. How they'd planned to renew their vows on their twenty-fifth anniversary, throw the sort of elaborate party her mom had always wanted. Unfortunately her father died before they could do it. "She has four unmarried sons whose weddings she could plan."

Jess shook her head. "Maybe she could help, but wedding planning is pretty much a bride thing. Sadly for us, Mom's become a Bridezilla without actually being the bride."

"Kelley's suffering from the same thing." He leaned closer and brushed his lips over her cheek. "Maybe we should just lock them in a room together and let them hammer it out themselves."

"Don't think I'm not tempted. Yet even if, by some miracle, we're able to work out all this wedding stuff, there're still all the underlying hard feelings simmering between everyone. I feel as if I'm walking through a field of land mines. I'm just so damn *tired* of it. It's exhausting. I'm at my wits' end. I honestly don't know how much more I can take."

Her words suffused him with a dread he didn't want to feel. Didn't want to so much as acknowledge. But one that he couldn't ignore. Although she didn't say the words, he sensed—no, damn it, he *knew*—that they had to fix the situation this weekend—or else. He halted and turned to face her then clasped her shoulders. She looked up at him and the dismal expression in her eyes cramped his insides with an unpleasant sensation that felt very much like fear. Fear that everything he wanted was somehow slipping through his fisted hands.

"We'll get this meeting over with quick, Jess—like yanking off a bandage. A fast meeting, then off they'll go and we'll resume our weekend."

Her bleak expression didn't change, twisting the knot gripping his insides even tighter. "Yanking off a bandage can really hurt, Eric."

His fingers clenched, pressing into her parka. "We're not going to let it hurt *us,* Jess."

The fact that she didn't instantly agree made him actually feel ill. Her gaze searched his, then she said quietly, "I don't want it to, Eric, but—"

"No buts," he cut in, not willing to even contemplate what she might have said next. "Everything is going to be fine."

He just hoped like hell he was right.

3

WITH HER STOMACH knotted with that "walking through the mine-field" sensation, Jessica entered the lodge. After everyone hung up their snow-coated jackets on the large rack near the door, they headed toward the lounge area. A number of tables were filled, and half a dozen patrons sat at the bar, most of them checking out the hockey game showing on the overhead TV. The bartender—who looked so much like Roland Krause, Jessica would have bet they were brothers—polished glasses behind the curved mahogany bar.

Once they'd seated themselves in overstuffed leather arm-chairs around a low, round polished oak table set on antlers, a waitress wearing a festive red Santa hat to top off her red-and-green outfit approached with a friendly smile.

"Happy holidays, everyone. What can I get you?"

"Scotch," said Marc without hesitation. "Straight up."

So much for hot chocolate. Obviously this was a meeting that required a stiff drink.

Jessica flicked a glance out the floor-to-ceiling windows at the swirling snow. "Aren't you the designated driver?"

"Yes. But since we're apparently going to be here for several hours—" he shot an "and it's all your fault" glare toward Kelley "—one drink is okay."

"Vodka martini," said Kelley, pulling a thick planner from her oversize purse.

"*Gin* martini," said Jessica's mom, in a tone that seemed to toss the first grenade toward Kelley. Jessica wasn't the least bit surprised that the two women didn't agree on what sort of martini was best.

After Jess ordered a white wine and Eric asked for a beer, the waitress headed toward the bar and an awkward silence descended on the group. Jessica cleared her throat and attempted a cheerful smile, but wasn't sure she succeeded. "Why don't we get started?" *So we can get this over with.*

"Excellent," said Kelley, consulting her planner. "First, we need to decide on an approximate number of guests so I can tell the catering manager at the Marble Falls Country Club which ballroom to block for us. The smaller ballroom holds up to one hundred guests, the larger one up to three hundred."

"The small one," Jessica said.

"The large one," her mother said at the same time, then frowned. "Although I'm not thrilled having the reception at the country club. The Ritz-Carlton is only an hour's drive from Marble Falls and the ballroom there is much more elegant. And it can accommodate more guests."

Jessica pressed her fingers to her temple in a vain attempt to stem the headache forming there. "Mom, I don't even *know* three hundred people."

"We have dozens of business contacts through the restaurant we need to invite, dear." She flicked a glance toward Eric. "No doubt Eric has a few as well."

"The Ritz-Carlton is out of the question," Kelley said, shaking her head. "It's too far, especially for a February wedding when the weather is so unpredictable. If there's a bad snowstorm, we'll end up with no way to get to the reception."

"Which is why the wedding should take place in June," Mom said, her jaw tilting to its most stubborn angle.

Kelley dismissed her words with a wave of her hand. "June is completely passé for brides. May is the perfect month—"

"Stop," Jessica said, holding up her hand. "I don't want to wait until May or June." She looked at Eric. "Do you?"

"I don't want to wait until tomorrow."

She nearly sagged with relief at his reply. Sometimes she truly feared he'd finally get so disgusted with all these issues that he'd decide she wasn't worth the aggravation. The mere thought made her feel physically ill.

He turned toward his sister. "The wedding will take place, as Jess and I planned, in February."

"But the weather—" Kelley protested.

"*February,*" reiterated Eric.

The waitress delivered their drinks and while Eric signed the bill to charge them to their room, Jess took a grateful sip of wine. Based on the first few minutes, this was going to be a *looooong* meeting.

"What's the next thing on your list?" Eric asked Kelley.

"We still haven't decided which ballroom we'll need."

"The large one," Jessica's mom stated firmly.

Jessica's headache grew worse. "Mom…I've told you that Eric and I would prefer a smaller wedding. Maybe around fifty people. Or less."

Her mom's eyebrows shot upward—as if she'd never heard this before—then collapsed in a frown. "Fifty? Impossible. That would barely cover our immediate family."

"Mom, there're only six of us in our immediate family."

"I mean our immediate *circle*—of family, friends, business associates and coworkers." She reached out and patted Jessica's arm. "You don't need to be concerned about the cost, dear. I've been saving for this day for a long time. The wedding is my gift to you." She flicked a look at Eric. "And Eric, too."

God, she hated when her mother did that—glanced at Eric as if he were something she'd just scraped off the bottom of her shoe, then tacked him onto the end of her sentence like an unpleasant afterthought. She'd discussed the matter privately with her mother several times, but each talk had degenerated into an argument with her mother harping that Eric was "the competition" and that Jessica should find some other man to marry—a doctor or lawyer would be nice. She'd even gone so far as to suggest that all the arguments were actually Jessica's fault for not introducing Eric to the family until they were already engaged.

Uh-huh. Well, she'd have to take the bullet on that one because she *had* kept Eric to herself for their entire six-month courtship. Because she'd *known* how her mother and brothers would react. Her brothers hadn't liked *anyone* she'd ever dated, and had scared off more than one potential boyfriend. As for Mom, she'd also found fault with every guy Jessica had ever brought home— except for her high school boyfriend, John Wilson. And the only reason Mom had liked him was that he was the spitting image of a young Paul Newman. Which was good. But John also had a roving eye. Which was not good. By the time she graduated from college, she'd learned that there were only two types of guys she should bring home to meet the family—the type she didn't want to date anymore as one visit, especially with the brothers, pretty much insured she wouldn't hear from him again, and the guy she wanted to marry.

She'd known from that first moment she laid eyes on Eric that he was The One, and every moment spent with him over the next six months had only served to reinforce that first impression. And that being the case, she sure as hell hadn't wanted to scare him off. She was just working up the courage to suggest he meet her family when he asked her to marry him. That had led to their first meeting with her family a week later basically becoming *Mom, guys, this is Eric. We're engaged.*

Although Jessica didn't meet Eric's family, either, until after they were engaged, that first meeting had gone much better. But that promising beginning had slithered right down the tubes when they'd brought the two families together for the first time two weeks later.

And the rest, as they say, is history.

"Now that we've settled the ballroom issue," Kelley's voice broke into her reverie, "let's move on to the color scheme."

"Butter-yellow," said Mom.

"Impossible," vetoed Kelley. "Too pale and springlike for February. Not only that—"

"I'm going to the bar to watch the game," Marc broke in,

clearly anxious to escape all discussions of things butter-yellow. Jessica envied him his freedom and wished she could join him.

Kelley turned to Eric. "Why don't you go with him, Eric? Unless you want to discuss the impossibility of butter-yellow?"

Everything male in Eric wanted to bolt from the chair and escape, but he wasn't about to abandon Jess. He turned toward her and she nodded. "Go ahead." She leaned forward and kissed his cheek, then whispered in his ear, "Go. Save yourself. No reason we both should suffer." Her teeth grazed his earlobe and his eyes glazed over. Damn it. All he wanted to do was get her alone. Finish what they'd started before the descent of The Families. He was one breath away from yanking her out of that chair, slinging her into his arms and escaping back to their cabin. Locking the door and telling the world and their families to leave them the hell alone. And by God, if this wedding meeting wasn't over in the next half hour, that's exactly what he was going to do.

"Besides, I like that you'll owe me one," she whispered.

An inferno of edgy need gripped him. Yeah, he'd owe her one and he couldn't wait to pay up. Still, he considered remaining with her in case an arbitrator was needed, but then it occurred to him that maybe she wanted some female bonding time. There was woman stuff that guys weren't supposed to be privy to— maybe wedding decorations were one of those things—what the hell did he know? Plus, this gave him an opportunity for a one-on-one conversation with Marc, something he'd never had with any of her brothers. From what he could tell, they always traveled in a pack. Like rabid dogs. Maybe if it was just the two of them, he'd make some progress. Jess with the women and him with Marc…maybe they could divide and conquer. It certainly was worth a shot. *Then* he'd get her alone. And naked. And put out this damn fire eating at him.

He stood, picked up his beer then leaned down to drop a kiss on Jess's curly, honey-colored hair. "I'll be at the bar if you need me."

He approached Marc with all the enthusiasm he would a coiled cobra. After sliding onto the empty stool next to his soon-to-be brother-in-law, he waited for Marc to acknowledge his presence, but his brother-in-law-to-be's gaze never shifted from the hockey game flickering on the TV. Hockey—just another strike against Eric in the Hayden brothers' eyes. They were all die-hard hockey—and football—fanatics while Eric preferred basketball and baseball. And tennis—which *really* didn't help his cause as the Hayden brothers all thought tennis was wimpy. Obviously none of them had ever played a grueling three-hour, three-set match.

Eric finally nodded toward the TV and asked, "What's the score?"

"Rangers are up, three to one."

Then more silence. Not a real chatty guy, Marc. Before Eric could think of another conversation opener, the bartender, who wore a Santa hat and a friendly smile, approached. "You need another beer?" he asked, eyeing Eric's nearly empty bottle.

Eric did a double take, then glanced toward the reception area where he spotted Roland Krause chatting with a guest. "Sure, thanks. For a second there I thought you were Roland. Are you related?"

The man grinned. "We're cousins. Everyone thinks we're brothers." He extended his hand. "I'm Steve. Steve Howell. Roland and I may look alike, but under my Santa hat, I have a lot more hair than he does."

After Steve had brought the beer and moved off toward the other end of the bar, Eric watched the game for a few minutes while another long silence stretched between him and Marc. Well, it was one way to avoid an argument—don't talk. At least the guy was scowling at the TV instead of at him.

Just then he felt the weight of Marc's stare. When he turned to look at him, Marc was—no big shocker—scowling.

"My sister doesn't look happy," Marc said.

Eric's head turned so fast toward the table where Jess sat he practically heard his muscles snap. She was taking a sip of her wine and seemed fine.

"I don't mean right this second," Marc clarified. "I mean in general."

Eric turned back toward him. "Based on your tone it's obvious you think that's my fault."

"Who else's would it be?"

"You want a mirror?"

Eric wouldn't have thought it possible, but Marc's scowl deepened. "What's that supposed to mean?"

"It means that *I'm* not the one making her unhappy. You and your family and the nonstop arguing are what's making her miserable."

"I guess it's missed your notice that *you* are what all the arguments are about."

A humorless sound escaped Eric. "Uh, no. I haven't missed that. You've all made that perfectly clear. Listen, I get the whole overprotective-brother thing. I've given more than a few guys the evil eye for sniffing around my sisters. But once Chloe and Lara found the men they wanted to marry, I was happy for them. They both chose good, decent guys. Believe it or not, *I'm* a good, decent guy."

"Says you."

"Yeah, says me. And says your sister. She's extremely smart and savvy—hardly the sort of woman to marry a creep."

"Smart women make stupid mistakes about men all the time."

"Well, she's not making one."

Marc slowly swirled his tumbler of scotch, took a swig, then said, "Your franchise restaurant can't compare to Hayden's."

Eric's fingers tightened on his beer bottle, but he swallowed his irritation. "They're *both* good places and Marble Falls is certainly big enough for more than one restaurant."

"She shouldn't have taken up with the competition."

The hell with trying to use any more polite subtleties. "That was her choice. And mine. And frankly, it's none of your business. If she and I can work through that—which we have—I fail to see why you and your family can't."

"What about your family? I haven't noticed them turning cartwheels."

"Maybe not, but any objections they may feel have nothing to do with Jess. My sisters like her. A lot. And they're happy for me that we found each other."

Marc's only reply was a stony stare into his scotch.

Eric resisted the urge to drag his hands through his hair in frustration. "Look, maybe I'm not the guy you would have chosen for your sister, but here's the brutal truth—it's not your choice. It's hers. And for all our sakes, especially Jess's, it would be nice if we could reach some sort of détente here."

Eric took a long pull on his beer and waited, but Marc still remained silent. Hopefully he was thinking the détente thing was a good idea, but based on his fierce scowl, that didn't seem promising.

Unable to stand the awkward silence any longer, Eric said, "I get why your mother is here, but how did you get roped into coming along? Are you the muscle?"

"I'm the driver. She doesn't like to drive in the snow." He glanced toward the table then tossed back a swig of scotch. "Last place on earth I wanna be."

"Last place on earth I want you to be."

A noise that sounded like a reluctant laugh passed Marc's lips. "How is it you can take off four days during one of the busiest weeks of the year? Business not good?"

Was that a hopeful sound in Marc's voice? Probably. "Business is great," Eric replied. "Definitely not the best time for me to be away, and it wasn't easy to arrange the time off, but Jess comes first."

The sound of Kelley's slightly raised and very terse voice caught Eric's attention. "It is absolutely essential that the band play a selection of current songs, Carol."

Marc shot a frown toward the table. "Your sister's a real 'my way or the highway' sort of woman."

Eric cocked a single brow. "Guess you'd recognize that trait since you're clearly a real 'my way or the highway' sort of guy."

The minute the words slipped out Eric wondered if they'd

undo whatever small progress they seemed to be making. But Marc nodded. "I guess I can be. Sometimes. At least with regards to my sister. And this wedding."

Shocked—pleasantly so—that Marc would admit as much, Eric said, "Same with Kelley. She doesn't like to waste time. She's disgustingly efficient. Knows exactly what she wants and isn't afraid to go after it."

"Does she always get it?"

"Almost always. She's very successful at her job. You are, too. Which means you at least have that in common. So maybe you can quit giving her the death stare every time you see her."

Marc studied him for several seconds with an unreadable expression, then said, "Jess told me Kelley raised you and your sisters from the time you were twelve."

"That's right." He debated how much detail he should go into, but figured since this seemed a relatively safe topic, he might as well run with it. So he told Marc about his parents' deaths, and how Kelley had quit college and been dumped by her fiancé. How she'd set aside her own life to raise three kids when she wasn't much more than a kid herself.

He finished by saying, "She's an incredible woman. I owe her a lot."

Marc slowly nodded, clearly mulling over the tale. Finally he said, "Must have been hard."

"It was. But we also had a lot of good times."

"I didn't know about her fiancé and all."

"Yeah, well, maybe if you'd take a few minutes to get to know us instead of writing us off as nothing more than 'the competition'—and maybe smile once or twice while you're at it— you'd figure out we're not so bad."

"I could say the same to you."

"Maybe," Eric conceded. "But I never wrote you off as the competition." He grinned. "I wrote you off as a scowling jerk."

Marc's eyes narrowed. "I'm not sure if I'm amused or pissed off."

"Why not go with amused?"

"I'm not sure I like you."

"Yeah, well the jury's still out on you, too."

"Still, this last half hour is the first time I haven't been tempted to toss you into a Dumpster," Marc said, his tone musing.

"Ditto. Just to let you know, you'd have a hell of a time doing so."

Marc nodded. "Figured as much." What might have passed for a flash of an actual grin flickered across his features. "That's why I like to hang with the brother posse when you're around."

"At the risk of taking a backward step here, it would take more than the four of you to get rid of me. I'm not going anywhere."

From the corner of his eye he saw Jess stand up. He glanced over, hoping the wedding talk had reached a friendly conclusion. One look at her pale face—dotted with twin flags of red on her cheeks, clenched hands and overbright eyes—disabused him of that notion. He was out of his chair in a flash and striding toward her.

"I can't listen to this anymore," he heard her say to her mother and Kelley as he approached, her voice low and unsteady. "I'm sick to death of this sniping, and neither of you listen to me anyway. What difference does it make that I'm the bride? Clearly none. So *you* two plan the wedding. I don't *care* what color the napkins are. Invite six thousand people if that's what you want. But I am *not* wearing that ridiculous dress." She jabbed a shaky finger toward a glossy magazine photo depicting a woman wearing a huge poof of a white dress. "I'll choose what I wear and if it turns out to be my flannel pajamas, then so be it.

"Bottom line is that I refuse to argue about any of this anymore. I'm *done*. And since I'm no longer involved in the wedding decisions, I'm going back to my cabin. And I suggest you all go home."

"Jessica," said Carol, her tone sharp. "You can't just walk away like this."

"I can and I am." Her voice broke on the last two words, and Eric could tell she was seconds away from losing it. He reached out to touch her, but she stepped back, shaking her head and hugging her arms around herself. "I. Am. Done. As for the wedding—I'll just show up at the church. Or, damn it, maybe I won't."

Without another word she turned on her heel and stalked from the lounge.

4

JESSICA HEARD ERIC call after her, but instead of stopping she quickened her pace, all her thoughts focused on one thing.

Escape.

She needed to put as much distance between herself and her mother and Kelley before she completely fell apart.

Snatching her parka from the coatrack, she dashed outside without pausing to don the garment. A gust of snow-laden, frigid wind pelted her and she gasped at the sudden change in temperature. At least six inches of fresh snow lined the path and the bitter-cold air seemed to snatch the oxygen from her lungs. Without breaking her stride, she struggled into her coat and mittens and tried to calm her rapid, shallow breathing—the first warning sign of the anxiety attack she felt gripping her in its talons. *Just relax. Breathe deep.*

Damn it, she *hated* feeling like this. Out of control, her heart thumping so hard and fast she could hear the staccato beats echoing in her ears. Her throat tightening, her fingers tingling from her too-fast shallow breaths, the tension constricting her muscles, the shivering that had nothing to do with the cold. She'd suffered such attacks after her father died, when the grief had relentlessly choked her, but she hadn't experienced one in several years. Until her engagement. Sadly, since then, she'd been forcibly reminded several times of exactly how they felt. Just like this. Like walls closing in on her and a mounting sense of being overwhelmed.

She needed to lie down, close her eyes until the feeling passed.

She felt like a coward running out like that, leaving Eric to deal with the fallout, but, God, she just couldn't take it anymore. She'd tried to be diplomatic. Polite. But her mother was driving her insane. And whatever last nerve Mom wasn't stomping on, Kelley trampled over. Sitting between them, she'd felt as if a big red bull's-eye were painted on her. Her mother had been over-bearing and rude, while Kelley's manner was demanding and brusque. Maybe she would have been able to stomach the tension, endure the discussion—translation: argument—to its end if she hadn't seen the wedding dress.

A half humorless laugh, half sob escaped her and she briefly squeezed her eyes shut, only to nearly stumble on the snowy path. The dress that her mother declared was perfect. Maybe—for some bride, somewhere, but absolutely not for her. That dress wasn't just a no, it was a *hell no.* Naturally her mother had disagreed. And then informed her that she'd already ordered it—because it was *soooo* perfect.

That's when all her pent-up anger had erupted like Vesuvius. If she hadn't left she would have lashed out and said things she'd regret once her temper cooled. She'd learned the hard way that things said in anger could wound deeply. And they could never be unsaid.

The memory slammed into her—the stupid, typical argument between a fourteen-year-old know-it-all girl and her aggravated father over too much time spent on the phone and not enough on homework. Angry words shouted out of teenage rebellion. And two days later, with the argument and her resentment still simmering between them, a heart attack. Her father was gone in the blink of an eye. The last words spoken between them had been said in anger. Eleven years later the memory still tore at her.

And so she'd escaped the lounge. Before regrettable words could be spoken—although she'd left a few seconds too late. *I'll just show up at the church. Or, damn it, maybe I won't.*

The words had slipped out before she could stop them. She hadn't meant them. Or had she? She couldn't deny that at that moment, she had. Coward that she was, she hadn't paused to look at Eric, but she'd sensed he'd gone perfectly still. And the same question that had plagued her for the last four months again raced through her mind: how in God's name could she resolve this mess and still keep her relationships with both Eric and her family?

She saw the cabin in the distance through the thickly falling snow and with a sense of relief, she quickened her pace. When she reached the door, she turned and saw Eric's bright red parka just now emerging from the lodge. Clearly he'd exchanged a few words with Mom, Marc and Kelley. She wasn't sure she wanted to know what those words were. Or what she'd say to him when he reached the cabin. She'd have less than ten minutes before he arrived to compose herself and she'd need every second of it.

As soon as she'd closed the door behind her, she yanked off her coat and let it fall to the floor. After jerking off her snow-encrusted boots, she immediately climbed into the bed and pulled the covers up to her chin. Shivering, she closed her eyes, tears leaking, unstoppable, from beneath their lids to slip down her chilled cheeks as she forced herself to empty her mind and concentrate on the slow, deep breathing exercises she'd learned after her father's death.

After a few minutes the tension and tingling sensation started to ease from her limbs. Her throat felt less tight, her breathing more regulated. Another few minutes and the anxiousness passed, leaving weariness and relief in its wake. She'd just sat up when Eric opened the door.

The instant his serious and concern-filled blue gaze locked on hers, a fresh supply of tears welled in her eyes. Damn it, this was supposed to be a *happy* time. Looking forward to their future together. Not fraught with all this gut-wrenching stress and hair-yanking frustration. She wasn't naive enough to believe their lives would be sunshine and roses all the time. But surely there shouldn't always be dark clouds and crabgrass, either.

Without a word he closed and locked the door. Removed his parka and gloves, toed off his boots. Then walked to the bed. Sat next to her. And drew her into his arms.

She went willingly, gladly, savoring his strength, the solid feel of him. Wrapping her arms around his waist, she burrowed her face into her favorite spot—the cozy nook where his neck and shoulder met, a place that usually felt deliciously warm but was now cool from the frigid weather. But one that still smelled delightfully of Eric—clean and masculine and *him.*

He pressed his lips against her hair and whispered, "You okay?"

Her throat closed, so she nodded. Then shook her head. Then shrugged. How could she explain how she felt when she wasn't certain herself? The only thing she knew for certain was that she was exhausted.

His arms tightened around her, as if he feared she might otherwise slip away. And a small part of her couldn't help but wonder if she would.

She wasn't sure how long they remained that way, holding each other in silence, before she finally lifted her head and leaned back to look at him.

Before she could say a word, he cupped her cheek in his palm and brushed his thumb over her skin. "You've been crying."

She attempted a smile, but knew it was a weak effort. "Oh, great. On top of everything else I'm puffy and blotchy."

"You're beautiful. And breaking my heart. I can't stand to see you cry."

"You didn't see it—just the horrifying aftermath. And I didn't really cry. It was just a case of freakishly leaking eyeballs."

He didn't crack even the slightest grin at her feeble attempt at humor. "You want to tell me what happened?"

She blew out a long sigh. "The usual—arguments, nastiness, tension. My mother and Kelley didn't provide you with the gory details?"

"I didn't ask for them. Instead I told them in no uncertain terms that I was as sick and tired of this as you were. That I wanted them to go home, leave us alone and not make any attempt to contact us before Tuesday unless there was a true emergency—one that involved hospitals and blood."

A humorless sound escaped her. "Hopefully Mom won't take that as an invite to check herself into the hospital for some ailment or another."

"If she does, ten bucks says Kelley tries to beat her to the punch."

She rested her hands against his chest, absorbing the thump of his heartbeat through his sweater. "I'm sorry I left like that, but I was just so...*ugh*. About to start screaming." She related the painful details of the color and centerpiece and floral arrangements and menu and monogrammed versus not-monogrammed cocktail napkin debates.

"I just kept sipping my wine, praying for it to end," she said, shaking her head. "And I was doing a damn good job of holding on to my patience until I saw the picture of that wedding gown, a gown, by the way, that my mother has *already ordered* for me." She shuddered. "Did you see it?"

"The one that looked like something Little Bo Peep would wear?"

"Yes! Thank you! All I needed was a curved staff and every sheep within a five-hundred-mile radius would flock to me."

One corner of his mouth twitched. "I think Bo Peep also wore a frilly bonnet. And lacy bloomers that came down to her ankles."

That dragged a slight smile from her. "Not helping. I told my mother that the only way I would wear that dress would be if she somehow managed to wrangle it onto my dead, lifeless body—and even then I'd probably resuscitate myself long enough to rip it off."

"And that's when the fight started?" he deadpanned.

A short huff of laughter escaped her. "Pretty much. Although it hadn't been particularly pleasant before that."

He brushed back a strand of her hair that she was sure looked matted and gross. "I'm sorry they came here, sorry I didn't insist they leave immediately. Sorry they upset you. I guarantee they won't be bothering us again before Tuesday."

Right. But what about after Tuesday? The nightmare would just begin again. Even though she'd washed her hands of the wedding arrangements, she knew she hadn't heard the last of it. And that in no way solved the resentment her family felt toward Eric.

Pushing those unsettling thoughts aside, she asked, "How did things go at the bar with Marc?"

"Better than at the wedding planning table."

"Not a real high benchmark."

"No, but I think we actually might have taken a small, tottering step forward. But then again, maybe not. He's not an easy guy to read."

"He never has been, especially not the last few months. I think there's something bothering him."

"Besides our engagement?"

"Yes, but he won't talk about it. Which means it must involve a woman."

"If so, he should watch out for that 'what goes around comes around' karma. It would serve him right if her family lived in Marble Falls and took an immediate dislike to him. But I've got my own problems without worrying about his." His expression turned serious and his gaze searched her face. "What you said before you walked out, about maybe not showing up at the church…was that just something that shot out in anger or did you mean it?"

A denial rushed into her throat, but she pressed her lips together to contain it. Because this was too important to simply offer him a placating answer. Because this was one of the reasons they'd come here—to talk about the state of their relationship.

At her hesitation, a muscle ticked in his jaw. "Well, *that's* the loudest silence I've ever heard."

"Eric…I—"

Her words cut off when he stood and paced in front of her. Then he turned toward her and dragged his hands down his face. "You're having second thoughts."

It wasn't a question. It was a statement made in a raw, hoarse voice that sounded ripped from his throat.

She rose and framed his face between her hands. "Not about my feelings for you."

"Just about marrying me."

"No, but…" She released a long sigh and lowered her hands. "I've now reached a whole new level of exhaustion, Eric. Do you know how many arguments we had during the entire six months we dated before getting engaged?"

He considered for several seconds. "No. Other than a few disagreements while figuring out our work situations, did we have any?"

"I can only recall two. Both of them silly misunderstandings, quickly resolved and completely forgettable. The rest of the time, it was…magic." Yes, romantic evenings filled with conversation and laughter that melted into sultry, sensual nights of discovery and exploration. Ice-skating and walks in the snow when they'd first met last winter had bloomed into springtime hikes and quiet evenings at home. Then summer, with private indoor and outdoor picnics. But then came the end of summer and Eric's proposal and the start of their current situation.

"I've lost count of the number of arguments since our engagement," she continued quietly. "I feel like I spend all my time fighting. If not with my mother, then with one or more of my brothers, or with you. I like *peace.* Quiet. Managing Hayden's is stressful enough—I can't handle having my personal life fraught with constant turmoil. I've never considered myself a quitter, but I'm just so damn *tired* of fighting."

He raised her hand to his lips and pressed a quick, hard kiss against her palm. "Then let's stop fighting."

"Based on the last four miserable months—which seem to grow more miserable by the day—easier said than done."

"No, it's not. We just need to stop fighting *each other.* If there's fighting to be done, let's do it together—*for* each other. Our families are causing the tension. It can't touch us if we don't let it."

"A great theory, and one we've discussed before. But as these last four months have proven, it's difficult to ignore one's family. Especially when you work with them. And live only a few miles away from them. And when they show up during your get-away-from-them weekend."

"Difficult, definitely. But not impossible. And they're gone now." He took her other hand then pressed her palms against his chest. "I love you, Jess. So damn much. Nothing…*nothing* is as important to me as you. You know that…don't you?"

She blinked back the tears burning behind her eyes at his words and nodded. "It's just that I'm so…disappointed."

"In me?"

She shook her head. "No. In this whole situation. In how badly it's turned out. I always imagined this one big, happy family scenario—gatherings, holidays, cookouts. And instead it's one big unhappy mess."

"As long as you and I aren't a mess, that's all that matters, Jess. Your mother and Kelley will just have to fight it out without us. After the wedding, everything will settle down."

"I keep telling myself that—"

"Good."

"—but I'm not sure I can stand this for another two months. At least not without the benefit of a morphine drip."

One corner of his mouth twitched, but remnants of worry still lurked in his eyes. "We have the next few days all to ourselves. No pressure, no arguments. Nothing to worry about except us."

He brushed his mouth over hers, once, twice, softly, and her weariness melted away, replaced by a sudden, fierce need to *feel*. A need to feel Eric. To recapture the magic between them. To rediscover how good they were together. To remember what they stood to lose if they were foolish enough to let it all get away from them. A need to forget everything and simply drown in sensation.

"Nothing except us sounds really nice," she whispered against his lips, slipping her hands over his shoulders and twining her arms around his neck.

He leaned back and his gaze bored into hers. "Do you love me?"

The uncertainty reflected in his beautiful eyes shamed her, filling her with a hollow ache she couldn't name that he'd felt it necessary to ask. That she'd made him doubt her feelings. While there was no doubt she hated this situation, there was also no doubt she loved him. And she was so afraid it was all slipping away.

A surge of fierce love rushed through her, coupled with an almost desperate need to reassure him, to not only tell him, but show him how much she loved and wanted and needed him. Now.

Rising up on her toes, she pressed herself against him and pulled his head down for her kiss. "Yes. God, yes. I love you. So much—"

His lips silenced hers in a hot, deep, passionate kiss that left her breathless. "Love you so much," she repeated, sprinkling kisses along his jaw to his ear where she raked her teeth against the lobe. "And I miss you. It's been so long…"

"So long," he agreed, tunneling his fingers through her hair. "Too damn long."

Her hands slipped beneath his sweater to run up his smooth back, and he groaned.

"Are you trying to seduce me?"

"Yes." She rubbed herself against him. "Is it working?"

"Absolutely."

5

ERIC LOOKED into Jess's eyes and his body hardened to instant attention at the heat simmering in her chocolate-brown depths. She certainly didn't need to put much effort into seducing him—she could accomplish the task with a mere look. A lone touch. A single word. A fleeting smile.

Need, sharp and edgy, scraped him, overwhelming him with the desire to yank her into his arms and spend the next few days blocking out the last few stressful months, specifically the last few stressful hours. All he wanted to do was *drown* in her.

If he lived to be one hundred he'd never forget the first time they made love. It had been after a dinner and movie date. His place. A cold March wind blew outside, a stunning contrast to the burning desire they'd both felt. No woman, ever, had felt like Jess. Had suffused him with such a complex mix of emotions, leaving him vulnerable yet stronger than he'd ever felt. One night with her had reduced every other sexual encounter he'd ever experienced into a distant and hazy memory. He'd known without a doubt that he'd never want or need to touch any woman other than her for the rest of his life.

Looking at her now, a powerful wave of tenderness flooded him. This woman meant everything to him. And he wanted, needed to show her that, make her remember how perfect they were for each other. How they absolutely, positively belonged together.

"Jess." Her name sounded like a hoarse rasp, filled with all the love and want and need she inspired. The instant their lips touched, he was lost. His mouth melded with hers in a deep, hot, wet, tongue-mating kiss that perfectly imitated the act his body craved to share with hers. Without breaking their kiss, he lifted her straight up and walked the few steps to the bed. When the backs of her legs hit the mattress, he trailed his lips and tongue down her neck. God, the way this woman tasted…a heady combination of heat and spice and vanilla that never failed to leave him hungry for more. No woman, ever, had tasted like her. Felt like her. The first time he touched her she'd all but left him shaking.

He interrupted their kiss only long enough to pull her heavy sweater over her head. She wasn't wearing a bra and the sight of her rounded breasts, topped with hard, rosy nipples rumbled a growl in his throat.

He kissed her plump lips again then dragged his mouth lower, down her scented neck, over her delicate collarbone while his hands skimmed down to her jeans, which he quickly unfastened. His tongue slowly licked around one plump nipple before drawing the taut bud into his mouth while his hands slipped beneath the lace of her panties to cup the sweet curve of her bottom. She gasped and arched her back, offering him more, an invitation he instantly accepted. While his lips and tongue laved and teased her breasts, he pushed the denim and her underwear over her hips. Licking a trail down the center of her torso, he lowered himself to his knees, bringing her jeans down with him. He helped her step out of her clothes, removed her socks then looked up the long, curvy length of her gorgeous body, into her eyes that glittered with arousal.

Reaching up, he teased her taut nipples, still damp from his mouth. She moaned and combed her fingers through his hair, arching into his touch. Pressing his face against her belly, he traced the tip of his tongue around the indent of her navel. He breathed deep and the musk of her arousal invaded his senses, making his head reel. His hands cruised down to her hips and he urged her down, until she sat on the bed, then ran one hand up her body and gently pressed her back until she leaned on her elbows.

Grasping her knees, he spread her legs, wide, his avid gaze

drinking in the sight of her glistening sex. He slipped his hands beneath her and dragged her closer, setting her thighs over his shoulders. Leaning forward, he gave her slick folds a long, lazy lick.

"Eric…" His whispered name ended on a feminine sigh, one that deepened into a groan when he slipped two fingers inside her and slowly pumped while his lips and tongue pleasured her, licking, teasing, sucking, flicking, swirling.

His other hand skated up to her breasts and he rolled her taut nipples between his fingers. She lifted her hips, writhing against him, seeking more, her breaths quickening into erratic puffs. He felt her body tensing, her arousal tightening, until with a sharp cry she came. With tremors still shuddering through her, he slipped a third finger into her wet heat and drew her clitoris into his mouth. She gasped and arched her back as she peaked again.

This time when the tremors subsided, he kissed his way up her body, then shifted her higher on the mattress. When he rose to his knees, intending to strip off his shirt, she leaned up on her elbows and shook her head.

"Oh, no," she whispered, her eyes glittering. "Now it's my turn. Stand up."

He shot a glance down at the bulge in his jeans. "Already done."

Her gaze followed his and she licked her lips, a gesture that did nothing whatsoever to calm him. "I meant on your feet."

After he obeyed, she rose from the bed to stand in front of him then grabbed the ends of his sweater and drew it upward. He raised his arms to help and by the time he'd dropped the garment to the floor, she'd unfastened his jeans. Dark need slithered through him at the knowledge that she clearly felt the same stabbing need as he.

Easing her fingers beneath his waistband, she pushed the denim and his boxer briefs down his hips, freeing his straining erection. His sigh of relief turned into a long groan when she instantly dropped to her knees and drew him fully into her mouth. No preliminaries, no teasing caresses, just a sudden, unexpected, deep wet engulfment.

A jolt of hot pleasure sizzled through him, and with a groan, he looked down and feasted his eyes on the erotic sight of Jess's plump lips gliding over him. Her tongue swirled, dragging a deep growl from his throat, while her hands, damn, her hands were everywhere. Dipping into the crease between his thighs. Cupping him. Teasing him. Trailing up and down the backs of his legs, over and around his hips. He sifted his fingers through her mass of shiny disarrayed curls and watched her lean back, until her lips only surrounded the head of his penis. The silky stimulation of her circling tongue and clever, magic hands drove him quickly to the brink of detonation.

"I won't last much longer if you keep that up," he managed to say between ragged breaths.

Instead of stopping, she made a low, rumbling sound of approval and once again drew him in deep. He tipped his head back and closed his eyes, shuddering as she repeated that long, slow, slick glide, again and again, until he was mindless. He held off coming by sheer will, but each erotic draw of her mouth, each long lick, each flick of her tongue pushed him closer to the edge. And when he went over, he wanted her with him. Wanted to feel all of her wrapped around him. Wanted to watch her come.

He gently urged her up then lifted her into his arms. With his gaze locked on hers, he lowered her to the bed and followed her down, settling himself between her splayed thighs. He brushed his erection along her silky, wet folds, then entered her in one long, deep stroke. The heat of her body clamped around him, dragging a groan from his chest.

Gritting his teeth against the intense pleasure, he withdrew nearly all the way from her body, then again sank deep, grinding his hips slowly against hers. He shuddered at the sensation of sinking into her tight, wet sheath, then withdrawing, again, again, the erotically slick friction jolting pleasure to his every nerve ending. His thrusts quickened, deepened, each one propelling him closer to the edge. Jess wrapped her legs around his waist, urging him deeper, countering each thrust, her fingers digging into his tense shoulders. The instant she arched beneath him, he let himself go, burying his face in the soft curve of her neck and pouring himself into her, each hot pulse of pleasure ripping a harsh groan from his throat.

When his heart rate returned to something resembling normal, he kissed the soft skin behind her ear then lifted his head. She slowly blinked and he looked into the most beautiful eyes he'd ever seen. And as happened every time he did, he fell in love all over again. "*That's* the way it should be between us. Always."

"Yes." Her fingers sifted through the hair at his nape, shooting a tingle down his spine. "I feel *soooo* much better."

"Me, too. Your fault."

One corner of her mouth twitched. "You know, I owed you one—"

"Consider yourself paid in full. I think steam actually pumped from my pores."

"Good to know. But as far as any weekend getaway score-keeping goes, I'm still ahead three orgasms to one. Which means I now owe you *two*."

"Sounds good to me."

She shot him a mock severe look. "At this rate I'll never even the score. You need to keep your hands to yourself and allow a girl to pay her debts."

"No can do," he said, running one hand up her torso to palm her breast and brush his thumb over the velvety tip. "Those thirty-two days damn near killed me. Never again. Besides, you're way too touchable. Even if I start out with good intentions, I'll soon be defeated."

"Hmmm. We'll just have to do something about that—and I know just the thing."

"Oh? What's that?"

"It's a surprise." She waggled her brows. "To go along with another surprise I have planned for you."

"Perfect. Because I have a surprise for you, too. One that involves a bottle of champagne and a picnic in front of the fire."

She lightly pinched his butt and rolled her eyes. "Way to ruin my surprise."

He smiled into her shining eyes, and she grinned back, creasing the dimples in her cheeks that he loved. *This* is the way he loved seeing her. Smiling. Happy. Relaxed. Eyes filled with love and mischief. Not with her face tearstained, eyes bleak, looking sad, weary and defeated as she had when he entered the cabin. Seeing her like that made him feel as if he had a hole in his heart, and it was something he intended to do his damnedest never to see again.

After dropping a quick kiss to each shallow indent, he eased off her and stood. Holding out his hand, he said, "Why don't you hop in the shower while I get the fire going? I'll join you in a minute. Help you wash your back."

"Just my back?"

"For starters."

"Are you trying to make me say yes?"

"Absolutely. Is it working?"

"Absolutely."

They exchanged a light kiss, then he watched her head toward the bathroom. Whew. No doubt about it, the woman had the sexiest, most incredible walk he'd ever seen. If there was an Olympic medal for Most Scrumptious Ass, Jess would bring home the gold.

Feeling more relaxed than he had in weeks, he quickly got the fire going, then pulled his picnic supplies from his gym bag— blanket, which he spread before the hearth, bottle of champagne, which he popped into the cabin's already filled ice bucket, plus the assortment of goodies he'd brought from the restaurant. Satisfied, he headed toward the bathroom where he heard the shower running and Jess singing. A grin tugged his lips. Just another quirky thing to love about her—the woman was completely tone-deaf. *I'll have to sing the lullabies to our kids.* He was fond of teasing her. *You can sing to them if we're mad at them.*

Kids…just another bright spot shining in his future with Jess, and something he'd never been able to see clearly with any other woman. But looking into Jess's eyes, he saw it all and a few years down the road, after they'd settled into married life, they planned to start a family. Two, maybe three kids. She was going to be an absolutely fantastic mom.

She hit a particularly bad note and a half groan, half laugh escaped him. Yikes. He needed to get into that shower and give her something else to do besides sing before the people in the other cabins called the main lodge to complain.

Heh, heh, heh. He knew just the thing to keep her occupied.

Smiling, he'd just started toward the bathroom when the phone rang. He shot a frown at the instrument and gave himself a mental slap for not requesting that all calls go straight to voice mail. If this was anyone other than Helen or Roland Krause calling to check on their accommodations, he was going to be seriously pissed off. It sure as hell had better not be one of his sisters or Jess's family. He reached the phone in three quick strides and snatched up the receiver.

"Hello?"

"Eric, it's Kelley. I wanted to tell you—"

"Hold it right there. Is anyone bleeding?"

"No, but—"

"Anyone on their way to the hospital?"

"No."

"Then I don't want—"

"But that's the point, Eric. No one's on their way anywhere. With the severity of this storm, travel conditions are hazardous and getting worse. The airport has canceled all flights and most of the secondary roadways are already virtually closed. There's also been a ten-car pileup on the interstate."

She made a short, impatient sound, then continued. "So the bad news is I'm stuck. Here. At the Happy Wedding Lodge. Yippee. I just finished registering and I'm in cabin number twelve—two down from yours. And before you complain about it, just know that I'm not any happier about this than you are.

Based on the weather reports coming in, I'll probably be stuck here all day tomorrow and maybe Monday as well."

"Is there any good news?"

"Nope. In fact, it just gets worse. In case you haven't connected the dots yet, this means that Carol and Marc are stuck here, too."

Eric pinched the bridge of his nose. Damn. His and Jess's romantic getaway plans were sinking faster than a bowling ball tossed into Mirror Lake. "You're right. That's worse."

"And just to put a cherry on top of this crappy snow-covered dessert, I just dropped fifty bucks in the lodge gift shop on essentials."

"What essentials? Your cabin should have all the shampoo-type basics."

"Chocolate. Chocolate bars, chocolate truffles, chocolate-covered pretzels, dark chocolate fudge and homemade triple-chocolate brownies. If ever there was a time that required chocolate, this disastrous outing is it."

He frowned. "I thought chocolate was your cure for man problems."

A few beats of silence followed his words. Then she gave a quick laugh that sounded somewhat forced. "Man problems, wedding problems, family problems—chocolate helps solve them all. Anyway, I just wanted to let you know I'm here. I'll try to keep out of your hair, but with so many plans to finalize and me being trapped here, the effort is *really* going to cost me."

"Well, bite the bullet. Cover your mouth with duct tape if necessary. I love you, kiddo, but I *really* don't want to hear from you."

"I know. And I love you, too. Most of the time. I'll just feed my chocolate addiction and try not to cave and call you." Her voice softened. "I know I can be a little…"

"Overbearing?" he supplied in a teasing tone.

She laughed. "Yeah. Sometimes. But believe it or not, I only want you happy. And Jessica, too."

"I know."

"I already said this at the lodge, but I'm sorry Jessica got so upset. I'll put on my halo and say that the fault was mostly Carol's, but I can see I didn't help matters. When it comes to overbearing, that woman makes me look like a preschooler." She hesitated. "And speaking of overbearing…how did things go at the bar with Marc?"

"I think 'overprotective' describes him better. Culling him from the Hayden brother herd was…enlightening. I think he may actually be human."

"Oh? Are you saying you…*like* him?"

"*Like* might be a bit too strong a word at this point, but I do think he's a decent, hardworking guy who cares about his family. Obviously he's misguided where I'm concerned, but as much as that irks me, it stems out of love for his sister, and being a brother, I can relate. I don't agree with him, but our conversation gave me some hope that things might turn around."

"I…see. Well. That's…interesting."

"You okay? You sound weird."

"I'm fine."

"Good. In that case, I'm hanging up. Don't call us, we'll call you."

"Words I'll try to live by. But be warned—Carol and Marc might not be so accommodating. You better lock your door and take the phone off the hook."

"Good plan. Bye."

He disconnected then switched off the phone's ringer, although with his sister literally only yards away and his future in-laws not much farther, he wasn't sure how helpful that would be. *Note to self: next romantic getaway will not be within driving distance of family. Or anywhere it snows.*

Right. Miami sounded good. Of course that didn't help him *now.* Damn. Snowed-in with the in-laws. Could it get any worse?

The instant the question popped into his mind he shoved it aside. "Don't jinx yourself, man," he muttered, then crossed the room to make sure the door was locked. He debated whether to tell Jess the latest development, but decided not to, at least not unless it became necessary—like if her mother banged on their cabin door. Without even trying he could think of about three hundred other things he'd rather do with Jess than have the "Kelley, Carol and Marc are snowed-in here" conversation.

He once again headed toward the bathroom. It was time to continue getting him and Jess back on track and do a couple of those three hundred things. Or four or five of them.

At least.

6

"YOU REALIZE the score is now five to two."

Wrapped in one of the soft, white terry cloth robes provided in the cabin, Jessica sat on the blanket in front of the crackling fire and gazed down at Eric whose head rested in her lap. Dressed in a robe that matched hers, which afforded her tantalizing glimpses of his broad chest and muscular legs, he looked sated and sexy and more than a little smug.

"Yup," he agreed.

"Which means I now owe you *three*."

"Yup."

"You don't look particularly unhappy about that."

"Nope."

"Hmmm. You're very monosyllabic."

He curved one hand around her neck and dragged her head down for a lush kiss. "Your fault. You render me speechless."

"At this rate I'll be in your debt for the next seventy-five years."

"Guess I'm stuck with you." He heaved an exaggerated sigh. "I'll try to take it like a man and not complain too much."

"Good. 'Cause no one likes a whiner." She plucked a grape from the platter of goodies on the blanket and lightly traced the fruit around his lips. Eyes glittering, Eric snagged her wrist and sucked the morsel—and two of her fingers—into his mouth. After she slowly slipped her fingers free, he said, "Yum," then took a grape and held it up to her. Mimicking him, she held his wrist and slowly drew the fruit and his two fingers into her mouth, swirling her tongue. Then sucked. Hard.

His eyes darkened. "You keep doing that and in no time you'll only owe me two."

She slowly eased his fingers from between her lips. After chewing and swallowing her grape, she said, "Oh, I'm going to pay my debt. In full." She slipped her hand inside the V of his robe and smoothed her splayed fingers back and forth over his chest, lightly grazing his nipples. "I have plans for you."

"The surprise you mentioned?"

She reached for her glass of champagne with her free hand. "That's right."

"If it's anything like this fantastic chest rub you're giving me right now, I'll love it," he said in a distinctly drowsy-sounding voice.

She looked down at him and saw that his eyes were closed. "Hey! You're not getting *sleepy,* are you?"

He peeked one eye open a slit. "Um…no."

"Uh-huh. Well, you *look* sleepy. And you *sound* sleepy."

"Your fault, sweetheart. Between the sex, the hot shower— complete with more sex, the food, the wine and now the chest rub, you have no one but yourself to blame."

"Then I guess I'll just have to revive you."

"Shouldn't prove too difficult. With one touch you pretty much do to me what rocket fuel does for the space shuttle."

"Excellent. Then my surprise should *really* send you blasting into orbit."

He peeked open his other eye. "Okay, that got my attention."

"Good." She lifted his head, eased out from beneath him and stood. "On your feet, lazy bones," she ordered, holding out her hands to help him up.

Once he stood he yanked her into his arms. "Anyone ever tell you you're really bossy?" he asked, nuzzling her neck.

"All the time. I deal with those individuals very harshly."

He bumped her pelvis with his. "Sounds…kinky."

"Hmmm. Feels like you're already more than halfway to being fully revived."

"Again, all your fault."

She laughed and eased from his arms. Nodding to the chair by the desk, she said, "All you need to do is set that by the fire, then sit back and relax. I'll be right back."

"Sitting back won't be a problem, but relaxing?" He shot a pointed look at the bulge beneath his robe. "Not likely with you around."

"Don't worry," she said, blowing him a kiss. "I'll take care of that for you."

"I think those are my new favorite seven words."

He made a playful grab for her, but with a laugh Jessica eluded him. After a quick stop at her overnight bag, she headed into the bathroom to ready herself for Eric's surprise. When she was done, she cast a critical gaze in the mirror. The black lace push-up bra definitely gave her cleavage a boost and the low demi-cup allowed just the tops of her nipples to peek out. Like the bra, the black lace boy-cut bikini panties covered just enough to tease. Perfect.

Or at least she hoped so. She'd never done anything like this before. But then no other man had ever owned her heart and soul so completely. It wasn't until she met Eric that she realized she'd always held part of herself back in previous relationships. But not with Eric. They just clicked on every level, their personalities and goals meshing perfectly together like letters in a crossword puzzle. Even the topics upon which they didn't agree made for interesting debates, but they agreed on all the important stuff. Besides, he was the most honorable man she'd ever met. And he made her laugh. And he was great in bed.

Definitely an irresistible combination.

Now if only this damn family feud would end—

She cut off the thought. Tonight, this weekend, was about her and Eric. No one else. They were going to concentrate solely on each other and their relationship.

After slipping on her black strappy four-inch heels, she donned her robe, then slipped the last of her props into her pocket.

Let the score-evening begin.

When she reentered the main room, she found Eric sitting in the chair, half-empty champagne glass dangling from his long fingers. With his hair tousled from her fingers, the trace of evening stubble darkening his square jaw and his robe gaping open at the throat to reveal his muscled chest, he looked deliciously rumpled and more sexy than any man had a right to.

She put some extra sway in her hips as she approached him, which he clearly noticed based on the way his gaze heated. When she stood directly in front of him, she leaned down and settled her hands on his forearms, which rested on the chair's wooden arms.

"Ready for your surprise?" she asked in her sultriest purr, then leaned forward to lightly run her tongue over his bottom lip.

"Are you trying to get me to say yes?"

"Absolutely." Another brush of her tongue along his lip. "Is it working?"

"Absolutely."

Straightening, she took his glass and set it on the floor, then slipped her hand into her pocket and withdrew two silk scarves.

"What're those for?" he asked, eyeing the material with interest.

"Remember how I said you need to keep your hands to yourself and allow a girl to pay her debts? Well, this is to ensure that you do just that." She looped the length of silk through the arm of the chair.

"You're going to *tie* me?"

"If that's okay." Her gaze wandered down his body in a full-blown ogle. Then she met his eyes. "Unless you want me to stop?"

"Hell, no. But you know I'll be paying you back for this."

She smiled. "I'll look forward to that." When she finished securing his hands to the chair's arms, she stepped back until two feet separated them. "Ready?"

"Oh, yeah. I have a feeling I'm going to like this."

She untied the robe's sash then slowly slid the garment from her shoulders and tossed it aside. His hot gaze skimmed slowly down from her loose hair, over her black lace bra and panties, to her high heels then back up again.

"Oh, yeah," he said, his voice a hoarse rasp. "I'm *definitely* going to like this. Striptease?"

"Lap dance."

His gaze heated from hot to smoldering. "Wow. Guess you read my letter to Santa."

"Maybe." She bent at the waist, set her hands on her knees, then slowly dragged her palms upward. "Have you been naughty or nice?"

"A little of both…"

His voice trailed off when she skimmed her fingertips over her breasts.

He cleared his throat. "Good thing you tied me. But I'm not sure these skimpy scarves are going to do the trick."

"I double-knotted them." Keeping her movements tantalizingly slow, she spread her feet, arched her back and drew leisurely circles with her hips. Then she slowly bent her knees and gradually ground down, then back up, her arms moving sinuously, hands sifting through her hair, gaze never leaving his. Based on the stark, raw hunger flaming in his eyes, there was no doubt he liked what he saw.

"Where the hell did you learn to move like that?" he asked, his eyes riveted on her undulating hips.

"I bought a DVD—*Lap Dancing for Your Lover.*"

"You mean you've been practicing this?"

Another slow downward grind. "For weeks."

"*Weeks?* And I've *missed* the practice sessions? No freakin' fair."

She wet her index finger with her tongue, loving the intensity of his attention, then dragged the moist tip along the lacy edge of her bra and was rewarded with a deep groan. Keeping her hips circling and her gaze locked on him, she slowly turned until she faced away from him. With her legs straight, she bent forward slightly and shot him a flirtatious look over her shoulder while lightly stroking her bottom. He groaned again, and shifted in his seat. His erection pressed against his robe and she realized she found this as arousing as he did. Certainly the naked hunger glittering in his eyes encouraged her to see just how hot she could get him. The thought of the benefits she'd reap—that they'd *both* reap—clenched desire low in her belly.

Keeping her movements torturously slow, she spread her legs then bent lower, until her bottom pointed directly at him. Watching him over her shoulder, she cocked one knee to the side, straightened her other leg, then glided her fingertips up the back of her straight leg. When she reached her bottom, she gave it a smart slap then puckered her lips and blew him a saucy kiss.

"Come here," he growled.

"Oh, no. A shortcut never leads to anywhere worth going."

"Yeah, but I may explode before we get there."

"Aren't you enjoying the show?" she asked in a throaty purr as she lazily repeated her last move on the other leg.

"Are you kidding? I'm so hard I'll probably never walk again."

"Hmmm…yes, you're looking rather…tense."

He strained against the ties binding him and lifted his hips. His robe separated, revealing the hard jut of his erection. "There's no 'rather' about it."

Her gaze drifted over him and heat sizzled along her every nerve ending. "Spread your legs," she whispered over her shoulder.

With his eyes all but breathing smoke, he obeyed. She straightened, and with hips circling, moved backward until her legs hit the edge of the chair. Keeping her back straight, she bent her knees, rested her hands on his thighs then lowered herself until his erection was nestled against her bottom. Then she slowly rotated her hips.

"Jess…" His voice was a ragged moan. She felt his muscles tense and his rapid breathing warmed the back of her neck. Then he leaned forward and pressed his hot mouth against her nape. "You're driving me out of my mind."

Tingles skittered down her spine from his lips against her sensitive skin. She changed her hip movement to a forward-back rocking motion that drew a groan from both of them.

"I can feel your heat," he whispered against her neck. "God… you're wet. You're as turned on as I am."

"Let's see how much hotter we can get."

"Any hotter and I'm going to spontaneously combust."

"Then you'll miss the best part of the show."

His teeth grazed the top of her shoulder. "God knows I don't want to do that. Bring it on, sweetheart. But if I go up in flames, it's all your fault."

"Noted." She straightened, then with an undulating sway, turned to face him. The fire burning in his eyes singed her, pooling more heat in her belly. His hands were clenched, his knuckles white, his breathing labored, his muscles clearly tight with expectation of what she'd do next. Heat seemed to pump off him like steam. Having him so utterly at her mercy, being so completely in control, and seeing how profoundly it affected him was…potent.

Keeping her legs straight, she leaned forward and gripped the back of the chair on either side of his head, caging him in. She then arched forward and brushed her breasts across his face.

He sucked in a sharp breath that exhaled as a growl. Setting a knee on the chair between his legs, she leaned down and slowly traced the outside of his ear with the tip of her tongue. He buried his lips in her cleavage and drew a deep breath. "God, you smell so damn good. Feel so damn good." His tongue flicked over her half-exposed nipple and her womb clenched. "Taste so damn good."

She continued to tease him, brushing her breasts over his face, circling her nipples around his mouth, nibbling on his earlobe, brushing her tongue over his bottom lip then gently sucking it into her mouth, all while her knee applied a gently rotating pressure against the base of his erection. His breathing quickened into a series of jagged pants and he lifted his hips and thrust against her knee. "I'm dangerously close to begging," he warned.

She slowly backed off, her own breathing unsteady. With her gaze fused on his glazed eyes, she untied his robe's sash and spread the white terry cloth wide. Anticipation pulsed through her at the sight of his rippled abs and that straining erection jutting halfway up his taut stomach. A single drop of pearly fluid glistened on the engorged head of his penis and with a single fingertip she spread the bead of moisture over him. Dropping his head back, he looked at her through half-closed eyes and rolled his hips toward her, seeking more.

She immediately backed off, and forcing herself to keep her movements leisurely and sinuous, she reached behind her to unhook her bra. After she'd let it fall to the floor, she cupped her breasts, reveling in his smoky gaze, his rapt attention. She tugged on her taut nipples then skimmed her hands down her torso. Hooking her fingers beneath her lace panties, she shimmied them down her legs then kicked the bit of material aside and slowly stood, running her hands leisurely upward.

With an animallike growl, he spread his legs wider and slowly thrust upward. Her womb clenched in response and she walked back toward him.

"Untie me." His voice was low, rough.

She shook her head, and eyes steady on his, leaned forward to grip his tense shoulders then carefully set her knees on the wide seat on either side of his thighs. He instantly leaned forward and drew her nipple into his mouth. A gasp escaped her and she shuddered at the wet warmth tugging on the aroused tip.

Reaching between them, she wrapped her fingers around his hard flesh. The scent of her arousal and his heat filled her head, making it spin. She positioned herself over his erection then slowly rubbed the velvety head along her wet, swollen cleft. That single touch ignited her like a match to gunpowder and she couldn't wait any longer to feel him inside her.

Grasping his shoulders, she sank down, a slow, slick impalement that shot sweet, hot pulses of pleasure through her. His growl of approval vibrated against her breast and he drew her nipple deeper into his hot mouth. She slowly rose, then lowered herself again.

"Eric," she said, her voice a breathless moan. "You feel so…" Her voice trailed off into a groan when he ground up, embedding himself deeper.

"So tight," he whispered, grazing his teeth along her neck. "So wet and hot. Don't stop."

She didn't, taking him in long, languid strokes that he met with increasingly demanding upward thrusts. She picked up the pace, lost in pleasure, both of them straining harder for the next stroke. Her climax exploded, and with a cry her body arched as the convulsions throbbed through her. With a dark growl, Eric ground his hips into hers and she felt him pulse inside her. Limp and panting, with aftershocks still rippling through her, Jessica melted against him, her head flopping forward like a rag doll's to rest against his shoulder.

"I'll untie you as soon as I can move," she managed to say between erratic breaths.

"Don't worry about it—I can't move a muscle anyway," he said, sounding as breathless as she was. "Good thing I've got a strong heart, otherwise that would have killed me." He turned his head and brushed his lips over her damp forehead.

"Yet I don't sense that's a complaint."

His huff of warm breath ruffled her hair. "Hardly. Best damn Christmas present I ever got."

She summoned the energy to lift her head and gazed into his slumberous, sexy eyes. "Glad you liked it."

"'Liked' is a pretty lukewarm word."

"Does that mean my debt is paid?"

"In full. In fact, I think now I owe *you* two."

She looped her arms around his neck and gave him a slow, deep kiss. After she lifted her head, she asked, "Do you think it'll always be this…magical between us?"

His gaze turned serious. "Yeah, I do. Because I love you just as much when we're not naked. You're the most incredible woman I've ever met—in bed, out of bed. Everywhere. All the time. And *that's* what makes it magical."

A surge of love washed through her, wrapping around her like a warm blanket. "I think it's been at least an hour since I told you I love you."

"Sweetheart, you just told me—a hundred times over—with that performance."

She waggled her brows. "Does that mean you owe me ninety-nine?" She leaned forward and nibbled on his earlobe.

"Are you trying to get me to say yes?"

"Absolutely. Is it working?"

"Absolutely."

She leaned back and looked into his eyes. The intense love staring back at her squeezed her heart, which he'd owned from minute one.

"How incredibly lovely that we have another three days alone here," she said, combing her fingers through the dark silk of his hair. "No interruptions, no phone calls, no families, no arguments. Just the two of us."

Something flickered in his eyes, but was gone so fast she decided she'd imagined it.

"No interruptions," he agreed. "Just the two of us."

7

"OH. MY. GOD. Is that my...*mother?*"

At Jess's incredulous question, asked in a horrified whisper that registered at least an octave above her normal voice, Eric halted in the act of hanging their snow-covered parkas on the coatrack in the lodge's lobby. He winced. Uh-oh. This didn't bode well for the relaxing, early-morning breakfast he'd anticipated.

After settling the coats on the brass hooks, he turned and followed Jess's slack-jawed, wide-eyed stare across the lobby toward the lounge area. And his stomach sank into his snow-encrusted boots.

Carol sat in profile to them at one of the low tables, a steaming ceramic mug set in front of her, chatting away on the cell phone held to her ear. Damn. He'd thought for sure they wouldn't run into any snowbound family members by eating so early. It was barely six-thirty, for crying out loud. Kelley would never show up anywhere before 10:00 a.m. unless a full-scale emergency was involved. She'd never been an early riser which was one reason she loved having her own business—she could set her own hours.

He figured Marc and Carol for late sleepers, too—restaurants closed late, so most of Eric's colleagues didn't jump out of bed at the crack of dawn. Eric normally didn't, either, but he and Jess had fallen asleep early without ever venturing out for dinner, and had awoken at dawn. After a bout of slow, soft morning sex, they'd both been starving and the few wizened grapes left over from their picnic the night before weren't going to do the trick. Since room service was only served in the lodge, they hadn't been left with much choice but to get dressed and haul their butts here through the nearly three feet of fresh snow that had fallen during the storm.

Yet clearly he'd miscalculated, because there Carol sat, chatting away, waving her free hand in the air. He frowned. Who the hell talked on the phone at six-thirty in the morning?

He sighed. "Yup, that's your mom."

He felt the weight of Jess's regard and turned to look at her. "You don't sound—or look—surprised to see her."

Clasping her hand, he led her toward the large Christmas tree so they were out of Carol's line of vision. "I'm not. Your mom, Marc and Kelley all got snowed in with the blizzard."

Her eyes goggled. "*All three of them* are here?"

"'Fraid so. Kelley's in a cabin two doors down from ours. Your mother and Marc have rooms here in the lodge."

"And you know this how?"

"Kelley called our cabin last evening while you were in the shower and told me."

She folded her arms over her chest and shot him The Look. He could hear the toe of her snow boot tapping against the hardwood floor. "And you didn't tell me because…?"

"Because I didn't want you looking the way you're looking right now." He reached out and lightly clasped her stiff shoulders. "I figured if you knew they were here, you'd be worried about them calling the room, or knocking on the door."

"And you weren't?"

"Can't say it didn't cross my mind, which is why I turned off the ringer on the phone. As for banging on our door again, I'd made it very clear to all of them that we didn't want any further interruptions." He captured one of her hands and brought it to his mouth to kiss her palm. "Once you tied me up, I didn't think about anything except you. I hoped we were here early enough to miss them." Craning his neck, he peeked around the tree toward the lounge. "Just our luck she's here so early."

"Mom wakes up every morning at five without an alarm.

Doesn't matter what time she goes to bed, she's up with the chickens. And she's a light sleeper. Which made it really hard to sneak in after curfew, and impossible to sneak in after 5:00 a.m." A quick grin flicked over her lips. "Worse for my brothers because they're all big and clumsy and never learned the meaning of the word 'stealth.'"

"Wish I'd known that before I suggested coming for breakfast. Who the heck do you suppose she's talking to at this hour?"

"Her sister, my aunt Liz. She lives in Florida and also wakes up at the crack of dawn. They talk every day at this time. My brothers and I keep telling Mom that if she'd spend as much time looking for a nice man who lived nearby as she does talking to her sister who lives sixteen hundred miles away, maybe she wouldn't be so lonely. And maybe she'd have more to occupy her time than trying to run our lives—although none of us said that last part to her face."

"Probably a good idea." He shot Carol a speculative look. She wasn't an unattractive woman. She'd been a widow for eleven years. Maybe she *was* lonely. Maybe that was the root of her overbearing nature. "Listen, if you think some male companionship would get her to concentrate on her own life instead of trying to interfere in ours, consider me on board the 'find Carol a man' bandwagon."

"Great. But that doesn't do us much good right now." Jess's stomach growled, so loud they both heard it. "I'm starving."

"Me, too." The scent of bacon wafted toward them from the Coldspring Room, and he lifted his nose to sniff the enticing aroma. Unfortunately the restaurant's double doors were situated directly behind where Carol sat.

"Mom only has coffee this early," Jess reported in an undertone. "She won't eat until around eight o'clock. If we keep to the perimeter of the room, maybe we can make it into the restaurant without her seeing us. Then we can get a table in a back corner, out of sight."

"Good plan. And maybe there's another exit in the restaurant. We might be able to pull this off."

"What about Kelley? What if she comes in for breakfast?"

"No chance. She never wakes up with the chickens. Marc?"

"Late sleeper. And if there's room service available, he's all over it."

"Good." He eyed her up and down, then said in a conspiratorial tone, "You ever had any sort of useful sneak-along-the-perimeter, military-type training?"

She considered for several seconds. "I was a Girl Scout in second grade. You?"

"Never a Girl Scout."

"That's a relief."

"But I did go to sailing camp one summer."

She looked toward the ceiling. "Great. If we happen across any yachts on our way to the restaurant I'll defer to your superior knowledge. Clearly we're well equipped." A mischievous gleam entered her eyes and she surreptitiously rubbed her palm against the fly of his jeans. "*Very* well equipped."

He sucked in a quick breath as his body came swiftly to attention. With a half laugh, half groan, he captured her wrist and dragged her errant hand up to rest on his chest. "Thanks. But I can't walk in a stealthy manner with a raging hard-on."

"They didn't teach you that at sailing camp?"

"No. But they did teach us how to deal with saucy wenches." He wrapped his arms around her and leaned down to nuzzle her warm neck. "Care to see my yardarm?"

"Are you trying to get me to say 'aye, Captain'?"

"Absolutely. Is it working?"

"Aye, Captain." She leaned back in the circle of his arms, lightly rubbed her pelvis against his and waggled her brows. "How's your mainsail?"

"Hoisted. You know, on second thought, maybe we should forget about breakfast and just head back to the cabin—"

"Oh, no, you don't," she said. "You'll have a mutiny on your hands. You promised me pancakes dripping with syrup. And eggs. And sausages. And bacon. And coffee, and—"

He halted her words with a quick, hard kiss then shot her a mock frown. "Then quit tempting me with your non-breakfast items or we may never get a meal." He took another quick look around the tree and noted Carol was still yapping into her phone. "Now or never. Ready?"

At Jess's nod, he took her hand, and keeping their gazes downcast, they headed toward the restaurant, staying close to the wall. Eric heaved a mental sigh of relief when they passed the area where Carol might well have seen them in her peripheral vision. They still needed to walk quite close to her to enter the restaurant, but they'd be directly behind her. Just a few more yards and they'd be safe.

"I've booked the ballroom at the Ritz for the first Saturday in June," he heard Carol saying as they moved behind her. Certain he'd misheard her words, he stopped. Jess halted as if she'd walked into a wall.

"Oh, they'll probably fuss at first," Carol said into the phone, "but what else could I do? Turns out the large ballroom at the country club was no longer available for the date they wanted in February, and the small ballroom simply won't do. I figured as long as we had to change the date anyway, why not make it June? June is the perfect month for a wedding—so much better than February."

Eric's every muscle went rigid with disbelief and a red haze seemed to dull his vision. He glanced toward Jess. She'd gone perfectly still and was staring at the back of her mother's head.

Carol was silent for several seconds, presumably listening to her sister. Then she said, "Putting off the wedding until June also gives me longer to make certain everything's perfect, and to hopefully get Jess more interested in planning all the little details. This should be a fun time for her yet it seems all she does is mope." After another few seconds of silence, Carol nodded and said, "Maybe she *isn't* sure. After all, their engagement happened so quickly—after only six months. I'm hoping the extra four months will give her time to know her mind. Maybe she'll reconsider her unfortunate choice. God knows she could have any man she wanted."

The surge of anger that roared through Eric seemed to implode inside his head. He couldn't recall ever being so furious in his entire life. In the space of a single heartbeat, his life flashed before his eyes—not his past, but his future. A future with his life being manipulated, being the victim of behind-the-scenes machinations and scheming, his express desires being ignored and circumvented. It wasn't a pretty picture. In fact, it was a really ugly picture. And the realization it left in its wake hit him so hard he nearly staggered.

He didn't want it. None of it. He wasn't going to let it happen. And he knew what he had to do.

As if from far away he heard Jess gasp then say, "Mom?" in a voice that reflected both confusion and outrage. Saw Carol start then turn around. Her eyes widened at the sight of them and a flush suffused her face.

She mumbled, "I'll call you back," into the phone then flipped it closed. Then she stood and faced them.

"Good morning," she said, offering a tentative smile, her gaze bouncing between them, clearly wondering what, if anything, they'd overheard. "I wasn't expecting to see you here so early. You usually sleep in, Jess."

"You and I need to talk, Mom." Jess turned to him. "I'm sorry to cancel our breakfast, but would you give me some time alone with my mother?"

Eric looked at Jess, but felt as if he were looking through her. He had to swallow twice to locate his voice. "Sure." He barely pushed the word through his tight throat. With a quick nod, he turned on his heel and strode away, not sure where he was going, but it didn't matter. He just wanted to get away. Before he said something he'd regret. Good thing he was too furious to speak.

Sure, he'd give Jess time, all the time she wanted. Didn't matter how long it took or even what she said. Because he was done. Finished. Couldn't take any more. Carol's words had snapped something inside him, something that he knew couldn't be fixed. It was time he faced the truth—and the truth was that what he'd overheard was the final nail in the coffin. This weekend with Jess was supposed to be about them. Just them. Getting things back to normal. Instead it had turned into the very thing they'd been trying to escape—the viper's nest their engagement had turned into.

He grabbed his coat from the rack, slammed his arms into the sleeves, then shoved open the door to walk outside, barely registering the cold and the snow that continued to lightly fall.

All she does is mope... It was time to be brutally honest with himself. Jess wasn't happy. She hadn't been for months. And neither was he. Not really. He just hadn't wanted to admit it, not even to himself. But now, there was no way he could deny it any longer.

Perhaps she'll reconsider her unfortunate choice. God knows she could have any man she wanted. Carol's words echoed through his mind, and his hands clenched into tight fists. Yes, she could have any man she wanted. He'd known that from the first minute he'd laid eyes on her. Just as he'd known he wanted to be that man.

June is the perfect month for a wedding. Maybe it was. But that didn't matter anymore, either. There wasn't going to be a damn wedding in June. And there wasn't going to be a damn wedding in February.

He was done.

When he arrived at the cabin a few minutes later, he went directly to the phone and punched the number for the front desk.

After Roland Krause identified himself with a cheery greeting, Eric asked without preamble, "Are the roads still closed?"

"I'm afraid so, Mr. Breslin," Roland said. "Is there something you need?"

Yeah. To get the hell out of here as soon as possible. He knew there'd be a fallout. And tears. And hurt, but he couldn't help that. The chips would just have to fall where they may. "Any word on when they'll be clear?"

"Well, the snow's still coming down, but I heard on the news that they're working on the interstates. Once they're plowed, they'll start on the secondary roads. We're pretty isolated here, so it'll be a while. To be on the safe side, I'd plan on being snowed-in here until tomorrow morning. Good thing you were plannin' to stay on till Tuesday."

Eric pinched the bridge of his nose. Great. "How about snowmobiles?"

"They're all rented at the moment."

"Dog sled?"

Roland chuckled. "Don't have any of those. Why don't you tell me what it is you need, Mr. Breslin? Chances are we'll be able to accommodate you."

Doubtful. But what the hell. Maybe the man had some cross-country skis or snowshoes—anything to get Eric the hell out of here. So he told Roland what he wanted. When he finished, Roland said in a solemn voice, "I see. Well, Mr. Breslin, as luck would have it, I believe I *can* help you." They spoke for several more minutes, then Eric replaced the receiver. He glanced around the room, his gaze falling on his overnight bag. He'd come back for his stuff shortly, but right now there was someone he needed to talk to.

He closed the door behind him and trudged through the deep snow. When he reached cabin twelve, he banged on the door. "Kelley, it's Eric. Open up."

Knowing his sister slept like the dead, he kept pounding and repeating his summons. A full two minutes passed before the door opened a crack. Kelley, her hair tousled, clutching the collar of her robe closed, and looking none too pleased, peered out at him.

"What are you doing here?" she asked.

"We need to talk." He made to enter her cabin, but she blocked his way.

"At this ungodly hour? I don't think so, Eric. Call me in a few hours."

"Now," he insisted, once again trying to enter, and once again her sidestepping to block him.

"Is something wrong?"

"Not something." He briefly squeezed his eyes shut. "*Every-thing* is wrong."

Worry instantly replaced her annoyed expression. "With you and Jess?"

A lump swelled in his throat. "Yeah."

"What happened?"

"I'll be happy to tell you as soon as you let me in—or am I supposed to stand out here freezing my ass off?"

When she hesitated, he rolled his eyes, his patience on a thin tether. "Good God, I don't care if your girly stuff is all over the place, Kell. Like I'm not used to that after growing up with three sisters and one bathroom."

She clutched her robe tighter. "Tell you what—I'll get dressed and meet you at the lodge in fifteen minutes."

"Forget it. It'll take that long to hike up there. They haven't shoveled the paths yet. Besides, the lodge is the last place I want to be. Jess and Carol are there." Anxious to get out of the frigid air, he shouldered his way inside. While Kelley closed and locked the door behind him, he strode into the room.

While removing his snowy parka, his gaze absently circled the room, noting the rumpled bedcovers, the cheery fire burning in the hearth.

The pair of men's snow boots next to the hearth.

He froze with his jacket halfway down his arms and narrowed his eyes. There was no mistake—those weren't Kelley's boots. Her feet were small and those boots weren't. His gaze darted around the rest of room. No signs of a man's clothing, but two wineglasses bearing traces of drinks rested on the night table. And it hit him that while he'd clearly rousted Kelley from bed, she hadn't looked the least bit sleepy when she opened the door. And the fact that the guy's boots were still here, meant *he* was still here.

His gaze shot toward the closed bathroom door then he swiveled around to face her. She stood near the door, her face flushed crimson. "You're not alone," he blurted out, unable to keep the surprise from his voice.

"Eric, listen. I…" She blew out a long breath and raked one hand through her tousled hair. "I don't know what to say."

"Actually, neither do I." His sister was thirty-four years old—her love life certainly wasn't any of his business. "Obviously I should have called first, but it never occurred to me you'd have company—"

His words cut off when the bathroom door opened. A tall man, fully dressed—thank God—except for his boots, emerged and walked toward him.

Eric actually felt his jaw drop. *"Marc?"*

"Eric." Jess's brother treated him to his usual scowl as he walked by. Marc stopped next to Kelley and took her hand. There was nothing scowl-like about the look he bestowed on her. And Kelley, who gazed up at him, jeez, looked like she'd just swallowed a lightbulb.

"Well I'll be damned," Eric muttered, staring at them. "I thought you two couldn't stand each other."

Marc turned and met Eric's gaze. "Seems we can."

Apparently. Clearly those sparks he'd detected between them were the result of more than animosity. "How long has this been going on?"

"Turns out we've had feelings building for each other for a few months," Marc said.

"But only discovered how deep they ran last night," Kelley added.

"Appears our feelings are stronger than either of us even suspected," Marc said, his gaze steady on Eric's. "You have a problem with that?"

Eric's gaze shifted to Kelley and his heart twisted at the light shining in her eyes. Shaking his head, he said, "As long as Kelley's happy, that's all that matters to me." He hesitated then said to Marc, "You know your mother isn't going to be happy about this."

"Probably not." Marc shrugged. "She'll just have to get over it."

Good luck with that. But it was just what Eric wanted to hear for Kelley's sake. He narrowed his eyes. "You'd better be good to my sister, you big, scowling jerk."

Marc blinked, then his lips twitched. "Same goes."

Eric's insides knotted tighter and before he could reply, Marc approached him. "I owe you the same courtesy you just showed me. I'm sorry I haven't offered it sooner. As long as Jessica is happy, that's all that matters to me."

He held out his hand. Eric studied it for several seconds, his stomach cramping with what he had to tell them. Damn. He didn't want to mess up this peace offering, but what choice did he have? He shook Marc's hand then drew a bracing breath. "Thanks. But there's something I need to tell you. Both of you."

8

JESSICA HURRIED through the lobby, a beehive of activity in the center of which a smiling Helen Krause buzzed. She offered the woman a quick wave but didn't pause, intent on getting back to the cabin as quickly as possible. Her breakfast with her mother had taken far longer than she'd anticipated—it was almost eleven o'clock. She'd hoped Eric might be waiting for her in the lounge or lobby, but she couldn't blame him for not hanging around for four hours.

An image of him, when he'd looked at her just before he left her outside the restaurant with her mom, flashed through her mind. She'd never seen such an expression on his face before. He'd clearly been extremely upset. As was she. But Eric had appeared almost dazed. Furious—like a volcano ready to erupt, yet somehow also looking as if he'd just lost his best friend.

She'd wanted to talk to him, but she had to deal with her mother immediately. And now that she had, she needed to tell Eric about the compromise she and her mother had hammered out. And hope that he'd agree to it.

She exited the lodge and struck out on the freshly shoveled path, a smile tugging at her lips at the sight of a family making snow angels and a group of shrieking teenagers in the throes of a snowball fight.

She picked up her pace, her rapid breaths blowing vaporous puffs in the cold air. When she arrived at the cabin, she closed the door behind her and blinked against the sudden dimness, a stark contrast to the bright white glare of the snow. She was about to call Eric's name when she made out his shape, sitting on the edge of the bed.

"Sorry I took so long," she said, quickly removing her coat then walking toward him. "Did you think I'd deserted…"

Her words trailed off as she drew closer to him. He was leaning forward, his elbows braced on his spread thighs, his clenched hands hanging between his knees. He looked up at her as she approached him, his expression more serious than she'd ever seen it. He rose slowly, as if some great burden weighed him down and concern suffused her.

"Are you all right?" she asked, lightly grasping his arm.

He stepped away from her touch, something he'd never done before, and uneasiness slithered down her spine. Obviously he was still very upset. Not that she blamed him. "We need to talk," he said.

Yes, they did. But the way he said those words, in that grave tone, and his somber expression, her uneasiness morphed into dread. Her intuition warned her she wasn't going to like what she was about to hear.

Forcing a half smile, she said in the brightest voice she could muster, "Of course we do. I want to tell you about my extremely *long* conversation with my mother, although I'll give you the condensed version—"

"Jessica."

She stopped speaking at the sound of that single quiet word. He *never* called her Jessica. It was always Jess or sweetheart or some other endearment. She had to swallow to locate her suddenly missing voice. "Yes?"

"The conversation with your mother isn't what I need to talk to you about." He nodded toward the chair by the fire. "Maybe you should sit down."

Her stomach plummeted to her feet. Sit down? Oh, God. Nobody was ever told to sit down because whatever was coming next was good. She shook her head. "I'd rather stand."

A muscle ticked in his jaw and she wanted to reach out and touch him, but she suddenly felt as if she couldn't move.

"About what happened this morning at the lodge," he began.

A feeling akin to panic made her rush to say, "I know it was awful, but—"

"It was worse than awful. It was...intolerable." He looked away from her for several long seconds and when he looked back his eyes were filled with both sadness and regret. "I'm sorry," he said softly. "So sorry to have to say this, but I just can't do this anymore."

Jessica tried to draw a breath, but it seemed as if his words had sucked all the oxygen from the room. She licked her dust-dry lips. "What do you mean by 'this'?"

"I mean the wedding. I can't do it anymore. It's over."

She didn't need to worry any longer about the lack of oxygen in the room because her lungs seemed to have shut down, bringing her heart along with them. A deafening silence engulfed them and she stared at him, certain she must have misheard, but one look at his face told her she hadn't. He was utterly serious. While she'd feared this moment might come, somehow, deep in her heart, she hadn't truly believed it actually could.

Her entire body started to tremble. "You can't mean that," she whispered. "I know it's been difficult, but—"

"But now it's impossible," he broke in. "We both know why we came here. The arguments, the stress, the problems were just getting to be too much. Well, this morning they became too much. I'm done."

Little black dots swam before her eyes and she had to lock her knees to remain upright. "I...see." The anguished words were barely audible. Yet as soon as she uttered them she realized that, no, she didn't see. Not *at all*. A kernel of anger sparked to life in her stalled heart, flaming brighter with each passing second until she narrowed her eyes at him.

"So that's it? It's all over? Just like that?"

To his credit, he looked as ripped apart as she felt. "I'm sorry. But I hope we can—"

"Can what? Stay friends?"

He blinked then frowned. He opened his mouth to speak but she rushed on, tears flooding her eyes with each word. "How can you *do* this? Where's the man who said he loved me more than anything? Who wanted nothing more than to be my husband? The father of our children? Who wanted to grow old with me?"

His frown grew deeper. "He's right here." He leaned toward her and peered at her face. "Oh, crap, you're crying." He moved to the nightstand and ripped half a dozen tissues from the box there.

With shaking fingers she swiped impatiently at the wetness coursing down her cheeks but the tears were instantly replaced by a new flood. God, how was it possible to hurt so much? She felt as if her heart were hemorrhaging. "You sound surprised," she said, her voice trembling and bitter. "Did you think I'd turn cartwheels when you broke our engagement?"

His tissue-laden hand froze halfway to her cheek and he stared. "What are you talking about?"

She snatched the tissues from his hand and scrubbed at her eyes. Her diamond glimmered in the firelight and she squeezed her eyes shut to block out the sight of the ring that had represented all her hopes and dreams.

His hands cupped her wet face. "Jess, look at me. Sweetheart, please…"

A sob caught in her throat. Great. Not only did he not want her anymore, but he was tossing out pity endearments. She opened her eyes and found him staring at her, his confused gaze intent on hers. "You think I'm breaking our engagement?"

She blinked at the incredulous note in his voice. "Are… aren't you?"

"No! God, no. Never. No." He peppered kisses all over her wet cheeks. "How could you possibly think that?"

"Uh, I guess because you were saying things like 'it's over' and 'I'm done.'"

He wrapped one strong arm around her waist and yanked her against him. With his other hand he dabbed at her tears. "I was talking about *the wedding.* Not *us.*" He cupped her cheek in his palm and looked deep into her eyes. "Jess…I love you so much. I would *never* give up on us. Ever." There was no missing the hurt that flashed in his eyes. "I can't believe you'd think I would leave you."

Her relief was so intense she felt light-headed. "I'm sorry. At first I couldn't believe it. But you were so upset when we overheard my mother, and so serious now with your 'we need to talk.'" She kissed him, once, hard, then leaned back to glare at him. "You could have made yourself clearer, you know."

"I thought I *was* being clear."

"Yeah—like mud."

"In my own defense, it never occurred to me you'd think I was dumping you."

She framed his face between her still-not-quite-steady hands. "As if you could." She hiked up her chin. "I'm not an easy woman to dump."

"Sweetheart, it would be impossible. How could I live without my heart?"

Her chin quivered. "Okay, that was a very romantic thing to say."

"And totally true. Ending our engagement never once crossed my mind."

"You scared me to death."

"I'm sorry." He brushed his mouth over hers. "Sorry I scared you, sorry I made you cry." He raised his head and searched her eyes. "Forgive me?"

"I suppose." She sniffled. "But only if you promise never to frighten me like that again."

"Promise." A glint of humor flickered in his eyes. "Good to know, though, that you'd have missed me."

"Ha. I wouldn't have missed you one bit."

"Yeah, that's obvious, Miss Waterworks," he teased, gently blotting away the last remnants of her tears with the wad of tissues he pried from her fingers.

"I wouldn't have missed you because I wouldn't have let you

get away. I have silk scarves to tie you up with and I'm not afraid to use them."

He grinned. "You've been reading my letter to Santa again." Then his expression sobered. "Jess, what I was *trying* to say about the wedding is that it's caused nothing but problems, ones that seem to multiply no matter what we do. So let's not do it." He cupped her cheek in his hand. "I want to *marry* you, so I can spend the rest of my life with you. A fancy wedding doesn't make a damn bit of difference to me. Saying vows to you does." Clasping her hands in his, he dropped to one knee in front of her. "Jess, will you marry me? I mean *marry* me—not have a fancy wedding with me?"

Another batch of tears rushed into her eyes. A half laugh, half cry rushed from her. "Yes. God, yes. Please, yes." He stood and caught her up in his arms and spun her around until they were both laughing and breathless. And then he kissed her, a deep, passionate kiss that tasted of love and happiness. After he lifted his head, she said, "This is exactly what I wanted to talk to *you* about. I shared a very long and exhausting conversation with my mother, but it did us both a world of good. We cleared the air about a lot of things and after a lot of arguing, tears and finally some laughter, we came to an understanding."

"What's that?"

"First, that I love you and am going to marry you. If she doesn't accept that, our mother-daughter relationship will be irreparably damaged. And second, that this is *our* wedding. Yours and mine. And that we're going to plan something very small and intimate. That we might even decide to elope. Or jet off to Vegas. But we're going to do what *we* want, when we want. I told her if she'd like to throw a party for us sometime afterward, that would be fine, but that I really thought she should save her money and take a nice singles cruise. Maybe she'd meet a nice man and could someday plan her own extravagant wedding."

"And she accepted that?"

"It wasn't an easy sell and she's definitely disappointed since she's been dreaming of my wedding for years. But in the end she finally realized that she needed to accept our decisions even though they might not be the ones she'd make. I made it *extremely* clear that there was to be no more interfering or manipulating. I don't think she understood how bad she'd gotten, but I made her see the light and she apologized, as well as promised she'd try her best to do better. She really is a good mom. I honestly think she's just lonely."

"So let me get this straight—you'd already decided that you didn't want a big fancy wedding before I gave you my whole sales pitch?"

She grinned at his grumpy tone. "Yup." She looped her arms around his neck. "Great minds and all that."

"Great. So how would you feel about getting married here? Today? Now?"

She blinked. *"Now?"*

"Well, not right this minute, but in about—" he lifted his left arm and consulted his watch over her shoulder "—two hours?"

She was about to laugh, but something in his eyes stilled her. "You're serious."

"Extremely. When I realized I couldn't take the fancy wedding thing any longer, I decided to take matters into my own hands. Those four hours you were with your mom? I spent them making arrangements."

A wave of cautious joy spread through her. "But we're snowed in. How could you possibly make arrangements?"

"You forget my very formidable wedding planner sister is here. Between me, her and Helen and Roland Krause, things are rolling right along. Apparently Timberline Lodge is a popular wedding ceremony spot."

"But who would perform the ceremony?"

"Helen Krause. She's an ordained minister."

"But we'd need our marriage license."

"It's in my wallet—where I've kept it, safe and sound, since we got it two weeks ago."

Warmth spread through her. "So it looks like all systems are go."

"Yes. Well, except for one thing."

"What's that?"

"The bride-to-be hasn't yet accepted my proposal. Will you marry me today?" He gently kissed her lips.

The floodgates opened and happiness spilled through her. "Are you trying to get me to say yes?"

"Absolutely. Is it working?"

She smiled into his beautiful eyes. "Absolutely."

AT FOUR O'CLOCK that afternoon, Jessica looked up at the soaring Christmas tree in the lobby of the lodge. The surrounding area had been transformed into a beautiful, romantic chapel-like setting with swags of pine and holly and dozens of flickering white candles. The hint of vanilla and pine scented the air, and gentle violin music played in the background.

A warm nuzzle to the back of her neck had her sucking in a quick breath. A pleasurable tingle shimmied down her spine and with a smile she turned.

"Watch it there, mister," she said with a mock frown. "My husband won't take kindly to you kissing my neck."

He handed her a glass of champagne then touched the rim of his glass to hers. "Your husband is the luckiest guy on earth."

"His wife's pretty lucky herself. Do you realize we've been married for almost two hours?"

"Happy anniversary."

She laughed then heaved a contented sigh. "The ceremony was beautiful, wasn't it?" Roland Krause had walked her down the short length of white carpet to Eric, who wore a dark suit, white dress shirt and red silk tie and greeted her with a dazzling smile. With Marc serving as best man and Kelley as maid of honor, and with her mother looking on, snapping dozens of pictures from the disposable cameras she'd purchased at the gift shop, Helen Krause performed the simple, lovely ceremony that joined her and Eric for life.

"Beautiful," he agreed, drawing her close with his free arm. "As is my bride." His warm gaze skimmed over her simple winter-white dress. She'd brought it along—as Eric had his suit—in case they went out somewhere nice to dinner during their weekend away, never dreaming it would serve as her wedding dress.

"You look pretty beautiful yourself," she said. "Especially right here…" She kissed his lips, a gesture she'd meant to be quick and light, but he hauled her tighter against him and gave her a kiss that made her head spin.

"Wow," she said after he lifted his head. "Whoever said the romance fizzles out after you get married obviously knew diddly-squat. And speaking of romance…" She gently nudged his ribs and nodded toward the lounge area where Kelley and Marc sat at a table in the corner, heads close together, talking and laughing. "Can you believe how happy they look? I've never seen Marc look at any woman like that."

Eric nodded. "Good. That's how Kelley deserves to be looked at."

"I'm glad she took our decision to get married today in stride. Marc, too."

"I basically had the same talk with them that you had with your mom. I know she was disappointed not to have a fancy wedding to plan, but in the end she just wants us to be happy."

She smiled. "Mission accomplished."

"Agreed. My only regret is that we didn't do this four months ago."

"Actually, looking back, I think those four months were good for us. My mom finally understands I'm no longer a child and you and I are stronger together for surviving The Family Feud."

"Can't argue with that. Of course, we might have a front-row seat to Family Feud, Round Two, courtesy of Kelley and Marc." He shot a meaningful glance toward the corner of the lounge area.

Jessica nodded. "I think you're right. I spoke to Marc earlier about Kelley. He told me he felt like he'd been struck by light-ning the first time he saw her."

"He's a goner." Eric touched his lips to hers in a slow, soft kiss. "I know exactly how he feels."

"Good to know." She chuckled. "Can you imagine Kelley and my mom clashing over *that* wedding? Fun times ahead there."

"Right. If by 'fun' you mean 'migraine-inducing.' But hey— that's their problem. They'll have to figure it out just like we did."

"Amen to that. Although, by the time any actual wedding planning rolls around, Mom might have other things to occupy her time. Have you noticed the way Steve the bartender has been looking at her? And the way she's been looking back?"

"Oh, yeah. There's definitely a mutual admiration happening."

Jessica smiled into his eyes and saw all the love and passion she'd ever dreamed of looking right back at her. "Looks like we have a candidate for our 'get Mom a man' campaign."

"Sure does. Between her and Steve and Kelley and Marc, I'd say our work here is done. And that being the case, how about we say our goodbyes and get our honeymoon started?" He leaned down and nuzzled the sensitive skin behind her ear.

With a pleasure-filled sigh, Jessica tilted her neck to afford him better access. His teeth lightly grazed her earlobe, eliciting a barrage of tingles. "Are you trying to get me to say yes?"

"Absolutely. Is it working?"

She gave a happy laugh. "Absolutely."

* * * * *

HIS FOR THE HOLIDAYS
Joanne Rock

For Jacquie and Kathleen,
who made my first Christmas story such
a pleasure to write. Happy holidays, ladies!
I'm proud to share a cover with you.

1

FIND MOOSE-SHAPED form for holiday lights.

Finish invitations.

Hang Christmas cards in foyer.

Test new cocktail recipes (ask Trish when she's free so I don't get toasted alone).

On and on it went. Heather Dillinger's preholiday party to-do list covered four single-spaced pages on her computer screen, her schedule of expectations and obligations as vast as her mother's guest list. Not that her mother had asked for Heather's help, but she certainly expected it the same way she'd assumed her Type A daughter would jump in and help every year since she'd turned—what, twelve years old?

The problem that came with a lot of competence—and perhaps taking a *smidge* of pride in the fact—was that Heather had snowballed into the family workhorse.

Which reminded her. She needed to find a recipe for a drink called a snowball. It would be pretty to serve a white concoction on a silver tray full of prism-like snowflakes—the closest she'd ever come to the real thing in Savannah, Georgia.

"Have you mentioned the party to Gary, dear?" Loralei Dillinger-Digby floated into Heather's home office on a cloud of White Linen perfume, her arms full of the lemon-yellow tulle she insisted Heather use on her summer collection of household furnishings. Heather's start-up fabric company, The Attic, was enjoying its second year in the black and her mother was working hard to put her creative stamp on that success, not realizing she influenced Heather's designs without lifting a finger. Loralei Dillinger-Digby had that effect on people.

"Mother, I'm *not* inviting my former fiancé." The list in front of Heather's eyes seemed to stretch and grow as she anticipated the inevitable next ten suggestions for the annual event that had morphed from a family celebration into a neighborhood open house, into an opportunity to showcase her mother's coveted historic house on one of the city's oldest thoroughfares.

The thought reminded Heather she needed to hunt down that snowball recipe very soon. The party was next week and it was already Tuesday. Sampling each attempt at the recipe beforehand would definitely be in order if she expected to make it through this planning with her sanity in check.

"Gary is a wonderful catch, Heather, and if he's not to your liking we might as well at least steer him toward someone we know."

"*We* won't be steering him anywhere." She clicked closed her to-do list to face her mother, only to discover Mom pulling samples out of Heather's swatch books faster than she scooped up sales at Neiman's. "What are you doing?"

"Trying to find a color that would complement Trish's eyes so you can whip her up something suitable to wear for the party. Don't you think Gary would just love her?" Her mother turned to wave a scrap of ice-blue silk and a roll of silver piping. "How about something along this line?"

Heather's heart squeezed tight at the suggestion—for so many reasons she could barely untangle them all to address every facet that bothered her. She'd broken off an engagement with a wonderful guy three months ago and her family couldn't let it go. They'd loved Gary—a golf pro with a summer home on Hilton Head that had her mother planning vacations a decade in advance—and Heather's realization that she didn't love the man had caused a huge family uproar. Bad enough she'd been personally devastated to realize she didn't feel as deeply about him as she should. But having to defend the choice every day while trying to run a business and planning the party had been seriously draining.

Screw the snowball recipe. She'd head directly to the bourbon.

"Mom, Trish is my sister—"

"Half sister."

"—and she'd never go out with my ex-fiancé, even if he wasn't totally wrong for her. He's a golfer. She's in a rock-and-roll band."

Her mother's grip on the silk tightened.

"You never learned that opposites attract?"

An image of a tall, dark and killer-looking military man sprang immediately to mind along with one hot weekend Heather had never been able to forget. Seductive memories swamped her in a fast-forward scroll the second she let thoughts stray to that man. She'd tried her damnedest to forget Lieutenant Jared Tyler Murphy since he'd left for a stint overseas without even waking her to say goodbye…

Hell yes, she understood exactly how much opposites could attract and it pissed her off to no end when she'd never been able to settle the score with him. She found herself thinking of him more recently since she'd broken up with Gary. Part of her blamed her inability to settle down on the fact that she'd never put her past to rest with Jared.

"You're right, Mom." She spoke through clenched teeth, unwilling to release her jaw for fear a year's worth of stress would come flying out of her mouth and Heather's workaholic tendencies truly weren't her mother's fault. "I wish Trish all the best if she'd like to date Gary, but I don't have the time to make a dress before the party."

Trish could handle their mother's insane suggestion in a minute with one withering look, so Heather didn't need to borrow stress over nothing. It was just the party and the family expectations that were getting to her, especially with Heather's canceled wedding date looming.

While her mother launched into a tirade about the need for a good dress, Heather turned to check her e-mail after the chime of a note arriving in her in-box. She didn't recognize the sender—

NiteStalker12—but she figured it had to be spam since she didn't know anyone with that screen name. Still, the subject line intrigued her.

Have you seen snow yet?

Probably an ad pitch for a ski weekend up north, something that was worth a read considering the alternative entertainment was her mother's wheedling attempts to interest Heather in the dress project. Didn't she know Trish would rather wear distressed denim and leopard print than blue silk?

But all thoughts of the dress, the party and her mother dissipated as she read the contents of the note.

Heather,
After our first snowfall this year, I got thinking about you. I hope I'm not out of line contacting you after all this time, but according to the articles I found on you and your business—congratulations on that, by the way—it sounds like you've remained unattached. If that's true and you want to see a snowfall firsthand, I'd really appreciate the chance to see you again this Christmas. No strings attached, obviously. I live close to a nice bed-and-breakfast and I can get you a room there so it's not awkward. I know this is out of the blue, Heather, but it is the season for making peace and I never could forget you....
Jared

At the end of the note, he included a few details—a phone number for a place called the Timberline Lodge and some flight times out of Savannah if she wanted to make the trek to Lake Placid, New York, to see him.

Her heart was beating so fast she thought she'd launch into cardiac arrest. Jared wanted to see her again? Well, déjà vu, since she'd just been thinking about him. But maybe that wasn't such a coincidence since they'd met during the holiday season.

"So I assume from the long, drawn-out silence that you're

coming around to my way of thinking?" Her mother laid the blue silk on Heather's keyboard before she could close the e-mail, but thankfully, her mother didn't take any notice of the invitation from the One-Who-Got-Away.

The only man to ever leave her wanting more. Maybe that's what had upset her most about Jared's hasty exit from her life. He'd gotten to her the way no other man ever had and it hurt to think he'd been able to walk away without looking back. Until now...

"Actually, I am." Heather didn't need to compare her four-page to-do list to Jared Tyler Murphy's sparse invitation five years too late. She'd already made up her mind that spending time with the ghost of her Christmas past would be too interesting to pass up. Especially in light of her former fiancé's inevitable appearance at the family holiday festivities. "I was thinking that you seem to have a lot of great ideas for the party and it *is* your party after all."

Her mother nodded, a smile curving lips carefully drawn in fuchsia pencil.

"I'm so glad you agree—"

"So I think it's only right you take the reins this year and do it all the way you'd like." Heather knew most of the work was done anyhow—her four-page list had been more than double that last week—but still she savored her mother's moment of obvious dismay at the possibility of being outmaneuvered.

"Honestly, Heather, I'm sure—"

"I just got an invitation to the mountains this weekend, Mom." She grinned, enticed by the prospect of escape from obligation and lovingly pushy relatives for a few days. And the idea of settling an old score tantalized her more than it should.

Loralei appeared ready to breathe fire as she drew her shoulders back and pursed her lips tight, but Heather fully acknowledged she might be exaggerating the moment. Trouble was, she had one-upped her mom so few times in her life she had to make the most of it.

"You're not serious."

Heather's gaze flicked back to the screen and the promise of a little sensual revenge on her partner from the best weekend fling imaginable. A weekend fling that had pretty much ruined her for all other men from a sex point of view since he'd never given her the chance to take the relationship to its natural burnout conclusion.

"Mom, I'm very serious. I'm going to Lake Placid to watch a real live snowfall."

And, with any luck, she'd come home next week with a little of that northern ice on her heart where a very real wound used to be.

JARED MURPHY'S breath whooshed out of his lungs and he could have sworn someone took a crowbar to the backs of his knees when he spotted Heather Dillinger. Five years had passed since he'd last seen her asleep in her bed, naked and spooned against him at five-thirty in the morning before he left for a yearlong stint in Afghanistan. But she still had the same effect on him even after all this time, a powerful surge of primal interest that left him struggling for a rational thought.

Five years ago, he had tried convincing himself it was the beer goggles that had made him think she was the hottest woman he'd ever seen. Now, stone-cold sober and freezing his ass off outside the small municipal airport, he knew better.

"Heather." He wasn't sure if he spoke her name or just thought it, but she looked his way as she cleared the fence, tugging a small overnight bag on wheels behind her.

His Georgia peach. And yes, he'd actually called her that in those shared forty-eight hours that had burned hot in his brain for months and then years afterward. Her hair was longer than he remembered, the wavy chestnut mass tied close to the ends with a green velvet ribbon that trailed over her shoulder. Her dark wool coat grazed her calves, the tie cinching her small waist and accentuating her curves even through layers of winter clothes.

"This is incredible." She pulled off a pair of oversize amber shades and smiled in a way that would have warmed any man's heart.

Except that, as he watched her peer around in wonder at the small parking lot in the middle of the woods, he realized she wasn't talking about their reunion being incredible.

She only had eyes for the snow.

He definitely had to get his head out of the past if he wanted any chance with this woman. They'd fallen into bed together too fast last time, unsettling all the traditional rules of dating. He wouldn't make the same mistake this weekend.

"You like it?" He took the suitcase from her as she watched a handful of new flakes land on her palm.

"It's fluffier than I imagined." She brushed the melting snow away and met his gaze for the first time. "Nice to see you again, Lieutenant Murphy."

Her blue eyes remained straightforward, but he thought he heard something a bit "off" in her tone. Did she have mixed feelings about seeing him again? Or maybe she just thought he had appalling manners since she was standing in a snow squall without a hat or gloves.

"It's Captain now, actually. And it's good to see you, too. Let me walk you to the truck before you freeze." He nodded toward a silver 4x4 he used around town and they made their way through a handful of other vehicles toward it. Seeing how many cars had miniature wreaths attached to their front grills next to his bare fender reminded him how little he'd celebrated the season in recent years.

Stowing her suitcase in the extended cab, he helped her into the passenger seat and figured this had to be the most awkward reunion of his life. They were strangers who'd slept together, people from totally different walks of life. But—bottom line— he *had* to see her again.

"So you live up here now?" She craned her neck to see the peak of Whiteface as he pulled out of the lot and onto the main route. Holiday tunes filled the cab.

"I'm from downstate originally, but the scenery is nice up here. My uncle had a cabin in the mountains when I was a kid and I always liked it. He left it to me last year and I've been finding local work so I can stay."

He still had family downstate, but he didn't have all that much in common with his sisters who were all married with kids. He'd sort of disconnected in his years overseas. This place now felt more like him and his first investment was already paying off nicely with the demand for ski properties increasing. He'd been purchasing plots around town to build new or refurbish old cabins.

"You're out of the military?" Her voice carried that cryptic tone again, the odd note he couldn't identify earlier when she'd said it was good to see him.

"Yes." He was proud of his time served, but he could definitely understand the high burn-out factor. The stuff he'd seen would stay with him his whole life. "I still fly a little. I'm on standby for a Medivac copter and I do some rescue work on the mountains."

"So you've been out of the service for a while?" She kept her eyes trained out the windshield, as if mesmerized by the miles of pine trees drooping under the weight of snow. They passed a handful of houses with inflatable snowmen in the front yard and decorated trees on their porches.

"One year." It had been strange adjusting to his life after he got out, but he didn't plan to share the sleepless nights and a sort of survivor's guilt he sometimes experienced. That wouldn't exactly launch this reunion in the right direction.

"It's been a long time since we saw each other," she observed lightly, folding her hands in her lap. The backs of her knuckles were red from the cold. "I was surprised to hear from you."

Jared sensed the need to tread carefully, unsure of the emotional undercurrents he suspected were at work between them.

"No more surprised than I was that you agreed to come up here." He still couldn't believe she'd said yes after the way they'd parted with virtually no goodbye. All these years he'd wondered if she'd held a grudge about that, but she seemed genuinely pleased to be here if a little distant. Reserved.

"The timing turned out to be fortuitous." She rubbed her hands together. "I only wish I brought gloves."

He steered the truck onto the long driveway that would take them to the Timberline Lodge, a five-star property that drew guests from all over the world.

"You can pick up some clothes at the lodge, or you're welcome to wear a pair of my gloves. I can pick you up some things at my place and bring them back here when we meet up for dinner." He pointed out the lodge as they neared the building. "I made reservations in the dining room here, but we can go somewhere else if you'd rather."

He didn't want to sound presumptuous about dinner or anything else for that matter. He was determined to prove to her he wasn't the same guy he'd been five years ago—a live wire who thrived on the thrill of the moment. He'd talked her out of her clothes long before he'd considered how wrong that was when he had to ship out forty-eight hours later.

These days, he wanted to show her there was a hell of a lot more to him than that. And it didn't hurt that having her here for the holiday might help him banish a few ghosts of Christmas past.

"You're leaving?" She tore her gaze away from the lodge to look at him. "So soon?"

She sounded genuinely surprised and he hoped he wasn't playing it too conservative. Just sitting next to her in his truck cab was seriously turning him on. And oh, man, there were some big-time memories associated with this woman. Her lips were slicked over with something shiny that drew attention to the perfect bow shape, the luscious indent in the center of the top lip calling him to take a taste.

He'd done that and so much more with her mouth before...

He cleared his throat and willed away thoughts that would make him start sweating if he didn't get a handle on himself.

"I figured you would want to get settled—"

"Then you must not remember me very well." Grinning, she wiped clean a fogged-over spot on her window that the defroster had missed. "I'm not the type to settle. I've only got a weekend here and there's so much I'd like to do. I'd be surprised if I'll even be able to sleep tonight."

She sent him a look that sizzled over him like a fresh sunburn, reminding him they hadn't slept for more than an hour at a time when they'd last been together. They'd both been keyed-up. Wild. Hungry.

But her glance disappeared faster than it had arrived and he wondered if he'd read into the whole thing. Damn but he sucked at playing the gentleman with this woman.

"In that case, I'll put your bag inside and let them know you're here while you think about what you'd like to do." He parked the truck and pocketed the keys. "Just name your pleasure, and we're there."

"Really?" Her blue eyes seemed to light from within as she considered the prospect. "I'm going to hold you to the promise of giving me my pleasure, but first I'm going to find out if this is the kind of snow you can use for a snowball fight."

She was out of the truck and in the parking lot a second later, her boots kicking up a snowy rooster's tail in her wake as she ran. He scraped his chin off the steering wheel at her deliberate use of provocative words—damn it, that had been deliberate—and pulled her suitcase out of the back. He had almost recovered from swallowing his tongue when a snowball pelted him hard between the shoulder blades.

2

HEATHER'S HANDS had warmed up enough to make only one snowball but thankfully, her aim was perfect.

It felt good to nail her former lover right in the middle of his sexy-as-hell shoulders, especially after the way he'd played it so cool with her from the moment she'd stepped off the plane. Just what exactly did he have in mind to invite her all this way after all this time? Heaven knows he hadn't sent out any sex vibes the way he had once upon a time....

"EXCUSE ME." She sauntered up to the mega-hot Army-man in camo who'd been watching her all evening from a darkened corner table on a patio overlooking dark Georgia marshlands.

He'd been drinking with another camo-clad hottie up until about half an hour ago when his buddy left the outdoor bar with a squealing blonde draped around him like a wet towel. Heather had thought Mr. Eyes-All-Over-Her would finally make his move then, but he remained in his seat, his boots propped on a nearby stool as he tipped back his beer and stared unapologetically at her.

The season had been warm that year and the managers had brought in a rock band that cranked out butchered holiday tunes while waitresses wearing reindeer antlers served candy cane martinis.

"Yes?" He didn't bother to stand, his manners definitely not of the old-school Southern variety. He rattled a low-hanging crepe myrtle branch between his fingers where the garland-laden foliage crept over the back of his seat.

"I can't help but notice you've been staring at me all night."
She'd like to think the martini she'd had earlier made her bold,
but she tended to act on instinct anyway, a habit engrained in her
head years earlier.

"You've been putting on quite a show." Camo-man grinned
and there was something wildly feral about the display of white
teeth in the dark. They were far from the dance floor here, and
this part of the patio had grown deserted as more of the bar's
patrons came under the spell of the oddly hypnotic, guitar-
charged Christmas music.

"Excuse me?"

His big boots slid off the stool where he'd propped them and
he unfolded himself from his chair to stand. She'd misjudged his
height from his slouch and now she felt the full impact of the
man, the muscle and the uniform.

She swallowed.

"You don't have to excuse yourself with me." He reached out
to touch her cheek with the back of one knuckle in a move that
was too familiar by half and yet the slow drag of his skin over
hers made her eyes flutter dazedly in response. "I'm liking everything I see."

Her heart rate kicked up a notch as her rational mind acknowledged he stood too close to her. Still, having zero experience with this level of immediate sexual attraction, Heather
found the magnetic pull too strong to step away.

"It's not polite to stare." Her mother's words leaped out of her
mouth before she could stop them, the automatic response
kicking in because her own thoughts were all deeply engaged in
wishful physical scenarios with the man in front of her.

His bark of laughter was the sort of blatant amusement she
often took at her mother's attempts to instill manners on the
world around her.

"Do you want me to stop?" His question was direct and to the
point and she didn't know if she could answer it honestly.

His dark eyes bored into hers, seeking the truth, and something about the way he posed the question assured her he would respect her wishes. He wasn't playing games.

"No." Even though she took pride in acting on instinct, this was pushing it. But damn it, that was the truth. This man's eyes were pure aphrodisiac. "But if you're going to stare I think you at least owe me the courtesy of acting on those powerful looks you keep sending my way."

His hand fell away from her cheek and she could tell she'd surprised him. He might not be playing games, but he'd expected her to play them.

"Not here." He withdrew his wallet and slapped a twenty on the table, securing it with his half-empty beer bottle. "Will you take a walk with me?"

He gestured toward the wooden boardwalk that led out into the marshes among the tall grasses. The walkways snaked all through the wetlands before winding up back at the bar that sponsored the outdoor entertainment every Friday night.

Heather knew what kinds of things went on out on those darkened paths even though she'd never ventured out there herself. Extending her hand to him, she gave the high sign to her girlfriends and nodded her consent.

"It's about time, Army-man…"

THE STINGING in her hands pulled Heather from memories of that unseasonably warm Savannah night and the man who'd seduced her with his eyes long before he'd touched her. She wondered where that man had disappeared since the Jared Murphy standing in front of her now bore little resemblance to him. Physically they were the same. But the eyes that had captured her right from the start five years ago were shuttered now. Distant.

That remoteness would make it a lot tougher to seduce him in order to take a little sensual revenge.

"You really need a pair of gloves." Apparently unconcerned about the snowball to his back, Jared lifted her hands and cupped them between his own.

The unexpected touch set off trip wires all over her nervous system, sending her whole body into hyperawareness mode. It didn't help that she'd just been daydreaming about their first meeting, a time when she'd allowed herself to be hypnotized by the delicious pull of sexual chemistry.

She'd been so wrapped up in those old memories she hadn't noticed him leave her suitcase on the dry sidewalk while he followed her into the snow-covered courtyard in front of the lodge.

"I've got a better way to warm up." She blurted the statement with all the finesse she'd used when she first met him and she'd parroted her mother's words. Of course, her comment now was a hell of a lot less starchy.

And she had to start somewhere if she was ever going to get him in bed this weekend.

Jared didn't speak for a long moment, as if weighing the wisdom of continuing the conversation. Now this facet of him, the brooding thinker—she recognized. He might have grown more aloof in the past five years, but at least now she'd spotted a hint of the fiery depths she remembered beneath the controlled surface.

"As a veteran of North Country winters, I think I might know a little more about warming up than you." Still cupping his fingers around hers, he drew their interlaced hands up to his mouth and breathed into the gap between his thumbs.

The warmth of his breath soothed her raw fingers stinging from those moments when she'd plunged them into the snow. Their eyes met over their joined palms and she felt the electric jolt of that connection clear down to her toes.

She swayed toward him like a hypnotized woman, her whole body responding to the source of heat that could set all of her on fire with the merest of prompting. She licked her lips in preparation for more.

"Is that better?" Jared's roughened voice cut through her romantic notions as he released her.

Her hands hovered helplessly in midair for a few seconds until she pulled herself together. What kind of seductress would she make when she fell into a swoon like some hapless teenager every time this man came near her?

She had to get the upper hand here, and fast. Heart racing with thwarted longing and more than a little bruised pride, Heather did her best to shrug off her dazed attraction so she could channel her inner temptress.

"Not bad, Army-man." She let the old nickname drawl off her tongue like a verbal caress. "But I'll bet we would have created a lot more heat with my method."

Tucking her hands safely into her coat pockets, she swished past him with a hip strut in full swing.

In your face, Murphy.

Her performance wasn't bad for a woman who hadn't flirted in years. But she would have her small slice of revenge if it killed her, and judging by the heart palpitations churning her blood into hot surges, she figured it very well might.

So THAT'S THE WAY she wanted to play.

Jared watched Heather walk away for so long he nearly didn't make it in time to hold the inn door for her. Damn it. He'd changed so much in the years since he had last seen her and he thought she would have, too. When he read about her linen business online there had been interviews with her that made her sound more…sedate.

But in person, Heather Dillinger was as much a firecracker as she'd ever been. He didn't know if he should be worried or insanely grateful at his good fortune.

Locking down the mess of reactions she stirred in him, Jared stalked past the huge decorated tree in the lobby to help her check in at the front desk.

The Timberline Lodge was a Lake Placid historic site, built as a great camp in the 1800s and converted to a bed-and-breakfast by owners who had fallen on hard times just before the Olympics came to the small town in 1932. Apparently the family had discovered a real affinity for the business, because the inn had been in continuous operation since then. The current owners, Roland and Helen Krause, had added several self-sufficient cabins to the grounds since taking over the operation, including five that Jared helped to restore when he first came back home.

"Jared Murphy, thank goodness you're here." Helen stepped out from around the reception desk to wrap him in a hug, the google eyes of her bright red reindeer sweater jabbing him in the chest. "Have you heard the forecast? We're expecting a major snowstorm."

"Really?" Heather stepped closer to the counter and Jared could see Roland was smitten in about two seconds.

The older couple had raised five kids of their own but still had room in their hearts to lavish affection on newcomers of all ages. At least, that's why Jared figured the Krauses showed up on site at his restoration projects every day with food from the kitchen and lots of approving feedback on his progress. They were first-rate people in his book and Jared hadn't been able to beg his way into paying for Heather's room for the weekend. They'd insisted his friends were family to them, end of discussion.

"It's a bona fide nor'easter." Roland leaned his elbows on the counter, the jingle bell on his Santa hat clanging on his shoulder as he made himself more comfortable. "I hope you brought a hat."

"Actually I'm in the market for one, but I saw lots of great stores along the water as we drove in." Heather signed her name in the leather guest register. "I thought I packed enough warm clothes, but it's hard to appreciate what this kind of cold feels like until you're in it."

When Roland discovered Heather was a Savannah native, he started regaling her with stories of a family trip down South when his children were young. Helen took the opportunity to pull Jared aside.

"Weren't you stationed in Savannah?" She had that knowing matchmaker look in her eyes and Jared hated to disillusion her that his only meeting with Heather had been more carnal than romantic.

"Yes, ma'am." He figured it would be better to offer up as few details as possible than stretch the truth.

"And you met her while you were there." Helen smiled away, her reindeer's eyes jouncing around as she practically bobbed on her toes at the idea of romance at the inn.

"Yes, but we didn't really have time to get to know each other all that well." That was true enough. "I just thought of her again recently and—"

Okay, this was where the truth stretching began since he'd thought of her many, many times before *recently*.

Shrugging, he didn't bother trying to salvage his story.

"I thought she might like to see snow," he finished lamely just as Roland had gotten to a punch line that had Heather laughing so hard she clutched the counter for support.

"Well I hope you show her more than just some snow-seeing," Helen advised in a conspiratorial whisper before she hurried back to her spot behind the counter and intervened in the start of her husband's next tale. "Roland Krause, that's quite enough for our guest who needs to shop for a hat and find her room."

Taking his wife's hint with the ease of a man who'd been married for more than half his life, the innkeeper straightened and pulled his Santa hat off his head before settling it on Heather's.

"The missus is right, but this will at least tide you over until you find something else." He affixed the hat at an angle so that the jingle bell fell right above the green velvet ribbon holding Heather's hair. "You make a right pretty elf."

"Thank you." Heather jingled the bell as if to test it. "I'm looking forward to this weekend."

Helen passed an envelope with a key over the desk to Jared.

"We won't let you leave until you've had a marvelous time, will we, Jared?"

He braved a glance in Heather's direction and wondered what a sexy Southern Christmas elf would expect from him in order for her to have a good time. The teasing look in her blue eyes communicated wicked intent.

"Not a chance." He thanked the older couple as he rolled Heather's bag away from the desk and deeper into the hotel.

Right out the back door.

"Are you sure you're going the right way?" Heather paused on the threshold of the door to check the packet containing her key card.

"The cabins are in the back. You can come up to the main building for meals, but this way you can watch the snow fall from all four sides and the fireplaces are wood-burning." He took a left at an intersection in the sidewalk toward the cabins he'd worked on. "Gas fires are pretty but—"

"Less atmospheric." She walked more slowly behind him and at first he thought she wanted to take in the scenery, but when he looked back to check on her he realized the walkways were getting slick as the snow fell in earnest.

Damn it. Could he be any more clueless? He was so busy running away from an overwrung sex drive that he'd ended up being downright rude. Leaving the suitcase, he jogged the couple of steps between them to give her his arm.

Just as he reached toward her, her boot skidded on the sidewalk, sending her flying forward. She careened into his arms and he caught her easily, but the quick step he needed to make caused his feet to slide, too.

He squeezed her tighter, protecting her if they went down. But he was able to find his footing again. He met her gaze in the swirl of white all around them and what he saw there shifted the ground out from under him faster than any icy walkway.

No teasing. No flirtation. Just simple hunger and want she didn't bother to disguise as anything else.

In other words—the exact same thing he was feeling as he held her for the first time in far too long. Her fragrance was exactly the same, a heady mix of floral and musk that had remained in a pink hair scarf she'd tucked into his pants pocket without him knowing.

He'd sniffed that silk dry in those first few months overseas, a tangible reminder of life and joy in a stark hell.

Something about that memory prodded him into action despite all the talks he'd had with himself about restraint. Bending over her, he covered her lips and damned the consequences.

3

HEATHER HAD NEVER thought of herself as having an addictive personality. But Jared's kiss made her rethink that position.

Far away in the back of her mind, some obnoxious little piece of herself shouted shrilly that she should be the seducer and not the seducee yet again. But, dear, sweet Lord. The shrew within probably just needed to get laid because a kiss this good didn't deserve to be stopped under any circumstances.

Her arms tightened around his neck, savoring the wall of solid shoulders beneath them. The heat of him around her fired away any chill at being outdoors in a snowstorm, his body a furnace of taut muscle and rigid angles. And speaking of rigid…

She was wrapped around him so thoroughly she felt the full extent of his desire for her, every impressive inch of him tattooed against her stomach.

He broke the kiss before things got any more carried away and he tipped his forehead to hers while she caught her breath. Or maybe he was waiting to catch his. She noticed their ragged inhalations rasped in synch.

"I swear I didn't ask you up here to take advantage of you." His words took a long moment to make sense inside her scrambled thoughts.

When they did, they stung.

"Since when would I allow myself to be taken advantage of?" Did she look like a woman who wasn't in control of her own desires? Okay, not counting the way she allowed her family to maneuver her. And even then, she drew lines when necessary.

She stepped back, out of his reach.

"I didn't mean—"

"Furthermore, if and when I let you take me, I can assure you it will only be to my advantage." She stressed the last word, turning his phrase back on him as she spun on her heel and walked away.

For all of two steps. Before she remembered she had no idea where she was headed. She'd never possessed her mother's flare for dramatic exits, but then, she had precious little practice since she preferred to run her life based on hard work instead of high emotions. Unfortunately her practical nature seemed to fly out the window around Jared.

"It's the second cabin on the left." He pointed the way, apparently guessing her dilemma. He already had her suitcase in hand and he held out his arm to her.

A nice enough offer since she would have fallen on her butt earlier if not for his quick reflexes. And decidedly strong arms, a mutinous voice in her head reminded her.

"Thank you." She took his arm for the rest of the trek, hoping against hope she could pull herself together and stay focused for the weekend.

She didn't come to Lake Placid just to see snow or escape the family resentment over her failed engagement. Her number one reason for this trip was to leave Jared Murphy naked and alone in his bed on Sunday morning so he would know how if felt to be abandoned and left wanting…

As they reached the cabin, Jared slipped the key card from her hands and used it to open the lock. Their arrival chased away her dark thoughts for the moment and she allowed herself to take in the charm and beauty of the place.

White clapboard siding made the cabin blend in with the snowy landscape, but the numerous windows were bracketed by black shutters and a small wreath with a red bow had been hung on each set of glass panes. The classic holiday decorations continued with a length of fresh greenery roped all around the entryway. Scented smoke puffed from nearby chimneys, lacing the snowy air with the smell of burning hickory or maybe pecan—something nutty and sweet. A six-foot toboggan rested against the cabin as if waiting for her to take it for a spin down one of the neighboring hills. Mountains, actually.

Peering over her shoulder she took in the pristine scenery once more. The inn property nestled on a mountainside as the faint smudge of sunlight sank deeper in the sky.

"Heather?" Jared held the door for her, waiting for her to enter the cabin and she experienced a twinge of guilt for her thoughts of sensual vengeance.

What if Jared had really gotten in touch with her to smooth over their past or make some kind of amends? He'd certainly chosen a charming setting and not some cheap interstate motel that smacked of a one-nighter.

"Sorry," she murmured, too confused to sift through what this weekend together might mean. For now she simply stepped into the cottage and out of the snow. "Wow. This is really wonderful."

Tugging off Mr. Krause's Santa hat, Heather peered around the cozy space with a practiced eye, enjoying the authentic touches to make the place look more like an Adirondack great camp.

"You like it?" Jared set her suitcase inside and pulled the door shut behind him before approaching the fireplace where a bundle of wood had already been laid.

"It's so full of warmth and character." She ran one hand along the rough-hewn boards that made the interior look like a log cabin.

At the far end of the room, Jared used a long stick of fat wood to light the fire inside a gray stone hearth. The living area furniture all faced the fireplace, the pieces just mismatched enough to make it look like a family homestead instead of a hotel. A pair of old skates hung on the wall, the silver blades polished to gleaming even though the leather was worn and cracked.

Framed pictures of Olympic events hung in a grouping near the entry while an antique game table sat to one side of the living room. The hallway that must lead to a bedroom was at the far end while the kitchen was situated on the opposite side, the appliances small and well-proportioned for the scale of the space. And although the gas range was antique-looking with cast-iron grills, Heather knew the model was modern.

"I'm glad you like it." Jared stirred the pile of sticks with the poker until the flame he'd fanned began to steady.

"If I tossed a few pieces of fabric across the couch, this place could be an advertisement for The Attic." She worked hard to incorporate this same kind of easy timelessness in her designs. An antique sensibility minus the fussiness.

Standing, Jared walked toward her, lighting sparks within her faster than he'd ignited the blaze in the fireplace.

Thankfully he dropped onto the arm of the couch a few feet away, sparing her wound-up emotions the agitation of his physical nearness.

"I read some about your business online. It sounds like you're doing very well."

The compliment pleased her, as did the interest she read in his gaze. Slipping out of her coat, she prepared to tell him about The Attic but the phone rang before she could speak. Frowning, she searched for the handset and found an old-fashioned black telephone with a round dial on a table behind the sofa.

"Excuse me." She picked up the receiver, expecting to hear from the innkeeper or his wife.

"Heather, thank God you're there. Why aren't you picking up your cell?" Her sister's voice blasted into her ear on the other end. With the vocal cords of an opera diva and the projection of a kindergarten teacher, Trish never had a problem making herself heard. "Never mind. What's important is that mom is trying to set me up with Gary. Have you heard about this?"

Heather tried not to let her frustration show in front of Jared. Not that she was angry with Trish, because heaven knew if her mother tried to set up her up with Trish's former fiancé, Heather would have wanted to vent, too. Especially since Trish's exes tended to be heavily tattooed, pierced and emaciated by the rock-and-roll lifestyle.

Mostly Heather was frustrated because her problems had followed her a thousand miles north.

"I know and I'm sorry."

"Don't you be sorry." Trish sounded offended that Heather would dare apologize and she roundly cursed family politics.

"If it makes you feel any better, she's mad at me for not sewing you a dress for the party so you could make a good first impression."

Trish snorted. "I think my nose ring was all the first impression Gary wanted from me."

"Yes, well, the fallout pressure from The Wedding That Wasn't turned out to be more than I could take, so I'm hiding out for a few days if you could just burn this phone number, okay?" She shifted uncomfortably, unable to leave the room since the phone in the cabin was circa 1940.

Jared stood to peer out the window at an incredible lake view Heather hadn't even gotten to enjoy yet. Damn it, she shouldn't let her family intrude on this weekend. When she wasn't seducing Jared into making him regret walking away from her, she could be outside playing in the snow.

"You? Being the bad girl for a change?" Trish squealed on the other end of the phone and Heather thought she slipped into that octave range that would make animals cringe. "Well, I can't wait to hear what made Little Miss Junior Peach Blossom turn rogue, but I'll let you get back to whatever hell you're raising up there at the North Pole or wherever you are."

In the interest of temporary peace, Heather said goodbye, ignoring her sister's—half sister's—implication that Heather could never raise hell.

As she hung up the phone, she glimpsed at Jared's back silhouetted against the window where the scarcest of daylight now illuminated the lake. She opted to skip mentioning the phone call altogether and joined him by the window, hoping they could resurrect their talk about her business. Maybe he hadn't even heard about the wedding she'd mentioned.

She didn't know how or when she'd get back to seduction tonight, but Trish's phone call had taunted her to follow through on the plan. Being a good girl had given her one broken heart, one broken engagement and a reputation as the Woman-Most-Likely-to-Answer-Her-Cell-Phone.

Tonight would be different.

JARED WAITED outside a store in the Olympic Village in downtown Lake Placid while Heather bought a hat later that evening. Over a foot of snow had fallen since she'd touched down that afternoon and the inches kept accumulating. He hadn't bothered to drive his truck into town since the village was walking distance from the Timberline Lodge. Heather had already made a few comments about the fact that he'd never be able to drive home tonight, implying he should sleep over at the cabin although she'd never said it outright.

Peering over his shoulder at her through the glass panes in the store's front window, Jared watched her charm the guy behind the counter in that effortless way she had. He'd gotten so much pleasure out of watching her that first night they'd met, observing how she turned heads everywhere she went. Not because she was exceptionally beautiful, but because of the comfortable way she carried herself, the ease with which she worked a room or bartered down the price on a knit hat. People wanted to make her happy, partly because her smile was an addictive drug that could bring a man to his knees, but more because she radiated a warmth of spirit that people could spot a mile away.

He knew he wasn't the only one who'd noticed this. That first night at the outdoor bar, he'd seen the way her girlfriends listened to what she had to say, the way she was always at the center of the group and still managed to be the first to reel in an outsider. The bartender looked to her for the group order. The bouncer flirted with her first. The band sent out a tune to her. And judging by how fast her cabin phone rang earlier, Jared guessed her family relied on her. She'd admitted her half sister had been on the other end but then she'd clammed up about the call, including a mystery wedding in the family.

Hell, he hoped it hadn't been hers she skipped out on this weekend. Maybe she'd just had a spat with a family member Bridezilla or something.

"What do you think?" Heather appeared in front of him suddenly as he heard the jingle of the store door chime while it closed.

She wore a sky-blue knit cap with a snowflake stitched on the front and gloves that matched. She'd taken her hair down from the ribbon that held it earlier, so the mass of chestnut waves spilled haphazardly over the shoulders of her dark wool coat.

"All you need are some ski poles and the locals would never know you're not a genuine snow bunny."

"I'm not even going to ask about snow rabbits or why I resemble one." She looped her hand through his arm and his insides contracted at the ease with which they moved together.

The kiss they'd shared earlier had never been far from his thoughts. Of course, fantasizing about what that kiss might have led to only hurt his cause to make Heather look at him as a man with more to offer than being able to last all night long. Damn it, he needed to make things right between them if he ever hoped to expel the memories of one crap Christmas after another. Even last year—when he'd first come home from overseas—he'd spent the holiday holed up in a stripped-down cabin to work on renovations in the hope of blasting away bad memories.

This weekend, he'd be making some new memories to replace those and who better to supplant all those dark thoughts than a woman who could light up the whole freaking village with one sexy grin?

"Ski bunnies are the visitors who are new to the slopes." He steered her past a couple of antique shops and a street vendor selling hot chestnuts. "They usually dress better than the pros who wear their gear every day."

"Kind of like the northern golfers who show up on Hilton Head with spiffy new clubs and no idea what they're doing?"

"Bingo." He tossed his pocket change into a bucket for a bell-ringing Santa, then stopped by the wooden toboggan run erected over the frozen lake.

"So you've just insulted me and my new snowflake hat." She peered up at the weatherworn contraption where kids climbed a winding set of stairs to the top with sleds of every color. "No wonder tourism is so much bigger down South where we are gracious and welcoming to our guests."

"You realize we only show up in the South so we can make fun of your accents, right?" He could listen to her talk all day long, and he had the feeling if he ribbed her about that sweet Southern drawl she'd only pour it on thicker.

"We just like to speak *s-l-o-w-l-y* to y'all as a subliminal cue to take a deep breath and relax once in a while before y'all keel over from the self-importance of your frantic pace." She smiled sweetly and pointed to the toboggan run. "Now, if you're done trying to make me out to be Ellie Mae in mittens, could you tell me what that is?"

She craned her neck to see where the network of wooden tunnels and archways ended but trees hid the outlet over the water.

"It's a sled run that shoots you out onto the ice." He figured they'd be better off out in the snow than in the all-too-heated atmosphere of her cabin back at the lodge, so he planned to push outdoor fun to the limit tonight. "Want to try it?"

She was already picking up a toboggan at the foot of the platform.

Jared paid for the rental and the ride and followed her up the stairs to the chute, taking the toboggan from her. At nearly six feet long, the wooden sleds were awkward but fast as hell.

They moved through the line quickly since the families were beginning to disperse now that it was almost nine o'clock. The sled run was lit all the way down to the ice, the snow shimmering in the reflected glow as they reached the top.

"Oh, my God." Heather watched as the kids in front of them fell off to one side on their way down the shoot. "Is this dangerous?"

"It's one hundred and sixty-six feet of fun, babe." He plunked the sled down at the top and waited for her to get on. "But just in case, you'd better sit in front."

"The front?" Her question was accompanied by shrieking from the next trail over as another group went down the twin chute.

"That's the safest place." He helped her get settled on her knees and then realized he'd need to wrap his legs around her if he wanted to keep her steady.

The position shouldn't be a big deal since she wore a long winter coat that tucked around her where she sat.

"Well?" She turned around to peer at him, her cheeks flushed pink from the cold. "Ready?"

He remembered other times he'd seen her fair skin suffused with color like that, right before she hit her peak...

"Yeah," he lied, straddling the sled and lowering himself to sit behind her.

"Oh." She let out a note of surprise at his sudden proximity, his boots tucking under the front of the sled so his thighs bracketed her hips. *"Ooh."*

She settled against him, leaning her back into his chest and shifting her legs to fold beneath her. The movement wriggled her butt right into his lap and he acknowledged all the snow in the world wouldn't be able to cool him off if they kept this up.

Ah—poor choice of words.

He ground his teeth against a surge of primal possessiveness.

"Hold on," he warned her, using his arms to tip the sled forward down the chute.

Gravity shifted, pushing them into their seats as they tore across the icy run. Heather screamed and wrapped her arms around his knees, squeezing him tight to her. It was probably the ideal date for a hormonal teenager, but damn it was killing him. Her hair blew back on one side of his face, the silky strands whipping in the wind and couching him in her scent. He slipped his arms around her waist to anchor her to the sled, his hands aware of the exact distance between his thumbs and the underside of her breasts.

Are we there yet?

Jared squeezed her hips with his legs as they flew over a small rise in the run that had them airborne for a few heart-stopping seconds. Heather murmured something that sounded like "Ohmigod, ohmigod, ohmigod" under her breath then squealed with delight when they touched down on the frozen ice and skidded to a stop midway across the lake.

For a tantalizing moment, they sat there, breathless from the run and seared together by the soaring temperatures wherever their bodies touched. If he shifted his arms or his weight a little bit, he could roll her right underneath him, his body perfectly aligned with hers...

"Don't let go." She whispered the words a fraction of a second before he would have bolted from the sled, her hands tightening on his knees.

He froze there, oblivious to the other tobogganers who must be coming down the chutes. Luckily their combined weight had propelled their sled much farther than the younger kids who took the ride, so they were fairly out of view beyond the lights of the run.

"I don't think—"

She turned sharply in his arms, the movement applying exquisite—excruciating—pressure between his legs.

"Then maybe you need to stop thinking so damn much," she chided him in a wispy voice that sounded as strangled with want as he felt inside. "There is such a thing as overthinking, Murphy, and the reason we got along so famously five years ago is that neither of us worked so hard at it that we got confused. Some things you need to just let happen."

His brain told him she was dead wrong. He'd seen the effects of *let it happen* mentality play out when his brother had gone into the service a year before him, leaving behind a new bride he didn't know was pregnant. Jessie had missed the birth of his son and alienated his wife because he'd married a woman he didn't know very well without taking the time to build a relationship first.

But Jared stopped listening to his brain when Heather brushed her lips across his, her body splayed against him with total abandon. She was every bit as wild and willing as he remembered, and he was as captivated as ever by that.

Heat blasted through him as her hips settled against his, her hands fumbling with the zipper on his jacket before she eased it down a few inches, just enough to expose his chest. A growling sigh wrenched up his throat at the feel of her fingers spread across his shirt.

He unbuttoned her coat, his leather gloves sliding on the fabric as he opened it wider. *Just for a minute,* he told himself. The lights shut off on the run behind him, signaling the close of the chutes and deepening the privacy of their corner of the frozen lake.

He cupped a breast in one palm, hating the barriers between them even after he slipped beneath her sweater. Still, her muffled moan into his mouth told him she found the caress of leather pleasurable so he kept the glove in place, fondling the tight peak of her breast.

"Take me," she mumbled against his mouth, her hips twitching with new urgency between his legs.

"Here?" He blinked through the fog of lust to gauge their position and saw her white teeth flash a smile.

"No. Take me home and then take me. Or take me anywhere. Just—" She nipped his lower lip with a damp bite. "Please let's go somewhere."

"Amen." He gave her nipple one last soft pinch before extracting his hand from her sweater. "I've got to turn in the toboggan, but if you wait for me here, the lodge is fairly close on the other side of the lake."

"Hurry." She eased off of him and peered around the ice before pointing to a nearby warming shed. "I'll wait over there."

He was already on his feet, cursing the raging erection that kept him from sprinting back to the sled rental place.

"I'll be back in five minutes, no more."

"Make it four and we can relive our last outdoor make-out session on the way home." Her hand drifted down his thigh and squeezed.

Memories of their walk through the Savannah marshes steamrolled him, flooding his head with images of Heather sinking to her knees…

"Four," he promised, heart sledgehammering his chest because he was an idiot to have thought this weekend could have led anywhere else but to bed.

His feet were moving fast in spite of the heavy desire flooding his veins because he was a man on a mission now. Heather might think they were just reliving the past this weekend, but he knew the outcome was going to be different from anything she expected.

4
_____

HEATHER WAS practically crawling out of her skin and they hadn't even reached the halfway point on their trek to her cabin.

Jared had been insistent about no quickies in the woods even though she'd made a couple of attempts to convince him otherwise.

"Talk about role reversal," he muttered under his breath as he tugged her up the next hill in the snow.

"What?" Her brain was so passion-fogged it only seemed to click along at half speed.

She'd forgotten how he could make parts of her ache with a fierceness close to pain.

"I remember a time when it was me trying to sweet-talk you into a close encounter in the woods."

Trudging through a drift behind him, she had to smile at the memory....

"NO ONE CAN SEE you except for me." Jared's words wound persuasively around her in the moonlight.

They'd walked so far away from the outdoor bar that the band's holiday riffs faded into a dull rumble. The breeze blew in off the marsh, enveloping them in the scents of briny water and mud. She had her back to the marsh, her spine pinned to a wooden railing that ran the length of the boardwalk snaking through the wetlands.

"You think knowing that I only have an audience of one is going to make me strip naked for you here? Now?" Her heart had developed an all-new rhythm around him, sort of a cardiac hyperspeed. In fact, all of her senses felt elevated to a higher pitch with him nearby.

"I thought we weren't going to play games with each other." His hands curved around her waist, his fingers on one hand brushing under her tank top while his fingers on the other dipped into the waist of her denim miniskirt.

She didn't know which felt better, but she knew she wanted more time to figure it out.

"I'm not playing games." Her fingers tunneled under the sleeves of his black T-shirt, savoring the rock-hard muscle of him.

She had to remember to write Uncle Sam a letter to thank him for the superb conditioning that resulted in such a magnificent male specimen.

"Then why can't you admit you want to get naked with me as much as I want to start peeling your clothes off?" His penetrating stare made his words a challenge.

Coming from any other guy, she could have balked at the level of he-man arrogance in that statement. But with Jared, that would have amounted to more game-playing and they'd said they weren't going that route tonight. Jared traced the hem of her panties around the curve of her hip and her knees buckled.

"I can admit it, but there's nothing wrong with me saying I'm not taking off my clothes in a Georgia swamp after midnight with a perfect stranger." A woman had her standards after all. "Maybe we could see each other tomorrow."

She could get naked with him then, after she'd had time to think rationally when she wasn't under the influence of hormones and peppermint schnapps.

"We could do that." His other hand splayed across her spine, covering an incredible amount of terrain. "Although I ship out of Savannah in—" he checked his watch "—twenty-nine hours. And technically it is tomorrow."

Her heart stuttered in her chest.

"That's not some kind of line, is it?" She hadn't grown up in a city home to both an Army and an air force base without hearing about that kind of ploy before. His hands stilled on her body.

"No games. I had a drink with a friend tonight because I'm Afghanistan-bound first thing Sunday morning. I'm looking at a yearlong stint."

The news sucked for him more than her, and after only knowing him for all of an hour, it damn well sucked in her book. But then, his intensity, his refusal to play games, his ability to lay all his cards on the table for her tonight made perfect sense. She'd found out earlier that he was a helicopter pilot—a dangerous job in a war zone. No doubt he was living for the moment tonight.

The silence stretched as she thought about that. About *him* and the reality of what he'd signed on for.

And in the space of another heartbeat, she made up her mind. She was already so hot for this man she was about to catch fire. Besides, didn't she consider herself a patriot?

Well, cue the "Star Spangled Banner," because Jared Tyler Murphy was one American soldier who would head off to his overseas assignment with all the fireworks he could handle.

"Then it looks like you're coming home with me, Army-man."

WHEN THEY REACHED her cabin, Heather handed Jared the key card, her nerves too jangled to use it. She felt as though she'd received a shot of that peppermint schnapps from all those years ago, her whole body humming with energy and pulsating sensations. She stepped back and bumped into a reindeer made of willow branches with a wreath around its neck.

Jared unlocked the door and pulled her inside before sliding the bolt. The sound of the security lock shooting into place had a finality that sent a shiver up her spine while she bent to plug in the lights on a tabletop tree decorated with red bows.

He turned to look at her, their eyes connecting for an instant before he pulled her into his arms and started pulling off her clothes. Her hat. Mittens. Coat.

"You're back." She smiled to see the laser intensity of his eyes, the heat steaming off of him as he watched her.

"What?" He didn't break his stripping stride as he turned his attention to his own clothes. Jacket. Shirt. T-shirt.

Clearly getting out of the Army hadn't affected his dedication to his workout routine. Her mouth watered at the sight of sculpted abs and sinewy arms.

"The look in your eyes that I remembered from five years ago. I wondered earlier where it went, but it seems to have returned."

With a vengeance.

The phrase popped into her head unbidden and she remembered her own plans for a taste of revenge. Right now all she cared about was having a taste of him.

"I wanted to move slower this weekend." He unbuttoned her blouse while he looked in her eyes, demonstrating extraordinary deftness with women's clothes. "I tried."

"I would have had to hurt you if you tried any harder." Her threat didn't carry much weight considering she melted in his arms.

"God, I missed you." He growled the admission into her neck as he lowered his mouth to kiss her there.

His lips covered a pulse point under her chin and he paused there, circling the throbbing vein with his tongue. She shivered at the heat of it, the tenderness of his words echoing in her ears.

I missed you.

She'd have to be made of stone for those words not to affect her. Wrenching herself away from the kiss, she placed her hands on his chest to hold him back, her pink polished fingernails appearing seriously outmatched by the strength of his pecs. She studied him in the dim light from two miniature lamps on either side of the fireplace. And damn it, she'd bet anything that he wasn't lying. He *had* missed her. Thought about her. Felt something for her.

And didn't that just shift her whole perspective?

"Kiss me." She heard herself say what she'd been thinking, the veil between actions and feelings stripped away along with the blouse he shoved off her shoulders. "Take me."

JARED KNEW a green light when he saw it and nothing would be stopping him now.

His lips found hers. Tasted. Savored and devoured by turns. Her tongue stroked his, her whole body pressed into him. Slipping a hand under her hair, he stroked her nape.

She made a sighing sound at the back of her throat, her fingers working the clasp of his belt. Restless. Hungry.

"Bed." He walked her backward toward the hall leading to the bedroom.

"No. Here." She tugged the belt free of the loops and started to work on his fly. "We've walked far enough tonight, haven't we?"

Her scent filled his nostrils, that floral blend from the silky scarf that had carried him through so many hellish nights stationed in a war zone.

"The lady calls the shots." He unfastened the pink satin bra she wore while she unzipped his pants.

"Mmm." She shoved aside his boxers and wrapped her hand around him. Her cool skin felt so damn good on his hot flesh.

He cupped her breasts in his hands, her pale skin tinged pink as he bent to lick a path down the valley between them. Her breath caught in her throat and her hand tightened around him.

The heat scorching through him spiked a few more degrees. He could run for miles without getting winded, but one touch from this woman had his lungs heaving as though he'd been doing sprints for an hour.

He backed her into the couch, only two steps away so that he honored her preference not to go anywhere. When her calves bumped into the sofa, he tipped her until she fell into the cushions.

Easing her hand out of his pants, he undressed her as fast as possible. And damn but he hoped he'd have more chances to enjoy the view. Now, he could only follow the dictates of his body that demanded Heather all around him as soon as possible.

When she was naked, he shoved off his pants, his eyes never leaving her. Her pupils dilated, and a soft moan escaped her lips.

"For me?" She ran her finger up the vein at the center of his shaft while he looked for a condom in his pants pocket.

A damn impossible task when his eyes were crossed. Thankfully he could find the thing based on feel. He came up with the packet and slapped it on the sofa beside her.

But first, he needed one quick taste…

"Oh!" She cried out when his tongue touched the slick heat of her sex.

Her fingers threaded through his hair, her whole body arching up off the couch in immediate response. He stroked her with slow swipes of his tongue, listening to the way her breathing shifted into high gear. She covered her mouth with one hand, muffling the soft whimpers of pleasure that hummed from her throat.

"Please." She panted as if to catch her breath. "I'm going to lose it in another minute and I want you deep inside me when I do."

He stretched over her, retrieving the condom. Heather kissed his neck, his cheek, his shoulder, anywhere she could reach while he opened the packet. She helped him roll it on, her knuckles brushing his abs. His muscles twitched in response.

He planted one leg between hers, parting her thighs. She whispered his name in a feverish little chant, urging him on when he was already half out of his mind for her.

He entered her in one deep thrust, and he watched as her eyes lost focus and her head tipped back in total abandon. Giving herself to him completely.

Her legs wound around him, her heels clamped on the backs of his thighs. She curved her hips into his, meeting his thrusts, her fingers clutching his shoulders.

His world narrowed until it was filled only with her. Her wants, her sighs, her body clenching his tight. He wrapped her in his arms, wanting her closer, wanting to feel every inch of her pressed into him.

Her spine arched with his touch and he cradled her thigh with his other hand, holding her steady against the heat, the force that pounded through him.

And then her whole body stilled. A high note vibrated in her throat, growing louder until an all-out scream wrenched free. She convulsed with her release, her muscles contracting so tight around him he thought he'd pass out from the pleasure.

Instead he followed her into mind-blowing bliss.

5

"TOMORROW WOULD have been my wedding day."

Jared blinked.

They'd made love a second time and Heather had given him the best sex of his life so he'd been feeling no pain afterward. Maybe he'd fallen asleep and just dreamed the strange words he'd thought he heard her say.

"Jared?" she called to him, finally propping herself up on one elbow beside him in bed. They'd made it to the bedroom the second time, but they'd only gotten as far as an overstuffed chair. Afterward, they'd fallen into the bed, exhausted.

"Yeah?"

"Are you even mildly curious about my wedding date that wasn't, or should I consider this weekend more of the strictly carnal variety?"

Crap. She must have been talking about her own wedding during the phone call to her sister—half sister—the day before.

"No." He sat up beside her, his head totally clear and ready to hear what she had to say. "I didn't plan on today unfolding like this. I had every intention of sleeping at my place and—"

"That's okay." Her hair was tousled and sexy as hell. There had to be five shades of brown in there depending on what kind of light she was in. "I wouldn't have wanted you to sleep anywhere but right here."

The sheet gaped away from her breasts and he knew one little tug of the cotton flannel would expose her completely. But damn it, that was not the direction he wanted his thoughts to take. And hell, had she meant it about a wedding date?

"You—were getting married?" The news blindsided him even after he'd given it time to sink in.

"Yes." She drew her knees up to her chest under the covers.

He'd started a fire almost an hour ago and the scent of hickory smoke wafted through the cabin along with the fragrance of fresh-cut pine from the garland draped over the wood mantel. The night had been just about perfect until she'd chosen to cut him off at the knees with that news. News which, apparently, he'd have to drag out of her now.

"When I wrote to you, I asked if you were still unattached." He planned to handle this one like a homemade explosive device.

That is to say, he wasn't touching it until he'd tiptoed around it first.

"And I wouldn't have come here if I'd been involved with anyone. Even if you had planned to sleep in your own bed."

She shot him a smile and he relaxed. Marginally.

"So what happened? Did you break things off?" He couldn't imagine anyone walking away from her—that is, unless the military had tapped him to serve overseas for twelve months at the minimum.

"I realized I didn't love him. At least, not the way I was supposed to."

Listening to her talk about some other guy didn't exactly fulfill Jared's agenda of making this a Christmas to remember. He'd invited her up here to revisit one of the best memories of his life and take away the emptiness of the Christmases ever since they'd met. But color him a sucker for punishment because he had to know more.

"So who is this guy? Someone you work with?"

She shook her head. "I met him at a charity golf tournament. He's a professional golfer. Sort of laid-back."

"Sounds too tame for you." Although, if Jared were honest about it, that's exactly the type of guy he pictured her taking up with after he left Savannah. Some rich Southern boy who would inherit an old mansion like the one she'd grown up in. Jared had seen her mother's place on their ride back to Heather's apartment that night after they'd left the bar.

"I'm not exactly a wild woman. You've seen my linen business. I sell pretty pieces of history. Very sedate stuff."

"That doesn't make *you* sedate." He brushed her hair back from her face, wondering how she could be blind to the things he saw in her after knowing her for such a short time. "People like being around you because you're a live wire. And selling antique linens wasn't enough for you, I noticed, since you expanded your business eighteen months after it began. Who knows how much your company might expand in five or ten years? That doesn't *define* you. You are as passionate about your work as you are about the rest of your life, and that makes people respond to you. Trust me, your golfer would have been in over his head."

Which made him realize that he was no better suited for her than this guy she'd dumped. But it also reminded Jared that if he let her go back to Savannah alone this time, he would never have another chance with her. It had been a miracle no one had snapped her up for good before now.

His chest tightened at the thought because, damn it, he wanted a second chance with her and he would do whatever it took to keep her here after this weekend.

"I like seeing myself through your eyes." She tilted her head to lay her cheek against his arm as he sifted his fingers through her hair. "It sure beats my family's view of me as the most capable and responsible one in the gene pool. But enough about me. Are you going to tell me why you sent me that invitation after all these years?"

And the hits kept on coming.

Just when Jared thought he had a grip on the currents at work here tonight, Heather changed the whole playing field. Now he needed to figure out—should he play it cool to keep her from running? Or gamble everything and confess that he was hoping for a Christmas miracle with this reunion?

AFTER THE INCREDIBLE way they'd made love tonight, and all the emotions this man could churn inside her with one sizzling look, Heather figured she owed it to him to at least ask why he'd wanted to see her again.

She couldn't ditch him in the middle of the night if there was any hope of a compelling desire to be with her. Three simple words—*I missed you*—had opened her heart to other possibilities.

"I always regretted that I didn't say goodbye to you." He stared into the flames crackling in the stone hearth across from the bed. He looked a million miles away.

Or maybe just five years into the past.

"I regretted that, too." She didn't mind admitting it, at least not now that he had confessed it first.

As soon as she formed the thought she remembered a time in her life after another breakup when her mother had told her that you couldn't keep score in a relationship. Was Heather still doing that? It had seemed like a rare piece of practical Loralei advice and Heather had meant to put the wisdom into practice.

"I didn't know what to say. My life at that point seemed a far cry from yours and I didn't think it would be fair to ask anything of you since we'd only just met."

"We did more than just meet." At least in her book, that constituted more than casual flirting.

"Which is why I couldn't get you out of my head."

He massaged her shoulder and her whole body hummed in sensual response. She'd been with him for less than twenty-four hours and already she was attuned to the possibilities of his touches. This particular touch had a decidedly provocative meaning.

In the back of her mind, she knew she should probably hang on to this thread of conversation. Hunt through the layers of meaning in what little bit he'd said to understand his motives for having her here.

But oh, sweet temptation, it was hard to maintain a conversation with his fingers sliding down her collarbone to trace the curve of her breast. Her eyelids fell to half-mast, her nipples tightening into hard points at the promise of his touch.

"I've thought about you a lot since then." One hand found her ankle beneath the covers and he cinched it, tugging her down until she lay on her back. "I've thought about doing this a lot, too."

His lips found one taut peak and rolled it between his tongue and teeth. The liquid heat sent shock waves of pleasure rippling over her, concentrating in her belly and sinking lower in her hips.

She'd never been with someone who held so much sexual sway over her. He made her hot and needy, out of control. That put him in a position of power she didn't want on a mental level. But oh, sweet stars in heaven, she loved it on the physical plane.

Love.

She shut down her thoughts, squelched a word she didn't want to think about. Instead she let his mouth ravish her and welcomed his hands roaming all over her body. He stroked her belly and drifted lower. Lower.

He cupped her sex in one palm, his fingers playing in the wetness. How could she be so ready for him all over again?

"How many times will you come for me tonight?" He did something magical with his finger, plucking at the most tender of places. "At least once more?"

Her body answered him in a way her words no longer could, her hips rising off the bed to meet his touch. Pleasure wound up inside her, concentrating wherever he stroked her. She made pleading sounds in a mindless hum of want.

He stroked and circled, his fingers closing in on what she needed and then backing off again until her skin flamed with hot desire. She reached for his arm, guiding his fingers near what she wanted, but he stopped her with his other hand.

Pinning her wrists above her head, he held her where he wanted her.

Something about the helplessness of the moment stirred her.

She lay in front of him, exposed and at his mercy, and the situation stroked something inside her that went deeper than any physical caress. She gave herself over completely.

Her orgasm shattered over her, tightening every muscle as the spasms clinched her again and again. His name wrenched free from her lips and he caught the cry in his mouth.

And while she lay there beneath him, bucking with aftershocks and murmuring his name, she knew she wouldn't just be hurting him when she walked away this weekend. Leaving Jared Murphy would require superhuman strength and there wasn't a chance she'd go back to Savannah any happier than when she'd left.

Because whether or not Jared ever admitted it, Heather knew they shared something special.

6

SOMETHING HAD GONE wrong the night before.

Jared didn't know how he knew that, but he understood it on a gut level. The sex had blown his mind. Heather had fallen asleep in his arms as though she belonged there. He should have been walking on clouds today, except that he hadn't really confessed why he wanted her here.

Would she run if she knew how tangibly he'd pinned his hopes on her? But if she was only returning to Savannah on Sunday night anyway, what did it matter if he sent her sprinting back?

Heather was still drying her hair so they could go for a walk in the newly fallen snow. They'd had breakfast in the cabin and even though he'd been tempted to keep her hostage in the bed all day, he thought he had better get to the point of why he'd asked her here soon.

Maybe the walk would present an opportunity. Now, while he listened to the blow dryer whirr away in the bathroom, he watched the family next door out the window as they trooped into the snow.

The father picked up the toboggan that rested by their door while the mother zipped a little girl's coat and tucked a boy's scarf around the kid's pudgy neck. Every one of them wore a reindeer scarf, even mom and dad. Something about that elemental bond grabbed him by the throat.

God, he envied that easy sense of family. He saw his brother struggle to be a part-time father after his marriage had buckled under the stress of too much time apart and Jared had no plans to go that route. He had put off that kind of happiness in an effort not to make the same mistakes, but at some point it had become easier to not take the risk.

And he'd never manage to take that gamble if he kept allowing Heather to think he'd invited her up here for nonstop monkey sex. But damn. He couldn't look at her without wanting her.

"Ready?" She appeared in the hallway wearing a pale green sweater layered over a pink thermal shirt.

He liked the girly way she dressed. No sophisticated dark colors or suits. She had curves and she showed them.

"I've been ready." He tossed her the hat and gloves she'd bought the day before. "Better bundle up."

The phone rang while she was putting on her mittens. He remembered her call from someone who sounded like family the day before and diplomatically made no comment.

"I'm not getting that," she announced, reaching for her jacket. She set it back down two seconds later and frowned.

"What if it's an emergency?" She seemed to ask herself more than him.

"Do you want me to step outside?" The phone started a fourth ring.

"No." She dived on it at the last minute, picking up and answering in a rush. "Hello?"

He turned his back on the conversation, hoping Joe Golfer Dude wouldn't call her here. He hated the idea that she'd been engaged and—damn it—today would have been her wedding day.

"I'm not going to plan this party from a thousand miles away." Heather's frustrated tone spoke to him more than the words he was trying not to overhear.

Scowling, he clicked on the remote to the TV, hoping some sports scores would distract him from her conversation about a life that didn't have jack to do with him.

Unless...

Unless he made a serious play for her.

He looked back at her where she spoke on the phone, her eyebrows crinkled in worry. Or was it anger? It bugged him he didn't know her well enough to distinguish between the two. He'd let a long-ass time elapse since he'd met her. Some of which he'd had reasons for, some of which he'd spent not wanting to seem like a stalker dude reappearing out of nowhere when she might very well have been married. If not for her business success and the articles he'd seen about her online, Heather might still be just a vivid memory.

The way she would be next week if he didn't figure out how to make her stay. How to make her understand that he wanted so much more than he'd been able to tell her back then.

"I had every intention of coming home to finish up the details, Mom. I just wanted to take some time away for a change. This event gets bigger every year and—"

Okay, he couldn't help but notice that snippet of conversation since it was clear she was getting upset. Her tone pitched a notch higher and when he stole a glance in her direction, she sort of paced in circles.

She needed to relax. Something he was good at helping her do. He smiled with satisfaction at his memories of last night. Too bad he hadn't flat-out told her how badly the past few Christmases had sucked for him and that his need to see her came with a core-deep knowledge that she could fill the parts of his life that were empty.

That was going to change today. No distracting her—or himself—with sex. It was past time for him to show her something about himself and his life here. Only then would she be able to decide if her future might have a place for him in it.

"ARE YOU SURE we're going the right way?" Heather tromped through the snow to some secret destination Jared had in mind, her legs getting a workout with two feet of snow on the ground.

Who would have thought something that looked so fluffy on the way down could be so heavy to trudge through?

They'd spent all day outside since her phone call from her mother. Heather had learned how to snowshoe, which was fun, but didn't compare to ice-skating. Maybe those two hours she'd spent on skates were part of the reason her thighs protested the drifts they walked through now in the middle of nowhere. Supposedly this would be a path back to her cabin at the Timberline Lodge.

"I'm sure. We're following that star." He pointed to a bright point of light in the sky even though night hadn't fully fallen. The sun set noticeably earlier this far north.

She smiled at the idea of navigating by the star, which seemed the right thing to do at Christmastime. The quiet trek through the forest provided welcome time for reflection, something her holidays had lacked the past few years.

After having spent such a wonderful day with Jared, Heather knew her love 'em and leave 'em strategy seemed horribly immature, a petty revenge to take on someone whose company awakened a new joy in the season for her after years of succumbing to the massive holiday party and demands of family and business. Holding hands with a compelling man—an Army helicopter pilot turned rescue worker—seemed like a much nicer way to spend Christmas.

But she'd been the one to make herself vulnerable last time and look how that worked out. She refused to be the one who lost her heart only to end up cold and alone on Sunday. Again.

Relationships aren't about keeping score.

Was she doing it again? Making tally marks next to their names to decide whose turn it was to give in?

"Too bad we don't have camels," she said, the quiet of the night made all the deeper by the two feet of icy insulation on the ground.

She didn't want to think about the fact that her holiday trip would end tomorrow morning and she'd have to figure out how she would handle leaving Jared. Her heart ached at the thought.

"We're almost there," Jared assured her, holding back a slender tree limb for her to pass under. "I actually took us a little bit out of the way to show you something first. I hope you don't mind."

"My seductive techniques must be sorely lacking if you can put off our return to the cabin to play tour guide." She'd enjoyed their time today, but she had tossed out a few comments to make sure he knew she was his for the taking anytime he wanted to head back to the bedroom. He'd resisted, insisting on showing her all that Lake Placid had to offer.

He halted his progress and pivoted on his heel to block her path. She fell into him at close range, her body thumping into his so they were chest to chest, his gaze glittering above her.

"Don't tempt me to show you how much it's costing me to wait." His hands gripped her by the elbows, steadying her. "And if I'm only going to have a weekend with you, I need to make sure I cram in a lot. That means I can't necessarily put what I want ahead of everything else."

Words escaped her for a long moment, the heat between them assuring her he wanted her. A thrill shot through her, sparkling over her insides like the moon on the snow. Sweet heaven, but this man did incredible things to her.

"Right." She couldn't match Jared in eloquence when he decided to speak his mind, although she still couldn't imagine what he wanted to show her in the middle of nowhere. "Then I guess we'd better get going."

They stood unmoving in a silent showdown for a moment, although what exactly they were battling for, Heather couldn't say.

"It's just up here," he said finally, calling over his shoulder. "You can almost see it."

Squinting into the distance, she could see the outline of some low buildings ahead, although there were no lights in the windows, making their features difficult to distinguish. But even with a bright moon and the last remains of twilight to illuminate the night, the surrounding shelter of pine trees didn't allow her to see anything special.

"Is this where you live?" She remembered he mentioned living close to the lodge and she wondered if he wanted to take her to his place tonight. Curiosity bubbled as she wondered what kind of home he would keep.

Everything about Jared seemed dark and mysterious since her

knowledge of his intimate preferences was wide but her under-standing of what made him tick was minuscule.

"No." He crushed any hope she had of dragging him into a nearby bed and having her way with him. "This is my build-ing project."

"I thought you flew a Medivac helicopter." She remembered he also said something about local rescue work on the mountains on his days off. "Just how many jobs do you have, Army-man?"

Stepping out of the trees into a large clearing she could see six log cabins of varying sizes and shapes with multi-gabled roofs and small porches. They looked like new construction al-though there was a definite old-fashioned appeal to the cottages. Space had been cleared that could fit at least six more of the buildings.

"This is more a hobby than anything, right now. My grand-father was a carpenter and he taught me how to build. In fact, I restored a few of the cabins at the Timberline Lodge when I first moved back here. Yours included." He led her toward the closest cabin, the moonlight picking out a few more details on the struc-ture now that they'd stepped out of the trees.

The windows were expanses of multiple panes in keeping with the old-fashioned appeal. Heavy stone chimneys bracketed both sides of each building. The porch rails were rough-hewn split timber and the steps up to the cabins were natural stone.

"And you liked that so much you decided to make your own village?" Peering around the small development she realized they were still close to the lake and that the property led down to the frozen expanse. Whoever had the rights to this land was sitting on a gold mine.

"I thought about building some houses like a Habitat for Humanity community, but Roland Krause—the innkeeper—con-vinced me I'd be better off using my grandfather's land for some-thing profit-generating so that I could finance more humanitarian buildings down the road and well into long-term."

This was his land. Jared Murphy possessed the gold mine and

the way he planned to use it tweaked her heart and conscience right along with it. She felt herself teeter on the brink of…oh, God.

Love?

The possibility blindsided her as much as the emotion behind it. She'd kept the lid on her feelings for Jared for so long that now, at this sweet provocation and the proof of his generous spirit, she fell headlong into what she'd tried to avoid five years ago.

"So you're going to sell these for a tidy sum and use the proceeds for more practical housing." Her boot collided with a stone and he reached to steady her.

He'd been doing that a lot this weekend. But then, she had reason to be unsteady in his presence after five years of fiercely mixed emotions. She blinked hard to process this new facet of him that she never knew existed. God, she hadn't known him at all.

The more she got to know him, the more she cared about him, wanted to be with him. That warmth of feeling would make it impossible to sprint out of his bed at dawn on Sunday. He deserved better, even if he didn't want her for keeps.

"Actually, Roland encouraged me to develop a hotel property like the Timberline Lodge, something that would continue to generate income for years." He released her waist now that she had her footing. "The lodge is just over this hill. Sorry if the trek has been a little long."

"That's okay." She fought to find her bearings, wondering why he'd show her his project in the dark and not, say, tomorrow morning. "The cabins are beautiful."

"Thanks." He helped her up the start of the incline, making sure her boots found traction. "You said some nice things about the materials around your cabin so I thought I'd show you these in case you were…I don't know…creatively inspired."

She stopped, her treads sliding a few inches.

"You want to recruit me for your project?" Did she understand him correctly?

She should be flattered that he wanted to work with her. It was a great opportunity to contribute to a community that needed a boost and could draw attention to her fabric business.

Furthermore, it would be fun. But she couldn't help but wonder if that had been an ulterior motive for inviting her up here after all this time. He'd never felt compelled to contact her while he'd been overseas or during the year he'd been back in the States.

The implications of his simple invitation...his assurances that he hadn't invited her up here to renew a hot relationship...it all made sense now.

"Only if it's something that would be a good fit for your business." He wrapped an arm around her waist, guiding her up the slope in spite of her sluggish feet. "I actually found your contact information on the Web site for The Attic while researching companies that specialized in design for historic properties."

The revelation pricked her heart with a powerful sting. He hadn't even been searching for *her.* He'd been trying to find a company to decorate his damn cabins.

All the fun she'd had today—the skating, the snowshoeing, an exhilarating run down the Olympic bobsled track—seemed tainted somehow. He'd told her from the moment he picked her up Friday that he hadn't been trying to get her into bed. But damn it, she'd been convinced he wanted to see her for more personal reasons.

She struggled to speak, to move forward. To pretend this news didn't cut her to the quick.

Yeah, he remembered her all right. Just not the way she'd wanted and dared to dream.

"One of my first jobs was decorating the historic home that belongs to my mother." Not that her mother had paid her. But at least Loralei had always been up-front about her motives. "Most of my business is selling antique linens that work well in historic properties, but I do some original designs as well."

"It blew my mind that some people think it's cool to use a two-hundred-year-old tablecloth." Jared grinned over at her in the moonlight. "Sorta makes you think twice about what you throw away if someone might pay five times the value for it in another generation or two."

They cleared the rise of the hill and she could see the lodge in the distance and her cabin only a hundred yards away. White lights shone in the windows of all the cottages, giving the place a festive glow she didn't feel.

On the plus side, however, was her realization that she didn't need to feel guilty about her seduce-and-run scheme.

Trouble was, she didn't know that she had the heart for it anymore.

JARED COULDN'T WAIT to get back to the lodge to propose his plan for a future together. He'd thought about her every second of his quick trip back to his place to retrieve some clothes for dinner tonight. He had nothing with him since he hadn't planned to spend the night before with her. He'd told her as much when they got back to her cabin and she'd assured him she was looking forward to trying out the hot tub while he was gone.

Now, speeding back to the inn, he was tortured by visions of her in the hot tub, slippery wet. He'd wanted to join her. Hell, he'd been dying to. But he figured a quick time-out to get enough clothes to take her out tonight would help him get his head on straight before he asked her to consider making a bigger commitment to a possible future.

He'd wanted to romance her yesterday, but she'd made it clear she had seduction on her mind. Since they had spent five freaking years apart he could hardly argue the point. Then today, he'd started off strong between showing her every fun thing Lake Placid had to offer. He wanted to ask her to consider life in the North Country over dinner tonight and he figured he needed as much ammunition as he could muster. He'd taken her to see the project he was building earlier so that his plans for the future would seem more concrete.

But something had gone very wrong out on the construction

site. Whether she didn't like the cabins or her woman's intuition sensed he was working his way up to asking her for a commitment, he didn't know. He did know that she'd pulled back afterward and that had him worried. She'd bolted into the bathroom as soon as they'd returned to the cabin, promising him she would be ready for dinner by the time he returned.

Should he have stuck around and tried to figure out what was wrong? He could have asked her right then to think about sticking around Lake Placid long enough to see snow on a regular basis. But he wanted to do things right this time after the way he'd left her five years ago.

Now, driving back through the village lit up with white lights and busy with last-minute holiday shoppers, he struggled to see the road ahead of him and not visions of Heather's slippery, wet body in a tub full of bubbles. But he couldn't even dream about joining her when he needed to figure out what was going through her head now.

He definitely needed some discipline when it came to her. There was no way he'd let himself set foot in that tub until he'd figured out what was wrong and told her he couldn't spend another Christmas apart….

THE ALARM CLOCK turned on the radio at five-fifteen, waking him up to holiday tunes a hell of a lot more optimistic than he felt.

He stared at Heather spooned against him, her big bed a decadent antique in an otherwise barren apartment. She'd only been out of college for a couple of years, but she had said she was working full-time and putting all her funds into building a business rather than making her apartment into a real home.

Not that Jared had noticed much of anything about her place besides the fact that she was in it. He was halfway in love with her by midnight on Saturday, but he told himself that his emotions were keyed-up because he was about to leave life as he knew it for at least a year.

Shutting off the alarm, he sat up in bed, wanting to wake her to see her gorgeous blue eyes on him one more time before he had to report in. His chest tightened with regret that he'd met her too late. If only they'd crossed paths sooner.

Angry with himself for this swell of emotion he didn't understand, he stuffed it all down and packed up his things. He needed to leave enough time to go back to base and dress. Pack. Hell, he needed to hurry.

He'd spent every last possible second with this woman who had blazed into his life Friday night like a comet. And he knew whether he woke her or not, the impression she'd made would be singed into his memories for the rest of his life.

His watch alarm blared an electronic beep, a backup he'd set to be sure he got his ass out the door in time today. Scrambling to shut it off, he glanced back at the bed to see if she'd stirred. She hadn't. Maybe a kiss goodbye wasn't meant to be.

He found all his clothes and dressed. There was nothing keeping him here because he'd made sure not to give her any information to get in touch with him while he was gone. It was better that way, he knew. Jared's brother had been overseas for eight months and Jessie had missed the birth of a daughter by a girlfriend he'd rushed to marry on his last leave.

With Jessie's crumbling personal life as a cautionary tale, Jared planned to leave well enough alone with Heather. He wouldn't make his brother's mistakes or foist off that kind of loneliness on Heather, no matter that his first instinct was to ask her to write to him. See him again when he came home.

If he came home.

No. This was the right decision. He sat beside her on the bed and stroked her silky hair where it spilled over on her bare shoulder. She gripped the pillow beside her head, fingers flexing in the down as she sighed in her sleep.

She slept hard and she played hard. He'd learned that much about her in the past thirty hours. He didn't always meet a lot of women because he tended to be more quiet and intense than the easygoing types who could lay on the charm and score every night. That didn't bother Jared, necessarily, but he appreciated Heather for seeing his interest and seeking him out. Damn but she turned him on.

She rolled to her back, her breasts lifting high over the top of the sheet for one breath-catching moment.

And just like that his brain tripped into imaginative high gear, thinking how easy it would be to slip under the covers right now and wake her up as he slid inside her. But they were out of time.

He bent to kiss her forehead in the darkened room, knowing damn well some lucky bastard would probably snap her up while he was gone. And while he wouldn't try to hold her back from moving forward with her life, that didn't change the fact that he would be leaving a piece of himself in Savannah, Georgia.

HE DROVE BACK to the main building at the Timberline Lodge, knowing damn well what he had to do. He'd started off the weekend thinking he had to test if Heather could be the missing piece of the puzzle that made his life feel so empty these past few Christmases. He'd tried telling himself it was the war, the posttrauma of war, the stress of getting acclimated to life outside the military, but now he couldn't pretend it was anything other than the loss of a woman he'd fallen in love with in the course of one hot weekend.

His cell phone rang as he pulled into the long driveway that wound through the woods to the lodge. The ID showed the inn, so he picked up expecting Heather.

"Hello?"

"Jared, I'm so glad I found you."

Helen Krause's voice on the other end of the phone surprised him. She seemed to be whispering on the other end of the line while a piano banged out "Jingle Bell Rock" somewhere in the background.

"What's up?" He hoped she didn't need him to fix anything. He'd made sure he wasn't on call for flying this weekend while

Heather was in town, but he'd done a fair amount of work for the Krauses over the past year.

"It's Heather." The two words commanded his full attention.

"What about her?" He speeded up his pace on the winding road.

"Roland just saw her pulling a suitcase up the path behind the lodge." She hesitated while the piano in the background ended the tune with a flourish and a round of clapping ensued, probably a special entertainment in the dining room.

"A suitcase?" He repeated the word blankly, wondering if there could be any reasonable explanation for her toting around her weekend bag.

"We don't mean to pry, dear, but we had a good feeling about her when the two of you checked in yesterday and we wanted to make sure—"

"You did the right thing and I'm going to build you that whole damn new kitchen you want for the inn to thank you." He didn't take the turnoff road down to the separate cabins but stayed on the main road to take him directly to the lodge. "I think I see her, Mrs. K."

Up ahead, he spotted a dark green coat and blue knit hat in the blaze of white lights decorating the front of the inn. Heather sat on her small rolling suitcase a few feet from the curb as if waiting for a ride.

"Don't you let her leave, Jared," Mrs. Krause counseled while a small group of voices broke out into carols in the background.

"Not a chance." He disconnected the call, determination firing through him as he rounded a corner past some lighted Christmas trees.

Heather stood, apparently spotting his truck barreling toward the inn. He didn't bother to park in the lot, pulling up beside her and turning off the engine. He shoved open the door and walked around the vehicle, facing her.

Heart in his throat, he knew what her packed bag signified. That didn't mean he had to accept it. He wouldn't accept it, because walking away from her last time had cost him more than even he had realized until recently.

No way would he make that same mistake twice. Clearing his throat, he nodded toward the suitcase.

"Going somewhere?"

7

"I CAN'T DO THIS."

Heather hated being such a Scrooge on Christmas when the sounds of carols from inside the inn drifted out into the courtyard. The whole place looked like a winter wonderland, more warm and welcoming than any holiday card she'd ever seen with the wreaths and bows adorning window after window and a wealth of tall pines covered in miniature lights around the parking lot.

"That's excellent news." Jared spoke softly, his gentle tone at odds with the dark emotions in his eyes, his big warrior's body tense. "Because I wouldn't let you do this even if you wanted to."

He grabbed her suitcase off the curb and faced her while she tried to gauge his mood.

"Do you want to talk in the lodge or back down at the cabin?" he prodded when she said nothing.

"Neither." She shook her head, hoping her cab wouldn't arrive too soon since she at least wanted to give him an explanation—more than they'd given each other the last time they'd parted company. "What I mean is, I can't stay here pretending that everything is all fun and frivolity between us when I had every intention of walking away from you tomorrow morning before you even woke up."

The plan had turned sour on her somewhere during their time together and she wouldn't sit across from him and smile over dinner while she plotted her exit.

He hadn't worn a hat and snowflakes fell on his dark hair, the lacy crystals doing nothing to soften the hard edges of him as his jaw tightened.

"You came here for revenge." He shook his head as if disappointed. "But then you decided you'd had enough fun with that plot, so you thought you'd bail out even earlier than planned?"

She swallowed her regrets enough to call up some indignation.

"Since your motive in inviting me up here wasn't exactly all hearts and flowers, I didn't think you'd mind. Or did you hope that I would be so thrilled at the prospect of new business that I wouldn't care you had an ulterior motive? Did it occur to you that I might not want to do business with a man who once walked away from me so easily?"

"You think I asked you up here for a business proposition?" He sounded genuinely surprised. Thunking her suitcase back on the curb, he stalked toward her, his dark eyes narrowing.

In spite of everything, her heart sped its pace, her body slow to get the message that Jared wasn't the man for her.

"I have good reason since you made it a special point to drag me into the middle of the woods to pitch your project." She'd been taken advantage of by her family enough times to recognize a maneuver when she saw one. Heather had been taught the art of the wheedle from a master, and next to Loralei, Jared was a novice.

"You're right." He confirmed her worst fears as easily as he'd trotted out of her bed to travel halfway across the globe.

God, she'd been a fool to come here.

And still her body contradicted her, straining against her will to be near him.

"I was trying to give you a pitch." He closed the distance between them, his hands settling on her shoulders. "And I did a piss-poor job of it if you came away thinking I wanted your help decorating the cabins for—well, just for the sake of a business relationship."

She tried to follow that reasoning and couldn't, but then she knew that having his hands on her had a track record of making her brain disconnect.

"Heather, I asked you up here because I wanted to show you what my life is about these days and who I am now that I'm not bound to the military."

Inside the windows looking out onto the courtyard, Heather noticed Mrs. Krause peering out at them, her bright Santa sweater a flash of color that was hard to miss. She hurried away again, leaving Heather to puzzle through what Jared was saying.

"And I respect what you're doing, but I can't do business with you when—"

"Heather, I don't care if you never want to work with me professionally." He said it in that no-games tone she remembered from a long-ago conversation when she had first been captivated by him and an approach to life so different from what she was used to.

"You don't?"

"I don't." He brushed a dusting of snow off her collar and tipped her chin up, the leather of his gloves smoothing along her jaw. "I just wanted you to see that you would at least have some potential work income to tide you over if you ever wanted to consider moving up here to be with me."

She blinked. Attempted to process that.

"Are you asking—"

Her cell phone rang in her jacket pocket, spearing through her thoughts and interrupting them.

"I'm sorry," she muttered, reaching into her overcoat to retrieve it. "I turned it on after I called a cab and—"

Jared pulled the phone gently from her hands and pressed the button to answer it.

"Heather can't talk right now. She's in the middle of the most important moment of my life." He thumbed the off button along with the power switch, never taking his eyes off her.

"I don't understand." She was so confused. She didn't want to return to the demands of her family early, either, but she couldn't stay and grow more attached to Jared.

She knew the moment he'd shown her those damn cabins that

she had fallen in love with him. Knowing that prohibited her from playing any stupid game of revenge, but it also meant she couldn't sleep with him on a casual basis.

"I didn't have a choice about leaving you five years ago. It would have been unfair of me to ask you to wait because we hardly knew each other. I didn't understand until years afterward how much our time together affected me, but waking up night after night thinking about you finally pounded it into my head."

A couple walked out of the lodge, laughing and kissing as they wove through the parking lot as one body. Heather envied that happiness even as she began to wonder if Jared's words meant there was still hope they might one day share that.

"I couldn't forget you, either," she confessed, knowing the time had come when keeping score didn't matter. She owed him the truth about how deeply he affected her. "You're the reason I'm not getting married today."

"Thank you." He cradled her face in his hands, his big body warming hers with his nearness. "I'm so glad you didn't end up with someone else, because I honestly don't know what I would have done if I couldn't have a second chance with you."

Her breath caught.

"Marry me, Heather. Move up here and be with me and— Hell, I'm doing this wrong and I've had five years to think about it."

"No!" She put a finger over his lips, an eagerness rising up in her chest in spite of her head's cry for caution. "I like where this is heading. I—I want to hear more."

"I want to be with you and I'm willing to go wherever you are. Here. Georgia. The Arctic. A tropical island. I don't care. I just want to have you in my life because I love you."

Her heart beat so hard now she couldn't even hear the dining room carols anymore, her whole world bubbling with new possibilities when she'd been five minutes from leaving Jared forever because she was too caught up in her wounded pride to understand what he really wanted from her this weekend.

"You invited me up here to court me."

The idea appealed to her every old-fashioned notion of romance. He grinned.

"I figured we had already successfully conquered the chemistry aspect of a relationship, so I tried my damnedest to show you we could get along out of bed."

The warmth in her heart bubbled into happy tears that spilled from her eyes.

"Except I kept pulling you back into it."

"I didn't exactly fight you off—"

"I love you, Jared." The sentiment rose up from the depths of her soul, the secret truth that had kept her from loving anyone else. "I didn't want to acknowledge that because no one falls in love during a one-night stand. Or—in our case—a weekend stand. But I guess I should have realized you meant a lot to me when I was still mad at you for leaving me years after the fact."

"I'd like to make it up to you." Jared waved to Mrs. Krause who had returned to the window to look out at them. The older woman brightened up like one of her trees, waving back at triple speed.

"I'd like that, too." Heather hoped at this point her cab was never coming. She could stay here staring into Jared's eyes forever. "You mentioned some very intriguing scenarios for the future."

"You mean the part about living in the Arctic?"

"Uh, snow is nice, but that might be a bit much even for me. I was thinking more about marriage, or did I mishear something?"

Behind them, the inn doors opened and the Krauses spilled out into the courtyard with Roland holding an overcoat over their heads like a tent.

"You didn't mishear anything." Jared kissed her long and slow on the lips, a kiss full of promise that made her forget about anything else but enjoying the shivery delight of his tongue stroking over hers.

When he lifted his head to look into her eyes, he smiled. "I don't have a ring right now, but I've got a couple of witnesses."

Roland and Helen arrived just then. The older gentleman smiled while his wife bit her lip.

"Heather dear," Mrs. Krause began, "let me just apologize for calling our local cab company to cancel your ride. I know it was wrong of me but you two looked like you could use a little time to talk and—"

"This time of year brings out the matchmaker in my wife, you know." Roland winked at Heather. "And we are awfully fond of Jared."

"I'm glad." Heather blinked away the seductive tenderness of Jared's kiss. "I don't have any need for a cab so you saved me the trouble of canceling it. As it turns out, I'm going to be staying in Lake Placid for quite a while."

"I've asked Heather to marry me," Jared informed his friends. "And I think I just received confirmation that she's going to say—"

"Yes." Heather wrapped her arms around his neck, throwing herself into his chest and into his life. "Yes, Army-man. You're the one I've been waiting for."

Helen squealed beside them and Heather suspected her husband tugged her away because by the time Heather let go of Jared, the innkeepers had disappeared.

"What about your family?" He pulled the cell phone from his pocket and handed it to her. "Do you think we should call them?"

Pleasure filled her that he would think of them. Her future with this man would be so full of happiness. Joy. Every day would be like Christmas with him in her bed and by her side.

"I've got a much better plan." She kissed his cheek and kept her arms around his neck, not sure when she'd be able to let go of him again. "How do you feel about a trip to Savannah tomorrow to help me pack a few things for my move up here?"

"You really don't mind leaving your family? Because I'm serious about moving down there with you. I don't have family ties up here."

"My business can move anywhere and I think you'll see why my family will be really fun to visit a few times a year." She couldn't wait to see Loralei swoon at the sight of Jared. "We can arrive just in time for a Christmas party my mother's been planning."

"Your mother, huh?"

"Yes." Heather adored her mother, but they would probably both extend their wings all the more with a little more room. "It will be a fun way for you to meet everyone at once."

"Even the ex-fiancé?" Jared quirked an eyebrow, but he didn't look the least bit worried.

Heather had the feeling he was going to handle the family far better than she ever had.

"I think my ex-fiancé will be glad to have you take his place after my mother tries to set him up with my half sister."

She had movers to call, clothes to pack, a business to transfer…and a man to ground her through it all.

"Heather?"

"Hmm?" She still couldn't let go of him. Couldn't believe that Christmas had brought her a little peace on earth and very, very goodwill toward this man after so many years of being a source of stress.

"No one will ever take my place." He stared at her with those no-games eyes, the ones that had followed her everywhere she went that night at an outdoor bar halfway across the country.

"Are you suggesting you'd fight for me?"

Leaning down to kiss her, he stole her soul with one brush of his lips.

"Right down to my last breath, angel."

* * * * *

DEAR SANTA...

Kathleen O'Reilly

1

WITH ELEVEN MINUTES to spare, Rebecca Neumann finished concealing the last pieces of Christmas contraband from her kindergarten classroom.

Though the big day was exactly a week away, the headmistress could come around the corner at any moment. The headmistress who insisted that Santa was nonsense and that the holiday was no holiday, a day like any other.

So the reindeer antlers were hidden under the piles of neatly graded and filed spelling tests. Verboten Dear Santa letters were stashed inside Rebecca's prized Prada bag. Blackballed holiday cards were stuffed beneath her FootSmart custom orthotics that would never see the light of another human being's eye. And the paper-plate snowmen were strategically covered by the flirty, little black Versace that she kept on hand for date emergencies. A woman never knew when the man of her dreams was destined to appear, and although never having been a Boy Scout, Rebecca had dated and dumped three of them, and cleaved to their motto like her own.

The clock ticked off another minute, and she took a last look around, checking for any telltale holiday paraphernalia.

Everything…looked…

No! Teddy! Teddy Ruxpin! A tiny piece of candy cane was dangling from his fuzzy bear mouth. According to Headmistress Cruzella (not her real name, but apropos, nonetheless), sugar was the worst of all sins of the young and impressionable. Sugar and processed grains were banned at Modern Manhattan Preparatory School, where "every mind is priceless," and the punishment for sugar possession was a ten-minute diatribe on nutritional education.

Furiously Rebecca pulled at the sticky mess, but it wasn't budging. No matter how hard she picked, it was still stuck.

Think, think, she just needed to think.

Okay, would anybody notice if she dumped Teddy in the trash? Probably. Ethan Wilder seemed really attached to the bear, and Ethan was Rebecca's last, greatest hope for the next generation. It would be her luck that she'd destroy his favorite toy, and curse his life-destiny forever.

Nah. She could erase the evidence but she had to maintain an efficient calm. After eight years of dodging Cruzella's rules and regulations, she'd gotten cocky. There was no transgression she couldn't sweep under the rug, no institutional infraction she couldn't whitewash away.

While keeping a careful eye on the clock, she plucked, pulled and wiped, clearing up everything but one stubborn bit of sticky candy. Eventually she knew she had no choice—Teddy was about to get buzzed. Stylishly, of course.

With bear in hand, she flew across the room, sliding to her desk in stocking feet. Right then, the door opened. As the lies sprang to her lips, Rebecca dug her shoes out of the desk while simultaneously stashing the bear behind her. Then she assumed an innocent smile, ready to face Headmistress Cruz.

Instead it was only…Natalie.

Rebecca dumped her shoes back in the drawer, and resumed breathing. "Give me a heart attack next time, will you?"

Natalie was the next-door kindergarten teacher, happily married with her first kidlet on the way, her face was always lit up brighter than a halogen bulb.

Sometimes Rebecca felt a twinge of envy, an unnecessary emotion that she rarely felt, and never admitted to. Rebecca's life goal was to marry a Prince Charming with a twelve-cylinder steed (preferably of Italian design), and live a life of luxury with a seat on the board at the Astor Foundation, and a new, state-of-the-art, homeopathic, ultra-luxe foot spa with jets and soothing, acupressure massage nodes.

Natalie's husband had a twelve-cylinder Jag, but Rebecca forgave her, since Natalie kept setting her up on dates with men who rated A+++ on the Rebecca Neumann Eligibility Scale. Unfortunately sparks never flew, the men were blah and something always felt wonky. But Rebecca kept trying; she had a mission.

Natalie looked at the bear, looked at the scissors, looked at Rebecca. "What are you doing?" Then she looked closer. "*Candy? Peppermint candy?* You've been at it again, haven't you? When are you going to learn, Christmas is a hanging offense at this school. Listen, I'll keep an eye on the door while you get rid of the evidence. You have thirteen minutes. That's what I came to tell you. Mistress Yvette is keeping them late in French class today. Le pop quiz."

"*A votre santé, Mistress Yvette,*" Rebecca murmured while efficiently trimming away the clumps of fur and tossing them into the trash.

"You're going to die, you know that, don't you? Cruzella catches you, and you're dead. Sugar! *Oy vey.* After that last bit at Halloween, with the candy pumpkins, you'd think you'd learn your lesson, but no—"

"Keep quiet while I get the last of this." Rebecca scanned her work, gave Teddy a sophisticated, slicked-down comb-over and threw him back into the toy bin, missing by a mile. Damn. Someday she'd master that shot.

Natalie picked up Teddy and slam-dunked the bear into the bin. "Why do you even try? You're too short."

"You're too pregnant, and you can still make the shot."

Natalie smoothed a hand over her stomach. "Yes, yes, I am, but I have the added benefit of a hormonal imbalance. Better than steroids."

Rebecca and Natalie pulled out two pint-size chairs from the tables. Rebecca sank gratefully into the seat and began rubbing her feet, already aching with another three hours of the school-day left. It was going to be a Four Advil day. And that was on top of the Three Advil day yesterday when Mrs. Capezzio insisted that sweet Richie did not scrawl his name all over the gym in permanent maker. Today on *Oprah:* Parents in denial. Rebecca shook her head sadly. "I'm worried, Natalie."

"About what?"

"I think being around overprivileged kids is messing with my head. Don't get me wrong, I yearn for the finer things in life, but I'm losing the delicate balance. The other day, Kaitlyn told me I needed collagen injections for my mouth, and I considered it. I don't need collagen injections. Do I?"

"No. Of course not, silly," answered Natalie with a quick glance at Rebecca's mouth, which Rebecca didn't miss, by the way.

The drawings above the blackboard weren't of monsters and bunnies, but designer fashions, formal dining rooms, pictures of South Beach winter homes and four Picasso-esque paintings of polo ponies. "It's these kids. I've dated men with less understanding of finance than little Claudio Gettleman. How a six-year-old can calculate earnings per share is really beyond me."

"He gave me stock tips the other day," Natalie admitted.

"Really? Did you invest?" The words slipped out before Rebecca could stop them.

"He *is* only six."

Rebecca grabbed the pen from behind her ear. "What's the name of the company?"

"B-I-O-N-E-X-T."

Carefully she blocked the letters on her hand, making her "N" with the three-step process they practiced in class. "You invested, didn't you?"

"No," answered Natalie. "Some. He gave me this whole spiel about engineering biological components—and it made sense."

Rebecca made a mental note to herself to call her broker that afternoon and then tucked the pen back behind her ear. The money was one thing—she could adjust to that—but the mind-set of the school was another. That was the one that kept her awake at night.

"This school is doing a huge number on them, depriving them of sugar, Santa, the tooth fairy. All the carefree things in life. Do you know that Cruz told Justin Lowenstein the tooth fairy didn't care if he lost a tooth because the tooth fairy didn't exist? Where's the justice in that?"

"You could quit."

Rebecca snorted inelegantly, a sound reserved only for her very best friends. "I'd die first. These children need me. Their childhood is zipping right past them. I was happy when I was a kid. No ADD, no bubble-gum-flavored Prozac. I'm the only piece of sanity in their lives it seems, certainly in this stylized mental institution. Present company excepted, of course."

Natalie popped a Tums into her mouth. "The kids do like the birthday parties you give. They think that keeping it a secret from their parents and the headmistress makes it extra special. Although I think Cruz is catching on."

"If she does, I can handle her."

"I hope so because now my class is asking for it, you child-corrupter, you."

"Go ahead, Natalie. Walk on the wild side."

Natalie laughed. "Oh, right. Classroom antics aside, you've never walked on the wild side. Your closet is littered with skeletons of skeletons that have never gotten a chance."

"Who needs skeletons anyway?" Rebecca shrugged it off. Her skeletons were all gone now.

"A skeleton is much better than a regret, do you at least have any of those?"

"Not many," answered Rebecca, because honestly, there wasn't much she regretted. She'd always gone after what she wanted with an élan that made her captain of the cheerleading squad, homecoming princess and president of the student body. No, not many regrets, except for…

"What?" prodded Natalie, whose dogged determination was probably the reason she got pregnant in like, two seconds.

"It was nothing." Quickly Rebecca tried to change the subject. "Isn't Cruz due about now?"

Natalie checked the clock. "You have over eight minutes. Just enough time to spill all the regrettable details."

"There's nothing to spill," Rebecca insisted.

"You're lying," answered Natalie, and Rebecca heaved a sigh. She was getting weak in her *old age* (not quite thirty-one, although if anyone asked, she was twenty-nine).

Natalie flashed her tough-girl look. The one she used when determined to get the truth—whatever it took. Rebecca held up a hand before she brought out the instruments of torture.

"Okay, fine. You want to know? It's completely nothing. There was this one day, this one guy in high school. Cory Bell. He looked at me. And I got this tingling in my fingers, my toes and the back of my neck. This was in my fully hymenated days, so I didn't quite understand the biology of tingles very well. Then Lawrence—who was captain of the football team—came up and took my books and walked me to class. Cory never looked in my direction again, but I've always wondered what would happen if… End of regret."

"That's all?" asked Natalie, which made Rebecca wish she'd made up something juicier.

"I don't get tingles very often. Bad circulation, I think," she answered, rubbing her feet.

Natalie's gaze turned wistful. "I had one of those. Once."

"What happened to yours?"

"He got incarcerated, ten years for grand theft auto. I consider myself lucky to have escaped. Think of it, instead of planning a Disney cruise for the little guy, I could be scheduling my conjugal visits."

"Think he's turned around?"

Natalie shook her head. "Ha. And Santa's going to drop down my chimney."

"Bite your tongue lest the reindeers and elves hear you and start offing themselves because you've dashed their Kris Kringley version of reality."

"You think this Cory person got incarcerated?"

Rebecca thought for a minute. "Odds are good. He wasn't at school long. Half a semester at the most. They said he had lots of problems. Foster kid. No parents. Hair too long, and eyes that revealed a level of experience far removed from the restrictive bonds of traditional adolescent behaviors. Every female has one of those boys in her closet."

Natalie wiggled her brows. "Would you have slept with him if those experienced eyes wandered in your direction?"

"No. I had plans, goals, aspirations. I still do."

"Would have been fun."

"So is jumping out of airplanes. Don't want to do that, either."

"And now?" asked Natalie. "What would you do today?"

Rebecca allowed a moment of introspection, savoring the idea. As a rule, she stuck to predictable men, and with the clock ticking, she couldn't afford to waste her prime-matrimonial years. But the single second in time had lodged in her brain, chiseled there for over a decade. Sometimes, late at night, when she was lying in bed alone…

Whoops. Rebecca shook her head, her blond page boy shaking artfully. "The fantasy is better. Besides, my tastes were never a black leather jacket. My standards are higher."

"Alec Trevayne high?"

Alec Trevayne. Now there was a man who rated A+++++ on her scale. She'd never met him in person, only drooled from afar when he pulled up in a bright red Bentley and dropped off Natalie's husband at a party two months ago. Rebecca lifted her hands innocently. "I can't help it if I'm seduced by such shallow things as a dimple, golden hair and abs made of steel."

"You said that about Jeremy Smithson when I set you up with him. Three dates and you dumped him."

"Snooze alarm, Nat."

Natalie got up and began to shuffle slowly around the room. Rebecca knew she'd be losing her partner in crime soon. Childbirth could do that to a woman, and Natalie was due in six weeks.

"You're too picky, Rebecca."

"You didn't settle. Why should I?"

Natalie leaned against the Wall of Presidents, a contented smile on her face. "No, I didn't."

"Thank you for the vindication. I'm waiting for true love, too."

"Is that what you're putting in your Dear Santa letter?"

The Dear Santa letter was Rebecca's annual Christmas tradition with her class. She believed in Santa as strongly as the kids. So the kids wrote their letters—wish lists, really—and then Rebecca took charge of mailing them off.

This year Rebecca's letter to Santa contained three wishes: a new, less volatile father for Pepper Buckley, a reading breakthrough for shy Isaac Gudinov and a fiancé for herself. "I also want you to know that I answered thirty-seven Dear Santa letters, all presents paid for out of my own pocket." Part of the Dear Santa program organized at the Thirty-third Street post office was the ability to write reply letters and send presents to kids, particularly to less fortunate ones.

Natalie shook her head, rubbing her alarmingly distended belly. "It's an inhumane heart that tries to bribe Santa Claus."

"Just want to make sure I'm making it onto the right list," she answered. However, Rebecca privately admitted that somewhere in the last few years, what had been a holly-berry outlook on the Christmas season, had become something of a routine. A desperate tradition that she kept up with, only because she couldn't bear to let it go.

Just then, the hallway filled with the sound of D&G sneakers, UGG boots and Roberto Cavalli hightops, signaling the end of her break. Rebecca slipped on her shoes and rose to her feet, a weary smile on her face.

No matter how much she complained and worried, and griped and moaned, Rebecca loved her job. There were some days, some rare days, when the kids would get it, would actually learn, and she, Rebecca Neumann, Girl Most Likely To Become A Trophy Wife, was responsible. Those elusive happenstances made all the "thou shalt have no sugar," nor any fun lectures from Cruzella worthwhile.

Rebecca sighed. "And now back to the trenches. I must don my armor and face the mini heathens with a happy smile on my face and a trill of delight in my voice."

Natalie waddled toward the hallway. "Maybe this time Santa will come down your chimney. Maybe you'll finally get a shot at dipping into the famous Trevayne S-H-O-R-T-S."

Kaitlyn stopped in the doorway. "I can spell, you know. That's shorts. My mommy and daddy don't think I can spell. She called him a D-I-C—"

Rebecca clamped a hand over Kaitlyn's mouth. "Precocious child. Come. Let's fill your mind with more intellectual drivel. It would be the highlight of my educational existence."

THREE HOURS LATER, with quitting time fast approaching, Rebecca finished grading the last round of math sheets. The crisp *clip-clip* of Cruzella's heels echoed through the marble hallways, and Rebecca pulled out her knockoff D&B clutch, an "I'm going home now" hint in case the headmistress decided to launch into a lecture.

Nina Marcel Cruz, known as Headmistress Cruz to all poor serfs in her fiefdom, was a stylish reed of a woman, with an innate fashion sense that made women jealous and men glad they weren't paying for it. Sometime after thirty, Cruz had stopped showing signs of aging, so Rebecca wasn't exactly sure how old she was, but the woman had founded Modern Manhattan Preparatory School in the boom days of the eighties, and since that first year, women had rushed from the maternity ward to put their children on the waiting list.

"Mistress Neumann."

Rebecca rose, pocketbook in hand, exit door firmly in her sights. "Yes. I'm just leaving."

"We need to talk." Cruz leaned forward, giving Rebecca a long, lingering whiff of Chanel. "I found these," she said, throwing the Dear Santa letters on Rebecca's desk. "Do you have an explanation?"

It was late, Rebecca was tired and all she wanted was to go home. But *noooooo,* Cruzella wanted to duke it out.

Fine.

Rebecca jerked open her desk drawer, pulled out her spare Prada bag, which she used for emergencies, and searched frantically inside. Empty. "You searched my desk?"

"The desk, the drawers and the closets, all fall under the oversight of this educational institution. Which I run," she added, hammering a finger on the calendar desk pad. "Modern Manhattan prides itself on not pandering to the fantastical myths that are told to children to foster their own sense of self-involvement and pull them further away from reality. If a parent wants their children exposed to the commercial extravaganza that is Christmas, there are any number of educational facilities that will cater to that belief system. We are not one of them, and I will not tolerate this flaunting of our mission. I want you to take these letters and return them to the children, explaining that this was nothing more than a simple exercise in letter-writing."

Cruz pursed her lips together (collagen-injected) and watched Rebecca, waiting.

She should have seen this coming, she should have been more careful. She could have hidden the letters at home, or better yet, in Natalie's desk. But she'd gotten overconfident and careless and now it was too late.

Those letters contained the trivial and materialistic desires of twenty-two children's hearts. They were written in scrawling, sometimes teacher-assisted handwriting, nothing worth losing sleep over. And she could explain it to them. She could look into

Pepper Buckley's somber eyes and tell her that this was only practice for the real world. No biggie.

She could gaze upon Ethan Wilder's open, honest face and tell him that Christmas is simply another day when the post office wasn't open. Easy, squeezy. Yeah, Rebecca could stand up in front of her entire class and proclaim that there is no such thing as Santa Claus.

Ho-ho-ho.

Her lips grew Sahara dry, and she picked up the stack of letters, her mind made up.

"No."

"I beg your pardon?"

Rebecca pulled herself together, her shoulders thrown back in best posture position. "No. I promised the kids I would mail these letters, and I will. I will not tell them this was a simple exercise in correspondence. It's Christmas." Rebecca could see the lecture brewing in Cruzella's eyes, but she was standing up on principle. She'd get the lecture over, apologize and then move forward.

However, Cruz was working herself into a late-afternoon rage. She stamped a heel on the floor. "We do not cater to the whims of fairy tales. Our teachers are grounded in fact and scientific method."

"It's only a letter," answered Rebecca, moving her tone to something light and conflict-free.

"So was the Magna Carta."

Rebecca's eyebrows rose. "You can't compare the two."

"You're fired, Miss Neumann."

Hello? Rebecca's mouth fell open. "What? You can't do this." She held tight to the desk, so tight her fingers turned white. Okay, maybe she had flouted the rules a bit, but *firing her?*

"I'm your employer. Of course I can."

No, she couldn't. Rebecca might be a mere kindergarten teacher, but she knew the law. "There's no documentation trail."

The headmistress's eyes were cold and calculating. "If this had been the first time I noticed your behavior, yes, but year after year, you have ignored the principles we teach in this school. It's all written up in your file. I'm not sorry, Miss Neumann. I don't have a choice. Not anymore."

"But the kids…" Rebecca trailed off, realizing the kids would be fine. Oh, yeah, they'd grow up thinking there wasn't a Santa Claus, they'd grow up to run Enron, and cheat on their golf scores, and fudge on their charitable donations. And it'd all fall on Rebecca's shoulders. She'd be the one responsible. Rebecca. No way. She had not yet begun to fight. "I'll tell the papers. The media will be incensed. I have the spirit of Christmas on my side."

Cruzella didn't even stop to breathe. More proof of her subhumanity. "I have five hundred of the best lawyers in New York on my side, along with the heirs to three of the major networks, two of the news cable giants and three of the newspaper barons in the city. How many major networks are there, Mistress Neumann?"

"Three." *Her fighting ideals were going…*

"News cable giants?"

"Two." *Going…*

"New York dailies?"

"Three." *Gone.*

"Have I left anyone out?"

"No," said Rebecca, who had spent four years as a cheerleader and knew that if your team sucked, fighting wouldn't get you squat.

"When they hear of your addiction to drugs and your scandalous doings with men, your reputation will be in tatters, and you'll never teach kindergarteners in this town again."

"I don't have a drug habit," snapped Rebecca, glancing down to make sure that her Advil was out of sight.

"I've seen the painkillers, Mistress Neumann. And then there's the scandalous doings with men."

"I don't have doings with men." God knows, she had given it her best shot, but somehow it never seemed to work out.

"Mr. Murphy tells otherwise."

"I have never, *ever,* kissed, fondled, caressed, groped, touched, teased, flirted with, or petted Mr. Murphy. He's lying." Mr. Murphy was the weasely science teacher who kept asking her out, which, of course, she had refused. Rebecca had meticulous standards in men. Mr. Murphy was a reptilian dweeb.

Cruz didn't seem to care. "Would you like to testify to that in court, Mistress Neumann? Go away. You don't fit in here. You have never fit in here."

There it was. The writing on the wall, in Palmer method cursive script. Rebecca swore, a particularly vile interjection, just to see Cruzella puff up in rage for one last time. Then she tucked the letters back in the Prada bag and hooked it over her shoulder. "I'll pack up my things."

"And don't forget those reindeer antlers. Tacky, tasteless and made in a third-world country by sweatshop workers."

Proudly Rebecca stuck the reindeer antlers on her head, and walked out, never looking back.

2

REBECCA SHARED an apartment with two of her sorority sisters from college. Both were on their way to matrimonial glory, brandishing two-plus-carat engagement rings whenever they got the chance. The plus side of the arrangement was that they were hardly ever home, and Rebecca saved enough in rent to subsidize her fashion habit.

She stalked into her apartment and kicked off her shoes, fighting the urge to cry, scream, or both. Her feet ached, her head ached, her stomach ached, and now she had no job. There was only one cure. Rebecca took out a pint bottle of bourbon, the liter of diet soda and started to pour.

One down, then two, and she still didn't feel any better. The phone rang, caller ID said Mom, and Rebecca didn't answer. She couldn't face her family. She was too ashamed.

Fired. What a miserable word. She pulled the pen from her ear and wrote it out twenty-five times on her While You Were Out Shopping… message page. She didn't deserve this. She had worked hard for her kids. Who was going to bake them cupcakes with extra buttercream icing when she wasn't around? No one. Who would be there to bandage bruised knees with a hug and a kiss rather than tincture of iodine? Not a soul. Give them extra candy on Valentine's Day? Not even Natalie.

Agh.

Rebecca propped her feet up on the sofa, flexing her feet, which sent shooting pains up her calf. She deserved the pain for being stupid. But how stupid was she?

What if, in the end, Cruz was right? What if Rebecca was

coddling them and they'd grow up to be spoiled adults ten steps removed from reality, just like her? What if Rebecca was the misguided one?

The phone rang again. Caller ID said Wilder. This time, Rebecca picked it up.

"Miss Neumann?" The voice was high and hesitant, even through the fiber-optic phone cable.

"Ethan?"

"Is it true? Austin's mommy called Daniel's mommy who called Megan's mommy who called my mommy. They said you won't be our teacher anymore."

Rebecca sank into the carpet, curling up against the couch. "I think so, Ethan. But you'll have somebody new."

"Megan's mommy said you had a nervy breakdown."

Oh, no, thought Rebecca, wishing the bourbon would do its job. "I didn't have a nervy breakdown. I told Headmistress Cruz that I believe in Santa Claus."

"There's no such thing as Santa. My daddy said so."

Rebecca rubbed a palm over her eyes. "Ethan, I need to get off the phone now. You'll be good? Don't give the substitute heck, will you?"

"No, Miss Neumann. Please come back. My birthday is next month, and I want cupcakes, but my mother said I can't have cupcakes because of the sugar."

"I'm sorry, Ethan," said Rebecca, a catch in her voice. Quickly she hung up the phone. She would not let her kids hear her cry. Not ever.

Not ever.

Not ever.

Because she was wasn't going to see them again.

Rebecca took the reindeer antlers off her head and threw them at the closed bedroom door.

"Hey!"

The door opened and Janine walked out, in boxer shorts, and a T-shirt with no bra. Which meant only one thing. Janine's fiancé was here, and they'd recently been indulging in afternoon nooky.

Rebecca swore and then immediately apologized. "Sorry."

Janine picked up the antlers. "What's wrong with you?"

Rebecca limped to her feet, and discreetly shoved the bottle of bourbon between the box of Splenda and the green tea bags. "Nothing. Long story." Her roommates would find out soon enough when she couldn't make rent.

Janine, still caught in the postcoital afterglow, didn't notice. "The UPS man delivered a package for you. It was huge."

Rebecca managed the expected smile.

Janine pointed to the corner. "I stowed it behind the TV. Go ahead, open it. I'm dying to see what's in it."

It was a giant gift box, with shiny green paper and a bright red bow, all Christmasish, and if one hadn't just been fired for said Christmas beliefs, one might have been totally excited. It was big enough, wide enough, deep enough.

Maybe…

Rebecca stared, her fingers crossed. Eventually curiosity turned into something more, and she tore off the wrapping. Then, *slooooooooooooooooooooooowly,* carefully, she lifted the lid.

And looked down to find…

A single sheet of paper.

Okay, not the brand-new, hot off the assembly line, homeopathic foot spa that she had coveted since her podiatrist first told her about it.

The paper was a handwritten note, with neat, tidy penmanship not seen in sixty years.

Dear Rebecca—

Because you've been good this year, I'm pleased to send you on a five-day holiday to the Timberline Lodge in Lake Placid, New York—all expenses paid, of course. I know what you want for Christmas, and there you'll find it under the tree.

Santa.

Santa.

Oh, that was rich. Even more pathetic, she could feel the old silliness springing up inside her. Gullible moron.

She reread the note four times, willing herself not to fall for it. This was a time-share opportunity, cleverly disguised with gleeful Christmas trimmings, probably a bad joke from Cruz.

However, she wasn't moronic enough to dismiss it completely, either.

Her first call was to the lodge, verifying its existence and asking if time-share opportunities were available. The old woman on the other end of the line sounded insulted.

"We're a family hotel with a long, well-documented history in the Adirondacks. No flim-flam here."

Satisfied with the sincerity of her response, Rebecca explained the note and then the woman chuckled. "Our Santa Claus packages are very popular over the holidays. We have a strict confidentiality clause if the giver requests it."

This time, Rebecca wasn't so quick to defend the existence of Santa. "And what if a creepy, stalker dude is the giver? Mr. Murphy, for instance."

"You have a creepy, stalker dude, missy?"

"No," admitted Rebecca, because Mr. Murphy wasn't that creative. "It wasn't my parents, was it?" Bob and Evie Neumann weren't the most luxury-minded of parents, but it wasn't completely out of the realm of possibility.

The woman laughed. "Could be."

Rebecca frowned, considering the uncharacteristic generosity. Her family had never been as flush with the green stuff as most of her friends, which perhaps, maybe, okay, probably, had influenced her more avaricious leanings. Her friends? "Natalie!"

"I beg your pardon?"

"It's just like her. This is a singles place, isn't it? Oh, no, no, no. Don't tell me. I want to be surprised."

"Yes, I'm sure you will be. You're confirming the reservation, then?"

"A lodge?" Rebecca still wasn't sure. She wasn't an over-the-river-and-through-the-woods sort of gal, but Natalie was usually spot-on, and she wanted to escape. If only for a while. If only to let the blood-letting inside her stop.

"We have a four-star restaurant, the suites have in-room whirlpool baths and fireplaces. A full spa—"

"Spa? With pedicures? And in-room foot tubs full of scented bubbles?" The world grew brighter.

"Sure. We can do that. And ice-skating, sledding, a movie theater in town—"

"Stop. You had me at the bubbles."

It was going to be the perfect escape. The perfect way to get her head together. She'd have a nice, relaxing vacation, and then figure out a way to get her life in order. Preferably something that didn't involve kids. Maybe retail? She would excel at retail.

"Look us up on the Web, Miss Neumann. You won't regret it."

"I'll be there on Friday."

Rebecca hung up, a bourbon-flavored smile on her face. Tomorrow she'd hurt, but right now she was happy. "Janine, I'm heading to the Adirondacks, and I'm taking the curling iron with me."

Friday, December 20th

THE SNOW WAS STARTING to fall in huge, blinding flakes, the road nearly invisible even though the wipers were moving faster than the wheels.

Eventually the road disappeared altogether, and Cory Bell swore. He lifted his foot off the accelerator and his pickup slid to a crunching halt. The last thing he needed was to be stuck with another one hundred and seventy miles to go. Hell. He hadn't even gotten out of the States, yet, and already the never-ending Christmas music was eating at his nerves.

When Christmas came, Cory headed north, running for the French-Canadian mountains where English wasn't the native language. He didn't like the holiday, didn't like being around people for it and chose to find a place where a man could disappear and nobody would care. Cory had learned early on that a disappearing act was the smartest thing he could do.

The windshield was nearly covered in white, and Cory cursed every meteorologist ever born. There wasn't supposed to be snow yet. Two days ago, they said it was supposed to be "unseasonably warm" until the storm blew in. When the windshield was completely blanketed, he knew that global warming hadn't kicked in here, at least not yet, and reluctantly he put the car back into Drive. There was a turnoff ahead for Lake Placid. He'd see what was there. All he needed was a restaurant, or a bar with people who saw, heard and said nothing. By the looks of the steely sky, he was going to be stuck for a few hours—at the very least.

THE LOCAL CABBIE picked Rebecca up from the train station and deposited her in front of a rustic snow-covered wonderland with huge firs lit up like golden Christmas trees. Timberline Lodge was an old-fashioned camping-style lodge, with two large stone support columns, towering timbers and an A-line roof that seemed to go on forever. It wasn't the quaint bed-and-breakfast she was expecting, but warm and—Christmassy. Was it what she needed right now? She wasn't sure.

The front door was twice her size, and she heaved it open, trudged inside, hauling her suitcase behind her.

Inside was just as cavernous as out. A stone fireplace climbed up one wall, running three stories to the roof. Rough-hewn timber columns were used to support it, so tall they must have been redwoods. Rebecca, who was used to feeling small, felt extra Lilliputian.

The furnishings weren't new; some had that homemade look—the real deal. And there might not be eight-hundred-thread-count sheets she had hoped for, judging by the looks of things, but heck, it was a gift, so who was she to complain?

She was stamping her pink UGG boots on the mat, when the door opened and a man entered behind her, his black hair blanketed in white snow.

"You work here?"

The voice was low, more of a growl, but Rebecca had faced worse every morning before 9:00 a.m., and all less than three feet tall. She straightened her mouth into a tight line.

"No."

"Didn't think so," he said, brushing his hair and shrugging out of his coat, tossing it onto the coatrack, and hitting it expertly.

She wanted to ignore him—she really should ignore him—but this one drew her eyes. He was a good head and shoulders taller than her, silky hair, black eyes, thick lashes that still held a few stubborn flakes of white.

The stubble-darkened jaw was square and hard, just another indicator that this man was not a cheery person, nor would he probably ever be. Such magnetic personality traits were the reasons that she kept looking, noticing the brown off-the-rack sweater. Off-the-rack had never looked so good. The blue jeans were old Levi's, faded, molded to lean hips and long legs. He was thinner than the current style dictated, but it looked right. He was lean, mean and had never owned a Bentley in his life. What a shame. A definite "C" on the Eligibility Scale, although she gave bonus points for smoldering sexuality. If this was any indication of the man quality at Timberline, she could get on board with this new plan. So what if the kids needed her? So what if she didn't have a job? After all, with the right husband, food and shelter wouldn't be an issue. And the right position at a philanthropic foundation could do wonders for other kids. New kids, underprivileged, rather than overprivileged.

Rebecca took a deep breath, hung up her coat (the nonathletic way) and stepped aside right as a tiny old lady came up to greet her.

"Miss Neumann, I'm Helen Krause. We've been expecting you. I was worried with the weather, thinking you'd be stuck somewhere on the roads."

"Not a problem for me," said Rebecca. "I took the train. Mass transit is my friend." Rebecca lifted her suitcase and the older woman waved it back down.

"Let Roland take care of that."

"Roland?"

"He's our doorman, as well as my husband."

Rebecca envisioned a ninety-year-old man trying to lug her four-ton suitcase up three flights of stairs and frowned. "I can do it."

Helen took the suitcase in her feeble, birdlike hand. "But you're a guest."

Rebecca reached out, ready to protest, but Mr. Lean, Mean and Bentley-Less stepped in between them. "Where's it going?"

Mrs. Krause smiled nicely, obviously not a devotee of the women's movement. "Follow me. Aren't you a dear man to help?"

The man grumbled something that sounded vaguely obscene, but fell into line behind the old woman. Rebecca followed, watching him move up the winding wooden staircase. Okay, there was more ogling, but he moved with an easy, athletic grace that was fun to watch, and filled her with a marvelous tingling sensation. What harm was there in that?

They went up three flights, down a hallway, around a corner, around another corner and then down another long hallway. Finally Mrs. Krause stopped outside a room and the man dropped the suitcase with a loud thud. Rebecca winced at the echoing noise. Yes, she should have packed lighter, but a woman needed her accessories.

Mrs. Krause beamed at the man. "You're staying with Miss Neumann then?" She turned to Rebecca. "I thought you'd be traveling alone."

"She is," the man answered. "I'm waiting for the snow to let up. Do you have a restaurant or place I could sit for a few hours? A bar would be great."

Mrs. Krause looked out the bank of windows, shaking her head. "The dining room will be open for tea shortly, but I'm not sure the snow will be stopping anytime soon."

"I'll be fine. You tell me where I can wait and be out of the way."

"The library's as nice a place as any. And there's hot cider and gingerbread cookies."

His eyes didn't look happy, but he didn't say anything, merely headed downstairs. The old woman watched him curiously, before turning her attention back to Rebecca. "You know, I'm not sure your room is ready. I asked the maid to put the portable foot spa in your room, and I don't think she's got to it yet. Perhaps you wouldn't mind waiting in the library, too? I'm afraid this weather has thrown everyone for a loop. The second shift maid couldn't make it in and we're a bit shorthanded."

Rebecca didn't mind at all. For a portable foot spa, she'd walk through hot coals. She smiled easily. "Not a problem, Mrs. Krause."

"Please call me Helen."

"Helen, then. And I'm Rebecca."

3

THE LIBRARY was a cheery place, if one could be swayed by such sentimental trappings. Rebecca could. The fire crackled in the fireplace, and a freshly cut spruce had been decorated with ornaments and tinsel, a lighted star topping it off. Everywhere was pine greenery, red velvet ribbon and mistletoe.

Any other time it would have been relaxing. Now it wasn't, because of *him*. Rebecca folded her hands in her lap and stared into the flames. The man sat on the stuffed sofa on the other side of the room, but she could feel him looking, breathing, emoting. Unrestrained tension rolled off him in huge waves—he didn't want to be here.

However, Rebecca was undeterred. She had coaxed first-year pledges into teasing conversations, she had bribed six-year-olds into confessing that they'd rocketed pencils into the ceiling tiles. And best of all, there wasn't a man she couldn't handle. Maybe a weekend flirtation was the best way to get the old Rebecca back.

"Nasty weather, yes?"

"Um," he answered, more of a grunt than actual vocal articulation. She almost corrected him, but then thought better. Not in the classroom anymore.

"Where were you going? Family for the holidays?" Judging by the worn black cowboy boots, he didn't look like the "family for the holidays" type, but then, she was the poster child for the "family for the holidays" look, and she was no fan of the experience. That's what happened when you trapped twenty-three Neumanns into a two-bedroom house. Actually it would have been okay except for Uncle Edgar, who never quite seemed all there, and talked twenty decibels too loud for average human ears.

"I'm heading to Canada."

"French, as a language, is severely overrated. You should consider Spanish instead. Not only more practical, but the climate is warmer, too."

His face was set like granite. An even bigger challenge. She cocked her head, smiled and she saw something flicker in the granite.

"You have family around here?" he finally asked.

"In Stafford Hill, Connecticut. This is a chance to get away for a while. Do some thinking. Maybe skiing," she lied. Everything sounded better than "I just got fired from the only job I've ever wanted, and actually I'm hoping to meet someone new."

He looked around the library. "Nice."

"I thought it sounded like an adventure," she answered, as if she were an adventurous soul. Oh, she, who brought eight pairs of shoes, all with three-inch heels (designed to show her short legs off to best advantage).

"Some adventure," he muttered.

"You don't want to be here?" she asked, going for the obvious. Better to understand the hostility and embrace it. Resolving conflict was a key job requirement when handling six-year-olds, and apparently surly men.

"Stuck."

"There are worse places to be stuck," she answered.

"Name one."

"Siberia."

This time he almost cracked a smile, not much more than a quirk of his lips, but mentally she cheered. Okay, the old Rebecca was coming back. She wasn't beaten down. She could feel it.

Normally she didn't try so hard, but the dark, somber eyes struck a raw place inside her. They were eyes like Pepper Buckley's, hollow and ancient. The pain there was like a loud ringing inside her head. Not that there was anything she could do, but she couldn't leave it alone.

The silence grew longer until a couple wandered into the room. Newlyweds, by the way they were ignoring the rest of the world. Hand in hand, eyes glued to each other. Until they spotted the mistletoe hanging from the chandelier in the middle of the room. Mistletoe made Rebecca happy, no question, because she was a world-champion kisser, and had parlayed an "accidental" mistletoe kiss into a full-blown relationship more times than she could count. However, watching others in the midst of moonstruck happiness wasn't really her thing. She was way too competitive.

The woman looked up at her lover, quirked a brow in invitation and then they kissed. Long, longer, endlessly, everlastingly, infinitely, skin-flayingly long. Thankfully no tongues looked to be involved. Rebecca felt her face bloom in uncharacteristic hotness.

She sneaked a peek at the room's other occupant, to see if he noticed, to see if he was uncomfortable, to see if he was getting turned on. He wasn't looking at her, he was staring fixedly at the fire, which was somehow worse. He was ignoring her.

Quickly Rebecca looked away before he saw her staring at him, and then he would think that she was the desperate type—which she wasn't *normally*.

The couple broke apart, took a cup of cider (which they shared) and wandered out, leaving Rebecca in an interminably fidgety state. She crossed her legs together and tried to look casual. Nearly an impossibility, but four summers of charm school training made every impossibility a possibility.

Rebecca got up and wandered to the bookshelves, looking for conversational diversions. There were a million diversions on the bookshelves. A collection of classical literature, thrillers, historical fiction and science fiction. She moved from row to row, trying to determine which one suited him best.

"They have a nice collection of Westerns here. McMurtry, Zane Gray. Do you like Westerns?"

He didn't even look up. "No."

Rebecca heaved a loud sigh, which, if he were a more sensitive type, would have been seen as a subtle rebuke. "Cup of cider?"

"With rum?" he asked hopefully, turning in her direction.

She scanned the table. "No, sorry."

"I'll pass."

She poured a cup for herself, took a sip and then leaned gracefully against the old antique table. "Where did you come from?"

He looked at her closely. "Curious, aren't you?"

"Simply making conversation. I love to talk to people, make new friends."

"I don't."

A second couple wandered in. A tall, modelesque woman, with her very own Adirondack Ken, complete with red-wool plaid shirt. Of course, it took them less than a minute to find the mistletoe. Rebecca clocked it. After seven minutes of R-rated tongue action, Rebecca made discreet choking sounds.

The man met her eyes, and laughed.

"Nice weather we're having. *Warm enough for you?*" she hollered to him.

The model pulled away from Ken, thankfully, and flashed a photogenic pout.

Rebecca wasn't cowed. "Do I know you? Didn't we do rehab together? Susie? Shirley? Or was it a 'J' name?"

The woman pulled at Ken's hands and the two left the room, off in search of new and more unusual public displays of affection.

"Little punchy there, aren't you?" the man asked. "I thought you'd be making new friends."

"Very nice," she answered, sounding punchy.

"Rehab, huh?"

"It just came out. Sorry."

"You could've left the room."

"So could you."

"Maybe I like to watch," he said, and Rebecca swallowed. Hard. She met his eyes and shrugged. "Maybe I do, too."

"Where's your Romeo?" he asked.

"Excuse me?"

"Why are you here alone? Somebody stand you up?"

"Christmas gift."

"A solo pass to a couples joint? Does this person *like* you?"

"This isn't a couples joint," she insisted, just as another couple entered the room. *Again.*

Rebecca turned to the stranger, her face contorted with misery. "I didn't *mean* to get pregnant. It was an *accident.* You have to believe me."

The couple wheeled around and left. Problem solved.

"You an actress?" he asked, his arms folded over his chest. Somewhere along the way, she had moved from mouthy pest to curiosity. Progress. Definite progress.

"Seventeen years of watching *General Hospital.* I teach school. What about you?"

"I build things."

"Big, officey things, or smaller, residential-type things?" she asked, curious. He looked like a builder. Probably drove a pickup. American made. Six-cylinder, possibly an extended bed. Nothing remotely sleek, or Italian. She really wanted to move him up on her scale, but he kept inserting barriers.

"Home renovation stuff. You teach really young kids, don't you?"

She'd heard that tone before, the easy dismissal. "Why do you think that?"

"You're too short."

"It's not nice to pick on a person's shortcomings."

"You said it, honey, not me." He got up, walked around the room, pacing. A man who didn't like being confined. No white-collar worker here.

"Nervous?" she asked.

"No," he said, still pacing. "I'm not used to sitting. Don't like all the holiday stuff." As he walked in circles, the room grew smaller. She was about to ask him to stop, but then another couple strolled into the room. The woman was pretty enough, but the man was wearing a cashmere sweater, Burberry, four-ply, and would have rated an A- on the Eligibility Scale if he wasn't wearing a redhead on his arm, too.

Crap. She'd been hoping for the Alaska Gold Rush, and instead she was stuck on the *Love Boat*.

Rebecca closed her eyes because this wasn't the way Christmas was supposed to be. You weren't supposed to lose your job. You weren't supposed to be alone. When she opened them again, she didn't bother to be polite. "I'm sorry. This mistletoe is taken. Find a room of your own."

The woman stared, slack-jawed. "I beg your pardon?"

"You heard me." Then Rebecca turned to the stranger, and kissed him.

It was graceless, classless and screamed of desperation. And wasn't that the truth? But as she kissed him under the mistletoe, the sounds of the lodge fell away, the scents taking over. The smell of burning wood, spiced cider, fresh pine and man. Rough, heady man. Rebecca knew Play-Doh, wax crayons and hand sanitizers, but this new and tantalizing aroma made her mind spin in circles, faster and faster. It carried her away, far away from the places she knew. This wasn't Ivy League, white-collar man. This was someone more seductive. More earthy. More basic.

It was exactly what she needed.

Eagerly she kissed him with everything she had, her mouth open and slack, inviting him to explore. She heard a groan, felt a hand at her waist, pressing her away, but then, glory be, he pulled her closer.

Her hand crept to his chest, finding a heartbeat under her palm. Strong and fast, even under the heavy wool. This time she moved into him, so that she could feel more than his heart. She wanted it all. The breadth of the shoulders, the safety of his chest, the heat of his hips. She'd never known what spontaneous sex felt like, had never felt the tingles in her spine, the ache between her legs.

Passion. This was passion. She could feel it in him as well. In the thrust of his tongue, in the urgent press of his mouth. Such a lovely mouth. She was going to have that mouth. She was going to have that man. She would ask him to her room. For a few hours. For a night. A decadent moan escaped from her lips, and it didn't matter what he rated on her scale. It didn't matter if he was stealing her away from her search for Mr. Right. Honestly, she didn't care.

He was the best Christmas present ever. Not a foot spa, not a hand-crayoned picture of Santa. This was better. This was a man.

A hot, hunky man.

Her way, her terms.

A noise disturbed her thoughts, and he lifted his head. The black pitch of his eyes gave nothing away, but under her hand, she felt the ragged breathing, felt the speeding heart.

There, under the shadow of the mistletoe, Rebecca smiled at him, a lurid invitation waiting on her tongue. She opened her mouth, but the voice behind her interrupted.

"Rebecca?"

No one knew her name except for Mrs. Krause. The deep voice wasn't old, wasn't feeble, wasn't even female.

Rebecca closed her mouth, and turned.

Alec Trevayne.

4

"REBECCA NEUMANN?"

Cory wiped his mouth and sized up the gent who had so inconveniently interrupted. Cold, hard cash. The guy reeked of it, from the cashmere coat to the tailored trousers, to the Italian wingtips. Cory took a step farther away from the woman, the name echoing in his mind. So familiar…

Not that it mattered. He knew what money could do. He knew how this situation would play out.

However, the woman surprised him. She stared at the dandy, then stared back at Cory, her light gray eyes wide with confusion. Cory wasn't used to playing the gentleman, but it was obvious the dandy wasn't as welcome as Cory had assumed, so he took a step closer to Rebecca, and reached out to her—like a boyfriend would. Before he could touch her, she flew out of the room like—well, hell, like a neurotic woman.

God.

"That was Rebecca Neumann, wasn't it?" asked City Boy, in a voice that dripped of fancy-ass England. Blimey.

"Who's Rebecca Neumann?" Cory asked, dodging the question with a question. *Rebecca Neumann?*

"I was expecting to meet her here."

"And you don't know what she looks like?" Cory folded his arms across his chest. London Boy might be broader in the pecs, but Cory didn't fight fair. Never had.

"It was supposed to be a surprise," the man finished lamely.

"Maybe she's not here yet. You know, the weather's really nasty. Got stuck myself."

The man didn't look convinced, but he wasn't going to argue, either. Not that Cory blamed him. Meeting a woman for the weekend, not knowing who she was, didn't say much for the guy. Unless this Rebecca was a hooker?

Cory shook his head. Nope. She was a kindergarten teacher, cheerleader, princess. No hooker blood there.

Cheerleader. That's where he recognized the name. The same girl? That same tight ass? *Definitely.* Would she remember him? Hopefully not.

Cory smiled and stuck out his hand. "Cory Bell. And you're?"

"Alec Trevayne. I'm sorry. This is quite embarrassing."

"Yeah, glad I'm not you."

"Was that your lady friend I walked in on? Sorry."

Cory coughed. "Mistletoe always gets to me. You know?" It was a vague answer, and enough to swing either way, depending on why Rebecca was running away from this guy.

The old woman who owned the place hurried into the room, getting Cory off the hook. "Mr. Trevayne? Is that you? We had a leak in the laundry room, so I'm afraid everything is upside down today. Did you find Miss Neumann?"

"Not yet," answered Alec, and Cory began to feel really sorry for the guy. Maybe he should tell him, ease some of the embarrassment. Nope. Cory knew how to keep his mouth shut and he had almost no sympathy for the human condition. Let him suffer.

Besides, his loyalty lay with Rebecca at the moment, mainly because she kissed him like it was her last day on earth. It's not that he had planned on getting laid today, but damn…he hadn't expected to find her tongue in his mouth, either. Cory wasn't a big believer in kissing, mouth to mouth was too personal for his sex life, but a woman's tongue, well, he wasn't stupid, either.

"I'll keep my eyes open for you. Good luck with the hunt," offered Cory, then he left the room. He should get out of this place. Snow or no snow. Leave Rebecca Neumann alone. But what if she needed him? protested his cock. What if she was avoiding the Brit for a good reason? Cory studied the snow falling steadily outside and swore. Then he and his cock took off, heading up the stairs to Rebecca's room.

Time to get some answers. But nothing else. Absolutely, positively, nothing else.

THE ROOM WAS EVERYTHING Mrs. Krause had promised, but Rebecca was too wound-up to notice. She had called Natalie four times on her cell, and each time all she got was voice mail. Natalie wasn't a big fan of the cell phone, but hopefully she would pick up soon.

Alec Trevayne? Here?

It reeked of Natalie's handiwork, which was normally a good thing, but now Rebecca wasn't so sure.

"Alec Trevayne." She said his name aloud, testing to see if the lip shivers would go away with rational thought.

Nah. Still there.

Her lips tingled, her heart was pounding and her lower nethers were tingling and pounding, all at the same time.

Alec Trevayne. Lust from afar. Bently-laden, Oxford-educated Alec Trevayne. For three months it had been her goal to have Natalie arrange a meet, and now, apparently, she had. He still looked good, and he had a great car, but the old thrill at the idea was no longer, chased away by other, more carnal ideas.

Think, think, think.

She was a schoolteacher. A former schoolteacher with a strong Teutonic streak of practicality, which did nothing to explain why she quietly shrieked when a knock sounded on the door. Rebecca got up from the bed, praying it was Mrs. Krause.

"Who is it?"

"Rebecca, it's the guy from the mistletoe. Open up."

Downstairs Alec Trevayne was waiting, perhaps confused, but nonetheless waiting. For her. Upstairs, right outside this door, was a veritable stranger. If it wasn't for those eyes... Dark, wounded and, yes, sexy as hell.

Was Rebecca willing to trade a lifetime (possibly) of pedicures and luxury automobiles for one night (possibly) with a man of questionable morals who could kiss a woman to paradise and back?

Yes, yes, yes.

After Rebecca opened the door, he strode inside and she was conscious of the clothes strewn all over the bed, the iPod, the portable exfoliator, the hair dryer, the curling iron, the four charging devices and the portable back massager that vaguely looked like something else, but really wasn't, although in times of crisis, a woman used whatever was on hand. Rebecca sidled in front of the bed, cocking a hand on her hip. "Yes?"

"Who's the guy that's looking for you? You ran out of there like you were scared of him. Are you?"

She considered lying, creating a fantastic cover story, but— no. Slowly Rebecca shook her head. "I'm not scared of him," she admitted.

"Why did you run?" he asked, a perfectly reasonable question.

She licked her lips, opting to hide behind the truth. "Because you were kissing me, and I was temporarily confused."

He looked at her, frustration evident. Then he looked up at the ceiling in that counting-to-ten posture she had often used herself. "So you're not afraid of him? I can leave here, and you'll be fine with him. Right?"

If this had been another man, Rebecca would have assumed a coy demeanor and subtly flirted until she got her way. But he was different from the men in her universe. And he could kiss.

That kiss. That life-altering, mind-shattering, lip-tingling, take-me-to-bed-now kiss. Subtle flirtation was completely unnecessary. She should be crawling under the covers, waiting for him to kiss her into gleeful submission.

Unless she was the only one whose world was rocked?

No way, Mr. Jose.

Rebecca corrected her posture and tilted her head back until she could look him square in the eye. When the dark gaze speared her, she almost caved, but quickly recovered.

"I want you to stay," she said, fighting the urge to stare at the floor.

The edge of his mouth curled up, and not in a pretty way. "You want to make the other guy jealous? Sorry. Find another schmuck."

Obviously her lurid propositioning skills were getting rusty because her lurid proposition had completely flown over his head.

"You don't understand. A friend of mine set me up with him—"

"And you don't want to be set up with him?"

"No, I did," she replied honestly. "But now I don't."

"What happened?" he asked, not quick to read between the lines.

"I want you to stay," she repeated.

"Because of one kiss?" he asked, and she wished he didn't sound so—startled.

"Yes."

"One kiss?" he asked again.

Oh, come on. What was he? Fishing for compliments here? Rebecca squared her jaw and looked him straight in the eye. "Yes. One kiss. Okay, I'm impulsive. I'm adventurous. I liked the way you kissed, and I wanted to sleep with you. Have sex. Make love. Do me. Screw me. Do the wild monkey, whatever euphemism is easiest for you to understand, that's good with me."

Her stomach cramped in two. This was worse than her bad-perm incident, worse than her first job interview, worse than the day the podiatrist told her it was orthopedics forever. This man couldn't reject her. Rebecca needed this weekend, this runaway weekend to forget about money, job security and food. This was about living for the moment. Alec was a life goal. This guy was a single moment of time. Right now, she only wanted the latter.

He just looked at her, blinked slowly, then frowned.

"And what about Alec? You'll keep dodging him?"

At least it wasn't no. "I didn't ask for Alec to meet me up here. This wasn't a date."

"I think he thinks it was a date."

"He's entitled to think whatever he wants, but as the other party cluelessly involved in this setup, I'm not responsible for his preconceived expectations. Only my expectations. I have my own expectations. I mean, I *had* expectations. Well, they weren't really expectations, more ideas, and Alec Trevayne isn't involved. At least not anymore."

"You have this much trouble with communication in the classroom?"

"No," she answered. She usually didn't have nervous neck sweat, either.

He stared at her skeptically.

"I don't want to think about work. I want to think about nonwork…and if you were interested in nonwork—with me."

"*I* don't think this is a good idea." But while his mouth said no, his eyes weren't so sure. She could see it.

"Fine," Rebecca stated, calling his bluff because reverse psychology was on the books for a reason. "Go on. Leave." She even opened the door.

His feet didn't move.

"Not leaving?"

"I'm still thinking."

"I'd prefer not to hit menopause before you decide."

His mouth quirked up on one side. "Okay. We have sex. Make love. Do you. Screw you. Not doing the wild monkey sex, though. That's a little weird. But I'm only stuck at the lodge for a few hours, maybe a night at the most."

Brutal honesty. Brutal, stick-in-your-eye honesty.

Rebecca hated that. "I don't remember mentioning anything more."

"I just thought you'd like to spend a by-the-numbers, romantic weekend with a guy who seemed like a good guy—once you get past the whole Brit thing."

"Can we leave Alec out of the room?"

The man shrugged. "Your decision to make."

"Yes. Yes, it is," she said, satisfied with her decision. And his decision, too. A good, safe two feet separated her from him, but the silence grew until it became a living, breathing elephant smack in the middle of the room. They were going to have sex. She was going to have sex with a stranger. She kept the panic carefully concealed from her face—another kindergarten-teaching survival skill.

Rebecca moved her head to one side, pseudoflirtatiously, and held out her hand. "I'm Rebecca Neumann."

CORY LOOKED at the outstretched hand. Perfectly silky white skin, polished nails that looked embarrassingly clean. He saw the nervous blink in her eyes, and saw a couple of hours of great sex flying out the window. Now was the time for sanity to return and he'd be stuck driving all the way to Canada with a hard-on because of some damned cheerleader fantasy.

"Cory," he said, taking her hand.

Her eyes blinked again.

"Cory?"

"Yeah."

"Cory Bell?" she asked, her voice rising a couple of octaves.

This time he blinked.

"Yeah."

"From P.S. 35?"

"You went there?" he asked, like he didn't know.

"Yes," she said, launching into full social-secretary persona. "Rebecca Neumann. You had a locker down the hall from me. Back against Mr. Espy's science lab." She shook his hand harder. "What a small world."

"Yeah."

Her hand stopped shaking his. "So what have you been up to since P.S. 35? Ha."

He racked his brains. Was he supposed to answer that?

Her eyes scrunched up, and he noticed that Rebecca Neumann wasn't eighteen anymore. There were lines around her eyes, the corners of her mouth. Laugh lines. Oddly enough, it made her sexier. Much more approachable. Much more touchable.

"Imagine seeing you again. After all these years. Like fate. Or kismet. Or serendipity."

He didn't know where this was headed, but Rebecca was still holding his hand. Okay. "No, just caught by the snow."

That seemed to make her happy, which was good, because he had already figured out that her buttoned-up sweater concealed a blouse, and possibly an undershirt, but he was up to the challenge, and his cock was starting to throb.

"Well…" she said, and there they were. Back to square one.

"Yeah," he said, and took a step closer, his free hand flexing. Buttons weren't really a problem.

Her bottom lip caught between her teeth, a move that would have been sexy if they were already having sex. Then the gray eyes turned dreamy. "Could you kiss me again?"

Kissing. Hell.

He'd known this was a bad idea—even if it was Rebecca. "I'm not big on kissing."

"But downstairs…"

Cory wasn't about to explain the reasons why he didn't like kissing. The sex, he was completely on board with, but impersonal and anonymous sex. Kissing? Nu-uh. She'd have to find another Prince Charming. And the road to Canada would be long, hard and painful. Cory shook his head, and dropped her hand. "I'll go."

That made her move. "No."

"Yes," he said in a firm voice because Cory didn't make exceptions, and he wanted to make sure she understood.

REBECCA LOOKED UP at him, and drew in a deep breath. A one-night stand wasn't quite what she had always fantasized about. This was different, but maybe different was right.

Fate was a powerful thing, opening doors, closing doors, and Rebecca was a big believer in the whole open-door theory. She didn't hesitate because she liked the banked desire in his eyes. Anything but the emptiness of before. She smiled, confident in her decision, and said yes.

Then he moved, reaching for the buttons on her cardigan and began to undo them one by one. She stood still, cold air biting bare flesh. First the sweater, next the blue cotton blouse. It slid easily from her shoulders. He smiled at the undershirt, and she wondered, but the silence was a magical thing, more evidence of great things to come. He reached behind her to unhook her Victoria's Secret bra. Efficiently he disposed of that, warm hands moving to the zipper of her slacks. In two seconds, the pants were gone and he was sliding the last layer of silk down her legs. She felt a strong urge to lock her arms across her chest, but vestal virgin wasn't the part she was playing. There wasn't a wedding ring on the line, only the chance to do something she'd never done before.

He backed her toward the oak dressing table, lifting her up, cold butt to cold wood. He started to remove the wool socks from her feet, and Rebecca stopped him before he could go further. "You're not big on kissing. I'm not big on sock removal."

His face was curious, but he shrugged. "Not a problem."

Then he began to undress, shedding boots, sweater, jeans. Each new divestiture exposed something new. A scar on his hip, a tattoo on his arm, a dusting of black hair on his chest. But two things were no mystery. The hard look in his eye, and the straining erection that seemed indestructible.

He came over, stood before her.

"Change your mind?" he asked, like he thought she would.

Stubbornly she shook her head, then watched as he sheathed himself with a condom. A condom. The universal symbol of actual penetration. Cory Bell was going to have sex with her. Sex. With. Her.

There was that single moment of panic. That time when she felt her blood chill, but then it was over.

This was Cory Bell.

The dark eyes watched her carefully, obviously waiting for panic, waiting for the vestal virgin to emerge. However, Rebecca was ready. She'd been waiting days, months, decades for this.

Rebecca Neumann and Cory Bell.

He pulled her legs around lean hips and then slid inside her. Rebecca gasped, not quite ready.

"Problem?" he asked casually, as if she'd broken a heel or dropped her change down the sewer. But no, he wanted to know if she had a problem with his cock being inside her. Thick, heavy, lively cock. This was what women threw their lives over for. This feeling. This fullness. This…joining.

"No problems here," she said, as if she had casual sex every day.

He studied her face, those experienced eyes looking into her, through her, but she lifted her chin. One corner of his mouth twisted, and then he shifted her legs a few inches higher. As he began to move, his gaze was as mechanical as his movements. He was detached about his lovemaking, his body going through all the right motions, but there was no emotion involved. This was down-and-dirty sex. Torrid, anonymous, tawdry sex.

Fate had decreed this, but Rebecca didn't like this new plan. His vacant eyes bothered her, ticked at her insides, and she opened her mouth to say something. But his thrusts were more potent, and the tingles in her breasts and thighs started to come alive, and her mouth fell shut as the pleasure center in her brain took over.

He made no move to kiss her, no move to touch her, other than the hot hands that lifted her hips. She moaned, low in her throat. His eyes narrowed at the sound, and a bead of sweat formed on the side of his face. Friction built between her legs as he increased the speed, almost painfully fast. She concentrated on that one drop of liquid, watched it slide down over his cheek. His chest was pumping now, so strong she could see the veins underneath his skin. There was life there, buried deep.

She cried out, a guttural sound that embarrassed her, but her body had moved past the point of no return. It was loose and lax, and she arched her back, her hips echoing his rhythm. It wasn't romantic, no hearts and flowers, nothing but backroom sex. The satisfaction of a biological drive.

Rebecca wasn't used to sex for pleasure alone, and she gasped as he hit a marvelously decadent spot.

Her body responded, her mind floating free from its objections.

She groaned, a protest basked in pleasure. A climax was building inside her and she wanted to catch it, but he didn't slow down, kept pumping again and again and again.

She arched even further, feeling him deep, deeper inside her, pushing, thrusting, tearing her apart.

Her hands clutched at the hard wood, clawing at nothing. Cory kept on, relentless, unceasing. She tried to speak, but there were no words. She needed to come. *Now.*

He ignored her, mindlessly thrusting. Her head moved from side to side, and she wanted to scream, but knew she couldn't.

There.

There.

There.

The orgasm crashed over her, and he froze, his head listing low. A moan broke from his lips, then his body jerked. Rebecca's legs went slack, her body reeling from the completion.

The room was spinning in a three-mojito manner, but there was no pain, nothing but golden rays bursting behind her eyelids. Man, if she had guessed this about Cory Bell before, she would have ditched high school Lawrence in a heartbeat.

This was...

This was...

Wow.

She'd never known that sex could be so—naughty.

"Wow," she whispered, staring up at the ceiling, watching the wooden beams rotating in front of her eyes.

She felt him pull out of her, and rose on her elbows, watching with dreamy eyes as he cleaned up. Efficiently, he began to dress, not even glancing in her direction. Rebecca might not have been completely back on planet earth, but she knew enough to realize there was more than one thing wrong with this picture.

As he tugged on his sweater, her conversational skills returned. "You're leaving?"

He still didn't look at her, instead focusing on his socks and boots.

"You're leaving?" she repeated, in a slightly less wobbly tone.

"The snow's letting up. I should hit the road."

Rebecca sat up straight, slid off the dresser, pissed and bare-assed naked.

Oh, no. Not. Now.

She tried to walk, her knees dipping before she locked them to stay upright.

"You're leaving?"

He stopped in mid-zip. "Look, you got what you wanted. Go back downstairs. I won't tell, he'll never know and you'll have the quiet, romantic weekend you're aching for."

"I don't want him."

"Don't lie. He's exactly what women like you want."

Rebecca took in a lung's worth of air, adding a full two inches to her height. She didn't care that she was naked, didn't care that her own juices were trickling down her leg. All she knew was that this man was not going to do *that* to her and then run away. She didn't care about Alec Trevayne. She only cared about this man, about how he could make her giddy with tingles. No way was he leaving like this.

This weekend was her Christmas, her only Christmas, and he wouldn't steal it from her.

She stalked over to the window, stared at the last remnants of the day, the snowflakes still falling fast and furious.

"You cannot drive in this weather."

"Rebecca, don't."

"Don't? Don't what? Don't yell, don't be angry?"

"No," he answered quietly.

"I will not be used," she said, blinking back tears.

"You used me."

"I did...not," she finished.

Cory didn't try to correct her, simply continued dressing. She watched him, arms folded over her chest.

Eventually he straightened, his gaze drifting over her body. Rebecca didn't move, her jaw locked in place.

"Do you want me to build a fire before I go? You'll get cold."

She was already cold, ice-cold, all the fire inside her spent. Rebecca shook her head. "Leave if you want."

He paused, then went to the fireplace, pulling some kindling from an old-style iron log basket. The second he lit the match, a knock sounded on the door.

"Rebecca? Rebecca Neumann?"

Cory looked up at Rebecca.

Rebecca looked at the door.

A slow, tight smile covered her face. She sauntered over, naked as the day she was born (except for the requisite socks), and threw open the door.

"Alec Trevayne? Hello, I'm Rebecca Neumann."

5

WHY COULDN'T SHE cooperate? This was a simple thing. He was leaving, she was staying, and she needed to get with the program. Cory rubbed at his eyes. "I should explain something to you," Rebecca said to the Brit. "We're both victims of a setup gone horribly bad. As you can see I'm pleased with my current lover."

Somehow Alec Trevayne managed an impeccable politeness, but how? Rebecca had the primest ass on the North American continent, but the Brit kept his eyes glued to her face.

Cory swore, grabbed the blanket from the bed and dropped it around her shoulders. He hovered nearby in case she decided to toss it off. Considering the hard line of her jaw, that seemed a possibility.

And, yes, Rebecca wasn't done. "I was given a travel package by Santa Claus. Yes, you heard right, Santa. When I got here, I discovered a man from my past, and we've spent the last few hours rekindling an old flame."

"There was no flame," Cory corrected, still hoping that Alec would be the stand-up guy he was supposed to be, while Cory could get the hell out of Dodge.

Alec looked at Rebecca, looked at Cory, then laughed nervously. "I should leave you two."

Rebecca nodded graciously, doing a great Queen of England impersonation. Damn, the two of them belonged together. "I'm sorry about the mix-up," she was telling him. "I'm sure we'll see each other in the city and have one of those awkward moments, and you seem so nice, and I hate to think that we can't be mature and laugh about this. Hahaha. I had no idea that Natalie invited you up here. We could've solved so many problems if Natalie had simply explained things to me."

"Things. Yes."

"Sometimes passion burns at the most inopportune times."

"Passion was not burning," announced Cory, his fingers curling into his palms. She was building a trap around him. A neat, skin-colored trap with tiny, white hands, soft, ripe breasts and the tightest—

"Don't mind Cory. He's shy."

At that, Cory knew he had to take a more active role in this situation. "Don't judge me by your standards. I don't greet strangers in the nude, no. But it doesn't mean I'm shy," he corrected, noticing the corner of the blanket starting to slip.

He turned to Alec, but the stand-up Brit was gone. Fled. *Damn it.* Cory slammed the door.

"Why the hell did you do that?" His watch said it was nearly seven o'clock. He'd missed a day and he needed to leave. He felt it, the panic, the anger, the need to run. She didn't understand. He *had* to leave.

"It's not any fun when you don't have a voice in the matter, is it?"

And now she wanted to play the victim? "Oh, come on, Rebecca. And fix the blanket."

Noticing her blanket-slippage was a tactical mistake on his part—he saw the beady gleam in her eyes.

"You liar," she said.

"I never lied."

"You said one night."

Do not argue semantics with a schoolteacher. So, he had lied. He had lied for her own good, for his own sanity. Cory moved to the window. "The moon is high. Technically it's now night."

She scoffed at his logic, the blanket slipping another inch, exposing the fine arch of her breast. Cory swallowed.

"You're a coward."

Yes, he was, and better that she recognized it now. "The last thing you need is a one-night stand."

"Since we haven't been together for one night, I'm in no position to know that, am I? I'm demanding my one-night stand. You know you want it, too."

One inch of taut, rose-colored nipple emerged. He'd been so careful not to touch her more than he had to. He deserved a medal for not touching her when he was inside her, but did she appreciate the sacrifice?

She cast the blanket aside, and Cory felt all the blood drain from his face. "Put on the blanket," he pleaded.

"It was easy earlier, Cory. This didn't bother you. You were all Mr. Hop-On-Rebecca. What's changed?"

Earlier, Cory had known the Brit was eagerly waiting down-stairs for Rebecca—it made the situation bearable. Now there was nobody downstairs. Well, there was probably somebody downstairs, but they weren't eagerly awaiting Rebecca. Now the only person eagerly awaiting Rebecca was Cory.

"Put on the blanket," he repeated, hearing the weakness in his voice.

She lifted it up from the ground, slipping it over one shoulder toga-style, no help at all. "You can't drive in this weather. No way. I'll get dressed if you'll agree to stay."

"That's blackmail."

"It's only blackmail if it works."

Cory hated the look in her eyes. Hope and excitement were shining there, blinding him. He stayed far away from women with those eyes, but most women with those eyes didn't lounge in front of him, smooth curves of peaches-and-cream flesh, and woollen plaid socks that honestly turned him on.

He was only a man.

Her smile grew wider, a victory smile, and Cory didn't have the heart or the willpower to disappoint her. All he had to do was be himself. She'd figure out the problem soon enough. He'd leave at first light, he promised himself. His fingers lifted, flexed, wanting to trace the line of her—

"We've got a deal," she stated, not even bothering to wait for his reply. She turned and quickly, efficiently put on her clothes. "We can order up dinner. Maybe a bottle of wine."

Wine. She wanted wine. Cory's throat was parched for whiskey, his hard-on was parched for something else entirely, and she was looking at him, ready for an evening full of chitchat.

The sounds of Christmas carols drifted in from outside.

It was going to be one holy hell of a night.

DINNER CONSISTED of buffalo wings, nachos, spinach dip, French fries, buffalo burgers and chicken fingers. Junk food heaven. Rebecca sat cross-legged on the bed and sighed in glorious satisfaction as she surveyed the food trays in front of them.

"Not a gourmet, are you?" Cory asked. He hadn't said very much while they ate and she wondered if she'd made a mistake by making him stay against his will. He looked comfortable leaning back against the pillows and eating nachos, but he was quiet. Too quiet. However, she'd just had Cory Bell take care of her life's one and only regret—she wasn't about to develop a new one.

"No. You?"

"I try to eat healthy when I can."

Instantly she was shamed. "I didn't get to eat much junk food when I was a kid. Everybody needs a vice." She slathered a fry in ketchup. "You have one?"

"Pretty much all seven," he said.

And she almost believed him. "Nah. I can spot greed."

"Your parents have money?"

"My students." Rebecca blew out a breath, as she remembered what she'd left behind. Maybe she already had a new regret.

"Why don't you quit if it bothers you?"

He sounded as if he was actually interested.

Could she tell him she'd been fired a mere two days ago? And if she did, would she look worse in his eyes? You betcha. It was a black mark, a flaw, a big splotch on her permanent record. So she chose to fudge the whole sordid jobless situation.

"I'm almost adjusted to it, and that only took me eight years. Some times of the year are harder than others. When the kids talk about skiing in the Alps at Christmas, or the annual 'I went around the world for my summer vacation' report, yeah, I get a bit envious, but hey, it's a living. You build buildings?" she asked, smoothly changing the subject. "Why?"

"Pays the bills."

"Very practical," she said, eyeing him with appreciation. "I always imagined you'd be out doing the *Easy Rider* thing, cruising across America, drifting whichever way the wind blows."

"Had enough of that early on. It gets old eventually."

"So why do you still dress the part?"

"Building isn't a desk job, Rebecca. It's dirty, grimy, and leather and boots are very practical."

"SURE, if you say so."

"What's that supposed to mean?" Cory asked, not liking the analytical tone she was using, nor the professor look in her eyes, either. He wanted the cheerleader back, the one who smiled pretty and didn't ask a lot of questions. Now she was a teacher. Cory had never liked teachers. They wanted to stick their nose where it didn't belong.

"You have a very stationary job. You cook for yourself, don't you?"

"Yeah, so?"

"You're settled, but you're trying to be all James Dean."

"Maybe 'James Dean' is what I want," he answered, jamming a nacho into his mouth so that he wouldn't have to talk.

"Maybe 'James Dean' is what you *want* to want, but 'settled' is what you *really* want."

He glared and she picked up the hint. "Fine," she continued, "spoil my fun. I don't get to analyze adults very often, except for Natalie of course, and she's completely boring."

"Natalie's the one who set you up in the Honeymoon Suite?"

"I think so, but I won't know for sure until she answers her stupid cell phone."

"I gotta tell you, I don't think she's your friend, Rebecca. This lodge is a trip to honeymoon hell. You're alone in a couples place."

"Not really," she said, with a pointed glance at him.

"Still a trip to hell," he insisted.

"The sex wasn't that awful," she answered, holding a French fry in the air, watching it limp to one side.

He gave her a hard look. "It wasn't awful at all."

"If you're into the whole furniture-banging thing," she said, biting the fry in two.

"Not your thing, huh?"

"Maybe."

"So why didn't you stick with the Brit?" It seemed to Cory that the Brit could give Rebecca everything she wanted, in spades.

"Alec?"

"You know more?"

"No, he's the only one."

"So why didn't you stick with him when you had the chance? Seems like he's the right guy for you."

Rebecca sounded like any number of confused women who wanted security, happiness and a man who she could count on—both in her bed and out. The Brit had driven through a blizzard to get to her. Had to give the guy credit for that. Cory wasn't the kind of guy to drive through blizzards for any woman.

"He's not the right guy," she announced.

"At least he doesn't make you nervous."

"What makes you think I'm nervous?"

"You get an eye-twitch sometimes. Relax, Rebecca. We don't have to do anything. After all, you're not into that whole furniture-banging thing," he said, not meaning to bring it up, but a man's pride was a sensitive thing.

"Maybe I like furniture-banging," she said, just to spite him.

"Never mind."

"Don't tell me never mind. Maybe I want to do some furniture-banging right now."

Cory held up a hand in peace. "Maybe you *want* to want furniture-banging, but you *really* want a wedding ring. I've seen your type looking through bridal magazines, not trolling the bars looking to pick up men for a one-night stand. Why are you so afraid to admit it?"

Rebecca shook her head. "Maybe I want to try it on. See if it looks good on me. I'm almost thirty, Cory. I don't know if I want to be me for the rest of my life. What if I'm missing something? Don't you ever feel that way?"

"You're not thirty yet?" he asked. She was on a personal life quest, and he was still doing math.

"Fine. I'm thirty-one," she admitted, and she didn't seem happy about it. "You're not Mr. Adventure, either, you know."

Cory looked at her, shocked. "I am."

"Please. You eat healthy. It's impossible."

"You make my life sound boring."

"Your life is everything you make it."

Once again she was leading the conversation into shark-infested waters, where the jaws of emotional trappings were snapping all around him. "Let's watch TV."

"Chicken-shit."

"*Bwak, bwak, bwak,*" he answered, not meeting her eyes, and then powered on the TV. Television was much safer.

PROBLEM WAS, Cory spent nearly fifteen minutes trying to watch the movie, but he wasn't interested. He'd replayed their sex video over and over in his head, and although he'd had one of the best orgasms in his life, she wasn't happy. It pricked at every bit of male pride he possessed.

Ha. She'd had a great time, but she didn't want to admit it because it didn't fit into her neat dollhouse existence.

He leaned over and began to unbutton her blouse. This was what she wanted, so damn it, he'd give it to her.

She looked at him, eyes wide and twitching. "Now?"

"Why not?" he asked because this was supposed to be a one-night stand. She was willing, he was ready. All he had to do was prove it to her. In fact—he took a handful of cotton and ripped—he wasn't close to boring.

Buttons flew across the room, and he saw the spark of adventure in her eyes.

He freed one breast from the pointless bra she wore and fastened his mouth around it.

She smelled like apple cider and something flowery and sweet, but her skin tasted like spice. Lush, potent, spice. His mouth sucked harder and he heard a low, feminine moan.

Success.

Cory lowered her back on the bed, slowly drawing down her pants. She shouldn't have dressed. He shouldn't have dressed, not when there was all this—

His hand reached down.

Moist heat.

Rebecca bucked when he touched her, but he hadn't even started. Not really. Determinedly his hand skimmed back and forth, and he watched her face. She had no idea what she kept bottled inside her. The eyes were a sensible gray until she got turned on. And then the devils came there, banking the silver with low fires. Her hair fell in a straight line, until her head listed to one side, the pale silk falling in her eyes like a wanton. And the mouth. No disguising the plump mouth and its intended uses. But they'd save that for later.

Later.

Cory cursed himself, drawing down her panties more roughly than he intended, but Rebecca didn't seem to mind. Her fingers were kneading at his shoulder like a kitten.

This time he drew her legs apart, watching as the sharpened, silvery eyes shifted to his mouth. He knew what she wanted. A kiss. A bond of more than bodies.

His fingers moved higher inside her, deeper, and she gasped. Her gaze moved off his mouth.

He bent his head, his mouth feasted on her other breast, pulling and laving.

Her back arched into him, her hips tilting in invitation. Her pelvis rubbing against the fly of his jeans. Rebecca was a fast learner, fast learning which things would drive him out of his mind. The jeans were gone, and then his cock was inside her.

Maybe it was nothing but furniture-banging, but it'd be the best furniture-banging she'd ever get. When he felt that slick glove surround him he felt a thousand devils burn within.

He had meant to screw her hard and fast. To show the perky tight-ass cheerleader that she wasn't the perfect angel she wanted to be. But that face...

It was as if it was yesterday, and he was back in high school. He felt that same pull. That same desire to make those angel's eyes look at him. See him.

Cory thrust inside her slow, smooth. She noticed the change, and watched him warily. Again he went inside her, deeper this time. Dark lashes fell against her cheeks, her eyes hidden. He sank into her again, willing her to look at him.

She did.

The wanton, cloudy gaze hit on his mouth, plump lips open, waiting, inviting. He shouldn't. He shouldn't.

There was a sick throbbing in his gut as he lowered his mouth, feeling her warm breath on his skin. He didn't listen to the voice inside him, instead he lunged into the kiss like a drowning man. There were many things that Cory feared, and this was one. Losing himself inside someone else.

He kissed her again and again, tasting the sweetness in her, plundering her mouth, drawing her light into his darkness.

It didn't work—the darkness was still there, but God, he kept trying. He pounded her. He wanted to own her. Wanted to...wanted to do so many things. But in the end, he knew he couldn't. The heat in his blood cooled, reminding him that when you trusted people, they could turn on you, pull you into the shadows and do despicable things that no person should endure. He wasn't going back there. Ever again.

He wanted to pull away from her, but she felt too good. Instead he thrust even deeper. Telling himself that he was only fucking her. And that if he said it enough, he'd believe it.

Over and over he moved inside her, feeling her move with him. Feeling her muscles, feeling her blood, feeling her.

It felt so pure.

Then her muscles stiffened around him, and he saw her eyes glaze over. When he watched her come, the punch in his gut was a thousand times worse than he'd ever expected. Instinctively his body reacted, tightened and he spilled himself inside her.

The innocent eyes stared up at him, seeing things, good things in him that weren't there. She, who'd never seen the darkness in humanity. He, who couldn't escape it.

No. No. No. No. No.

Quickly Cory withdrew from her and began to dress. He needed to leave, he needed to leave now. Rebecca watched him from the bed, and he didn't want to meet her eyes, but his eyes didn't obey. His gaze kept wandering over her, seeing the places where he'd touched that slight body, where he'd trod. Red marks marred her arms where his hands had gripped too tightly. There was a purple bruise on her breast where his stubble had been. She had the look of a woman well used.

For the second time that evening, he put on his boots, ready to go. He waited for her to stop him, but there was a new look in her eyes. She wouldn't stop him anymore. Rebecca Neumann had finally wised up. He wasn't the kind of guy who was going to stick around, not for anyone.

"Not bad furniture-banging there, huh?" she asked, her mouth still swollen from his kiss.

Damn her. Cory stood, taking one inopportune step toward the bed. "I'll leave now," he stated stupidly because he still thought she'd stop him. Instead she stretched like a cat, and Cory felt the tortured urge to pounce.

Her eyes dared him to pounce.

It was the challenge that did him in. Cory'd never been one for a challenge. He walked out before he'd do something she'd regret for a very long time.

6

REBECCA FIRED A pillow at the door, which accomplished nothing, but proved her foolishness. As if the previous ten hours hadn't.

Some Christmas present. Four orgasms, one hickey and a bad case of stubble burn. And those were only the physical symptoms. Still, she'd known exactly what she was getting into.

A one-night stand.

She got up and stood near the window, watching the late-night sky light up with stars. The whole scene was like something from a fairy tale, a Normal Rockwell painting come to life. But right now, it sucked eggs. Big eggs.

The fire was crackling happily, uncaring of her foul mood. It was 2:00 a.m. and she wasn't going to sleep anytime soon. This was Christmas, this was her vacation. Why couldn't something go right for a change? Was it too much to ask?

Five minutes later there was a quiet knock on the door. This time Rebecca grabbed a robe from the bathroom and went and opened the door.

Cory—not that he looked happy to be there.

"Road's still blocked?" she asked, trying to be casual.

He nodded curtly. "Nobody was at the front desk—guess everybody's down for the night. If it's all right with you, I'll sleep on the floor."

And somehow they'd moved beyond the one-night stand to the no-night stand. "The chair might be more comfortable."

His eyes cut from hers to the stuffed chair. "I'm used to the floor."

In the top of the closet she found some blankets and an extra pillow. She tossed them in his general direction. "I'm going to soak my feet. I hope the noise won't keep you awake."

Actually she hoped it would keep him awake for hours upon hours, but that wouldn't gain her points on the sophistication scale, so she turned on her heel and went off into the bathroom. As far as she was concerned, Cory Bell was on his own.

THE WHIRRING SOUND kept him awake. She said she was soaking her feet, but she'd been at it way too long.

The floor was hard, but Cory wasn't a stranger to hard floors. When you slept on the floor, it was easier to get away fast.

Some habits died hard, some habits never died at all.

He stared up at the ceiling, wishing for anything that would numb the damned knot deep in his gut. Everything irked him. The holidays, the trees, even the twinkly lights. If it wasn't for her—no, scratch that—if it wasn't for the snow, he wouldn't be here at all.

Cory pulled the blanket up tight and closed his eyes. He might not be able to sleep tonight, but he'd be sure that she would never know.

REBECCA RAISED HER FEET from the bubbles, but even the soothing scent of cucumber and melon didn't help. What the heck was wrong with her? Was she deficient in some way? Never. Except for fallen arches, she was absolutely perfect.

Okay, he was right. She wasn't cut out for one-night stands. Maybe that was why she was sitting here giving herself a pedicure at 3:00 a.m., wondering what was wrong with her? Darn it, did he have to be so cold, so uncaring, so…one-night-standish?

Arg.

She picked out the pale mauve nail polish, but forgot about the metal towel rack overhead. She hit it. Hard.

"Ow."

"You okay?" Cory called from the other room.

So now there was care and concern for her well-being? She glared at the closed door. "Lovely."

"Don't want you to get hurt."

"Oh, no. No hurt here."

"Sure you're okay?"

"Peachy."

"Was that sarcasm?"

"No sarcasm."

"It sounded sarcastic."

She gathered the robe around her and flung open the door. "There. Was. No. Sarcasm."

"You're angry."

"No, I'm painting my toenails and unless you have a secret desire for a career in the beauty industry, you'll leave me alone."

He sat up, pushed the blanket aside. She was both relieved and disappointed to see that Cory had gone to bed in his clothes. "I'll help."

Rebecca took a step back, hiding her feet under the robe. Her feet were the reason she never wore sandals, never wore flip-flops, never exposed her naked feet to men—ever. They were ugly. "You can't paint toes."

"I do great interior and exterior work. How hard can a toe be?"

"Ten."

He scoffed. "How hard can ten toes be?"

"Why are you doing this?" she asked, giving him a suspicious once-over. When she'd walked in, his face was paler than earlier, and his eyes, well, his eyes looked nervy.

"I couldn't sleep. You're pissed."

"I'm not pissed," she stated for the record.

"Whatever," he said, not quite listening.

Rebecca was used to regaining lost attention. That, and she wanted his eyes less nervy. "I'm a little pissed."

Some of the color returned to his face. "A little?"

"I'm a little more than pissed, but this isn't that bad, comparatively."

"You fall into rages often?"

"You haven't met some of the kids I teach."

"Monsters?"

"I got fired," she said, her toes peeking out from under the robe. That got his attention. "From your job? Was this recent?"

"Two days ago," she admitted, though it seemed like four lifetimes ago. Still, it felt good to say it aloud.

"Then I think you should really let me paint your toes." His face wasn't filled with sympathy and his eyes held their normal flat darkness, but the air turned. The night was softer, warmer. Some of the old ghosts had left the room.

Maybe it was time. Out of all the men she'd ever lain with, Cory Bell was the man least likely to run screaming from her feet.

She settled herself on the bed, her feet tucked safely under her, and he took the nail polish from her hand. She watched, waiting for him to admit defeat and hand it back. He didn't. For the first time she noticed the deep scars on his right hand. Four neat half-moons scored in the middle of his palm.

He saw her look and closed his fingers over the marks. Then he unscrewed the lid and pulled out the brush, and she laughed.

"You have to shake it first."

And he shook it all wrong. Rebecca took the bottle, shook it correctly, then handed it to him.

"I bet you were hell in the classroom."

"I was a sweetheart. Except when they deserved it. And then—"

"You want me to paint your toes or not?" he asked patiently, waiting for her to produce her feet from the safety of white terry cloth. He was going to see her fallen arches.

It's not that they were huge banana boats. They weren't. A tiny, trim size six. Everything about her she could live with, except for her arches. Flat feet. Done in after eight years of gymnastics and cheerleading. It wasn't a big flaw, and somehow that made it worse. It wasn't an elaborate stretchmark, or an extra pound of flesh that she could exercise away. It was prosaic, and ordinary, a physical characteristic that couldn't be hidden under full-coverage concealer. And she hated it.

Suddenly his eyes were too knowing, too aware. She couldn't do this. She held out her hand for the polish. "Here. I'm not going to make you do this."

"Why not?"

"I changed my mind. I don't need to paint my toes."

"Why not? You've got somewhere else to go?"

"I just don't want to."

"Maybe I do."

"You don't."

"I want to do something for you. In the big scheme of things, painting your toes seems like a wise choice."

It was her moment of truth, to finally show someone her flaw. He was waiting, watching her expectantly. Okay, maybe it wouldn't be so bad, and they weren't ever going to see each other again. So what if he laughed? First she pulled out one foot, then the other.

There was no laughing.

Silently he took the brush from the bottle and started painting her little toe.

It was an amazingly anticlimactic moment after a lifetime of apprehension. Rebecca studied his bent head and wondered at the thoughts there.

She didn't talk while he worked, just watched him with cautious eyes. He concentrated so carefully, his hands not shaking, and every now and again, he'd bite his lip. In high school, she'd heard rumors, and as an adult, she'd seen that rigid, disciplined demeanor before. The first time, it was a small boy in her class. Eventually he'd been taken away from his father, yet Rebecca never knew the details.

She longed to put the life back in Cory's eyes, longed to stroke his hair, longed to hold him close and keep him safe, but she realized she was about twenty years too late. So she began to talk, simple things at first, the story about how she ruined her mother's garden by using hair spray on the roses, the time she thought she could sing and how she decided to run away to Juilliard, until her father said she had a voice like a wounded hyena. Cory laughed at that, she saw it. He started to talk, too, not like her confessions, but stories about the renovations that he'd done for people, stories about his trips to Canada, never sharing anything about his childhood at all.

After a while, she stopped talking and merely watched him, silently, jealously, wishing for Christmas miracles that never would occur.

Saturday, December 21

AT FIRST LIGHT, Cory rose and dressed, keeping the promise to himself. It was easier to escape in the dawn, when most everyone slept like the dead. Rebecca was a restless sleeper, a cover-stealer and a clinger. He hadn't slept that well in years.

He paused by the bed, watching her, her eyes closed, her face so peaceful and full of dreams. She was glorious and sexy and everything he'd wanted her to be. She pushed aside the blankets, exposing a long length of bare thigh, and he almost stayed. Almost climbed back into bed, burying himself in her body, burying himself in her heart.

But people like him, the ones who lived in the sordid shadows, didn't get the cheerleaders of the world. They never would. One day he'd wake up from a nightmare, and she'd ask about it, and he would lie. And the lies would go on from there. The knot tightened inside him, telling him to run. There were some secrets he'd never share.

He swore quietly, pulled on his coat and left.

REBECCA KNEW the second Cory left her side. She kept her eyes shut, listening to the rustle of clothes, fighting the sting of one wayward tear that seemed to want to escape. No regretful tears over a one-night stand. She'd bet that that was one of the rules. The door closed and Rebecca buried her head in the pillow.

WHEN CORY GOT downstairs, the lodge was awake, people ready and waiting for Christmas. The seconds ticking past, bringing the holiday closer and closer. It wasn't Christmas specifically that made him antsy, any holiday would pretty much do it for him. Any time when families got together and outsiders were treated, well, like outsiders.

When he was a kid, he'd tried to do the right thing, knowing one wrong word, or look, and he'd be cast from the house faster than you could say "emotional difficulty."

That'd worked for a while until 1984. His fourth foster family, the McGraws, had had him for nearly two months. Then Mrs. McGraw had left the house for a long weekend in Atlantic City, leaving Cory alone with Mr. McGraw, who was the first pervert Cory had come across. Less than twenty-four fun-filled hours later, Cory hit the streets. Fuck me once, shame on you. Fuck me twice, shame on me.

After that, he'd gotten tougher, smarter, faster. When situations got dicey, Cory was gone, out the door, no looking back. This time, he had to get past a maid rushing up the stairs with a breakfast tray. And Mrs. Krause who was carrying a pile of towels. She spotted him and stopped.

He tried to avoid looking guilty, but Cory had looked guilty his entire life. "Morning."

"Leaving so soon?" she asked, cutting right to the chase.

"Yeah. Figured I'd move out as soon as the roads were plowed."

"They are clear. Mr. Trevayne said his goodbyes an hour ago. Too bad you're leaving, though."

"Yeah. You have a nice place," he offered.

"If you're heading toward town, maybe you can take a couple of guests to the train station. They were looking for a ride."

Cory glanced away. "Sorry. Going the opposite direction."

Mrs. Krause clicked her tongue.

"I should get out of here," he stated, because he could feel her niceness drawing on him, pulling him back toward the warm confines of the lodge, of Rebecca.

"Be careful of the ice. Mighty slick. Could drive right into a ditch and disappear altogether."

And that was the idea. "Thanks for the warning." Cory gave a halfhearted wave and headed out the door.

As soon as he was gone, Helen Krause hollered for her husband. "Roland!"

Roland Krause came from the kitchen, scratching his head. "You don't have to yell. Not deaf yet."

"Cory Bell just left. Tell me how far he's going."

The old man gave her a knowing wink. "Not far without the battery cables."

"You think he'll check it?"

"Probably. But with all the young hooligans running around in this area—whoo-ee, makes me wish I was forty years younger—"

"When you were one of those young hooligans."

He patted her on the rear, and she felt a blush in her cheeks. "I could chase you around the living room if you'd like."

"Not now, Roland. We have guests."

"All right, Helen. For you, I'll wait. Forever if I have to."

Helen watched her husband walk away, still doing her heart good after all this time. She sighed, quit her mooning and returned to work. There was still much too much to do.

"MY, MY. Back again?"

Rebecca greeted him at the door in the terry-cloth robe and this time, her red wool socks. He tried to ignore the *thump-thump-thump* in his chest.

Which immediately put him on the defensive. "Don't start. They took my battery cables. Tell me what kind of whack job disables cars in the middle of a snowstorm?"

She folded her arms across her chest. "Battery cables, huh?"

"You want to go down there and see for yourself?"

"No, I believe you," she answered in a voice that called him a liar.

Ah, hell. He should have known she wasn't the "forgive and forget" type. Rebecca Neumann looked as if she could hold a grudge forever.

"Okay, I shouldn't have left like that. I'm sorry, but I'm doing the right thing here. You should understand that. I'm doing the right thing." The hard slate-gray of her eyes didn't seem to comprehend the truth in his words.

"I don't need you to do me any favors."

"And you don't need my problems, Rebecca." It was the understatement of the year.

Time to start over, he decided. She was leaving on Tuesday. He could stay a day, maybe two, if only to show her that he wasn't worth the effort. Cory planted a small smile on his face. "Look. I'm still stuck, so let's make the best of it, okay? What do you want to do today? Sky's the limit, and well, actually the weather's the limit, but I'm game to whatever you want to try." There weren't many options, and in Cory's mind, most didn't involve clothes. It was a win-win all the way around.

"Let's go outside," she said. He examined the froufrou paraphernalia she had littered around the room. Outside?

"In the snow?"

"Well, duh. We could walk to town."

Cory made a rude noise. "Bunch of antique stores? No, thank you," he said, still thinking an afternoon lying in bed would be prime. "We could go ice-skating," he offered. A compromise and better than antiques.

"I can't skate."

"Good. You can learn."

"You can?"

"Hockey. Junior high. Put a stick in my hand and I can fly."

"So you could teach me?"

"Hockey?"

"I think I have to learn to skate first. You'll have to teach me."

"I can't teach."

"I can't, either, but they did pay me for it."

She had that sultry gleam in her eye, and he knew she'd beaten him. Maybe deep in his black heart he'd wanted her to beat him.

Fan-tastic. Today was whatever Rebecca wanted. "I'll try, but if you break your ankle or something, I'm not liable."

AFTER BREAKFAST, they went to the lake situated close behind the inn. There was a small crowd, couples, a few families, but most people seemed to have stayed in.

Rebecca eyed the ice nervously. It seemed very hard, very cold. "Maybe we should go back."

"Now who's being a chicken-shit?"

"My blood runs deep yellow."

"I thought you wanted to do this. Do it." He dragged her out on the ice, skating backward, guiding her around in a slow circle. It was like a glorified car-tow.

"You should move your feet," he told her.

"But then I'll fall. Car-towing is good."

"Come on," he said, his voice warm and coaxing, and for a second she caught a glimpse of Cory the Seducer. How many high school girls parted with their virginity because of that crooked attempt of a smile? The dark eyes never quite bloomed alive, but sometimes you saw a flash of humanity, a flash of a man who should've been.

Her feet stuttered in perfect time with her heart. Then one foot slid in front of the other.

"Do it again," he said, still coaxing, still seducing.

Rebecca kept moving along, a shuffling gait more suited to a senior citizen's walker than ice. She didn't enjoy being gawky or flawed, especially in front of other people. But she didn't do it for her, she did it for him. The momentary flash of his smile made all the embarrassment worthwhile.

"See, you're skating," he said, a complete overstatement. Then he let go of her hands. She screamed and promptly fell on her butt. He moved behind her, steady arms hooked under hers, easing her upright. Just as she was ready to fall again, he quickly propped her back up.

Rebecca felt the need to restate the ground rules. "No letting go. I don't like falls. They hurt."

He shrugged casually, a man accustomed to pain and falls.

Rebecca didn't want him to hurt. She wanted to ease the falls and heal the pain, but she knew she couldn't. Cory wasn't her Charlie Brown Christmas tree. She couldn't wrap him in a blanket and bright ornaments and have him suddenly come to life, because life wasn't a thirty-minute TV special. Scars didn't heal. They stayed. They burned, and they never went away, no matter how hard you tried. This, Rebecca knew only too well.

For a while, Cory towed her around, but sometimes he did let go. The first time, she froze. The second time, she skated. Two glides before falling, but it counted all the same. As a childhood educator—former childhood educator—she knew the power of positive reinforcement, no matter how small and insignificant the accomplishment.

"Excellent," he announced, his face ruddy from the cold, but the eyes were endearing. He had no idea how powerfully he was growing on her. Cory Bell from P.S. 35 was an adolescent girl's fantasy. Cory Bell, the man, had grown into much, much more. Even if he did have a tendency to run.

She lost her balance, tilting into him, possibly—probably—on purpose.

He stared at her mouth, and she heard his indrawn breath. She wanted to feel his mouth, breathe life there, into his heart. He lowered his head, and she waited. Just when she could feel his warmth, feel the whisper inside him, he drew back, his eyes guarded once again. "That's probably enough for today."

Rebecca tried to smile, possibly—probably—failed. "Sure."

As he removed his skates, she again noticed the scars on his palms. Maybe there wasn't anything that would help. Maybe she should give up the fight, but that wasn't Rebecca. She'd always been blessed (or cursed) with what her mother called "razor-sharp focus." Frustrated, Rebecca began removing her own skates. With the skates safely returned, he walked ahead of her on the narrow path to the lodge, giving her his back. She'd dealt with abused kids, she'd seen what worked, what didn't. But he wasn't a kid anymore, and she wasn't sure how to handle a man who buried his pain so thoroughly.

Rebecca trudged through the deep snow, feeling the cold build up inside her. Why couldn't he open up to her, admit that he was having fun? Because he was stubborn, that's why.

So, she had no choice. She gathered a fistful of snow and rolled it into a rocklike ball of ammunition.

Rebecca fired.

Dead hit, right on the back of his head.

Perhaps there was a smirk on her face when he turned. Quickly she wiped it away.

"What was that for?"

"Having some fun."

His eyes narrowed. "You fight dirty, Miss Neumann."

"And your point would be?"

He laughed. Low and full of retribution. She should have been fearful, but Rebecca had her jets firing. Those same jets had made her homecoming princess by a landslide, snag James Anders Hardy from bitchy little Monique O'Neal and beat out snotty Heather Patterson for the Modern Manhattan Prep job. Now, Rebecca was two seconds away from a full-blown connip-tion, and as anyone who had experienced Miss Neumann's class knew, a conniption was a moment to be feared.

She watched as he picked up some snow and trudged forward. One step, two. Closer to her. His eyes weren't nearly so empty now.

"Bring it on," she mocked.

He reached for her, and promptly dumped his handful of snow inside her coat. Down her shirt.

Rebecca gasped, her nipples sharpened into frigid icicles. Deftly she shook out the snow, but there was no feeling in her chest anymore. Rat bastard.

He snickered, dancing away from her, her fists flying.

She grabbed more snow, packing it tight, wound up the pitch, and let it fly.

He ducked.

Damn.

Cory advanced, hands held up. "Truce."

Rebecca, noticing the curve of his mouth and heated light in his eyes, felt the exquisite thrill of victory, and stuffed her hands in her pockets. "Fine."

He hooked a finger on her coat and pulled her toward him. She shouldn't have seemed so breathy, so girly, so…eager, but this time when he lowered his mouth, she was ready. Oh, she was more than ready. The hard bark of a tree bit against her back, the hard feel of Cory crushed against her front, and everything in between was starting to melt. She knew he could kiss, knew how good he could kiss, and frankly, it confused her why he avoided the whole kissing thing.

As far as Rebecca was concerned, two people could stay here, mouth to mouth, forever. As long as it was Cory. As long as it was her. A sigh welled up inside her. Longing and loneliness combining forces to overwhelm her. She had never imagined she was lonely, aching for this. But now…she never wanted to be alone again.

Cory lifted his head and stared, the pulse throbbing in his throat. His dark eyes were rabbit-still, and she could see the panic radiating from within him. She didn't move, didn't speak, merely waited for the instant to pass. She would wait as long as necessary because no man had ever made her want so badly.

The wind danced through the branches of the tree above them, snow falling to the ground.

I know what you want for Christmas, and there you'll find it under the tree.

The words from the letter came back to her, and she felt the magic. The air shivered with it, whispering in her mind, stunning her with it. This was her Christmas present. He was her Christmas present. A bubble of laughter welled up inside her. She'd been so wrong to doubt for one second the magic of Christmas.

She smiled up at him, still waiting.

"Sorry. Didn't mean to do that," he said, the light completely dimmed from his eyes. She felt the laughter inside her dim, as well. Now wasn't the time for sorry. Now was the time for the "I've been waiting forever for you" speech. Now was the time when the cupids and cherubim plucked at their harps and lyres, and carolers burst into glorious song.

She waited for the moment, but the moment passed.

Instead Rebecca bit the inside of her mouth, hard.

7

BEING SURROUNDED by all this "happiness" and "joy" was starting to make Cory jumpy, as if he was inside some undercover operation, pretending to be something he wasn't. Rebecca made him want to pretend.

When the sun rose on Sunday morning, he didn't even think about running away. Didn't even act like he wanted to. She just rolled over next to him, throwing an arm over his side, keeping him close. Cory went back to sleep. Dreamless sleep. He didn't need dreams, he was sleepwalking through one. Happily.

He knew she saw things in him—some real, some imagined—and somewhere he'd stopped worrying about it.

Rebecca would be leaving soon.

They had until Tuesday morning, Christmas Eve, and then she would leave for her parents' place and he'd be on his way to Canada. Until then, he would stay. Have a good time. It was sex, nothing more, then he'd dash out the door without saying goodbye—the patented Cory Bell method of retreat. Goodbye wasn't a word in his vocabulary.

He woke again and watched her sleep. He kept repeating the plan in his head, but it felt off, like driving in a nail and missing the stud. As he stroked the softness of her hair, he knew that for now he wasn't going to worry. Now he was going to pretend that his past had never existed, that the scars in his palm had never existed, that the black hole inside him didn't exist, either. At the moment, the only thing that existed was her.

She woke a few minutes later, and they took a shower together, before Cory brought up breakfast from the dining room. She'd just finished eating when her cell phone rang. Cory glanced at the display, didn't want to seem overly curious, but didn't want to see some guy's name, all the same.

It was Natalie. Rebecca ignored it.

"Why aren't you picking up?"

She flipped off the phone. "Sometimes it's better not to know."

Yeah, ignorance worked a lot for him, too. He understood that. He wasn't sure what the plans were for today, but the way she was rubbing her feet, it seemed like ice-skating was out. He suggested a sleigh ride later in the afternoon, and judging by the way her eyes lit up, that was definitely on the agenda.

Gee.

In his rational mind, he was all sarcastic and smarmy. In his not-nearly-so-rational heart, he knew he wouldn't deny her anything.

"How do you know Natalie?" he asked, curiosity finally overcoming caution.

She pulled three sweaters out of her suitcase and held each one up to the mirror.

"We worked together."

"She's a teacher, too?"

Rebecca decided on the blue one, and then lined up four sets of boots. Yes, the woman loved her shoes.

"Tell me about your kids," he said, after pointing to the pair with low heels. Thankfully she didn't argue.

He kicked back on the bed and watched her morning routine. After the shower, there was the skin treatment, then the makeup, then the hair. Rebecca was not speedy in the morning. He thought it was cute. While she towel-dried her hair, she started to talk, laughing sometimes, the sound making him smile. He'd gotten to where he'd ask her ordinary questions about her life, just to hear that laugh.

"Well, mainly they're spoiled, with demanding parents, and more money than any one family should have. They have toys that cost more than some apartments. And when they do something wrong…" She laughed. "Never tell a parent their child is not perfect."

But all that complaining didn't match the serene look on her face.

"Why do you do it?"

"I don't anymore," she reminded him.

Semantics. Cory rephrased. "Why *did* you do it?"

Rebecca pulled the towel off her hair, and started to brush. A hundred strokes. He counted. "Because stuff happens."

"Like what?" he asked, hoping to coax another laugh from her.

She took so long to answer, he thought she hadn't heard. Finally she moved to stand in front of the bedroom mirror, and slowly she began to brush again.

"There was a kid I knew once. Every year they had Christmas at her grandparents' house. Twenty-three relatives divided among two bedrooms. It was total chaos. Anyway, one Christmas morning, early—she always got up early on Christmas morning—her second cousin, Marty, cornered her in the bathroom. He'd always been really skanky, creepy, and in trouble with the law, but everybody wanted to believe he was good inside because he was 'family.'"

She stopped brushing, paused and then started again.

"He bent her over the sink and raped her. And told her not to scream, so she didn't. Not once. She kept waiting for someone to come and save her. They never did. And when he was done, she was pissed. Man, she was so pissed. Spitting mad. And she wanted to hurt him. Like he'd hurt her. She told him that Santa Claus would get him for what he had done. He laughed, told her that Santa Claus didn't exist, and walked out the door. He knew she wouldn't say anything. She was only nine, only a little girl. She'd looked in the mirror. Looked at herself. There was this emptiness in her eyes. Something was gone and she wanted it back. She never got it. But she tried."

He sat quietly, frozen in place.

Rebecca turned away from the mirror, hairbrush in hand. When she looked at him, her blond hair was still damp from the shower, and there was an emptiness in her eyes.

Rapid-fire images shot like machine-gun fire in his brain. Silent screams, milk-white flesh and innocence lost. Carefully he dug his nails into his palms, focusing on the pain there until the pain inside him was gone. It was a trick he used a lifetime ago.

He'd never thrown up, never allowed himself. But he wanted to now. His mouth was full of rage and terror and partially digested scrambled eggs. None of which would do her any good. Quickly though, his control returned and he swallowed it all.

Instead of cutting half-moons into her palms, Rebecca didn't play the victim, she fought back. She became head cheerleader, homecoming queen and a teacher who most likely stuck her nose where it didn't belong.

Then Rebecca smiled tightly and went back to brushing her hair.

What was a man supposed to do? Cory wanted to comfort her, pull her into his arms and tell her that everything would be all right.

The hell it was. He knew that nothing would ever be right. So did she, but she didn't want pity any more than he wanted it. They had survived. Life went on—but it had changed for him.

"Do you still want to do that sleigh ride today?" she asked.

Rebecca seemed to want casual conversation, while he was still trying to keep his guts inside.

"How does she face Christmas every year?" he asked, his voice quiet. He had to know, had to understand her, had to go deeper into the dark places that he hated to delve. This was for Rebecca.

She shook her head nervously, the blond strands flying as she brushed faster. "She has to. She won't let anybody steal her Christmas. Not anybody."

"She ever tell anyone besides you?"

"Nah. She's tougher than she looks. Her business, nobody else's."

"What happened to the guy?" Cory asked in a whisper.

"Murdered in a Florida prison. Seems inmates don't like deviants any more than Santa Claus."

His fists unclenched. "I'm glad."

"Me, too. No kid should go through that."

"No, they shouldn't." She didn't say any more, and he knew the subject was now closed. Rebecca didn't look back. Ever.

He watched her with new respect, watching as she never missed a step. He'd always judged her through his high school eyes and overlooked her, dismissed her. He'd never been more wrong.

"So when are you going to get your job back?" he asked.

Rebecca brushed her cheeks with pink powder, back and forth.

"I'm thinking of moving to retail."

That brought Cory to his feet. There was no way. "You can't do that. You can't give up on your kids. There are people that need you."

"Nobody needs me, Cory. Those kids will be fine."

She was so confused. Clueless about it, but that didn't change the fact that Rebecca Neumann was one of the few things right in the world. And he'd make sure she got her job back, if he had to go there himself...

Whoa. Hold it, Bell. He wouldn't be seeing her in New York. Tomorrow was it. Their last day. The snow was still falling, but Tuesday was Christmas Eve, and she was leaving for Connecticut.

Rebecca Neumann, one of the best people to have ever come into his world, was going away.

She was putting on lipstick, and he wanted to put a sledgehammer through the wall.

His fingers flexed into his palms, he took a long breath, his heart slowing down.

Although Rebecca was leaving, that didn't mean he couldn't make the most of the situation. She wanted Christmas. He'd give her an amazing Christmas. It might not be Tiffany snowflakes on Fifth Avenue, but no matter how big she talked, Rebecca wasn't Fifth Avenue, either. He'd still make it special.

So for the final time, Cory had a new plan. His eyes met hers and he tried to smile. His was a weak, half-assed smile, but after thirty-one years, he hadn't yet mastered the art of looking happy.

REBECCA WASN'T SURE what was up. Didn't all men want perfection? Undamaged goods? But when she'd confessed her secret to Cory, he hadn't run. When she'd done everything right, he ran. She showed him the worst parts of her soul and he acted as if she was his best girl ever.

Talk about throwing her system for a loop.

However, she went along with it. After she finished getting ready, he kissed her. Long, lingering. No passion, all tenderness, enough to bring a tear to her eye. She wiped it away before he saw.

Downstairs, Mr. Krause was dressed up in a Santa suit, wandering around like he owned the place, because, well, he did. Rebecca expected Cory to take off. Instead he came up, shook the old man's hand and wished him Merry Christmas. It was oddly awkward, like when Maximillian Guerlain had played Abraham Lincoln for the President's Day play. Her heart twisted.

However, right now there was a sleigh ride to look forward to. A sleigh ride she knew he would hate.

"We don't have to go," she offered, getting embarrassed by all his niceness.

"I love sleigh rides," he answered, lying his ass off.

It was cold outside, but she didn't feel it—she was warm and happy. Marvelously, gloriously happy. Two tall draft horses guided the sleigh, huffing their way along the mountain path. As they rounded a bend, Lake Placid appeared, nestled between the hills. She watched Cory, daring to brush the dark silk out of his eyes. Instead of pulling back, he quirked his lips in a half smile.

The afternoon went on from there, roasting marshmallows by the fire in the main hall. He teased her that her mascara would melt. She slapped him on the thigh, but oops, missed, her hand lingering. His eyes darkened; she shrugged innocently.

Supper was in the room. Salad and baked chicken, only in deference to what she now termed his sissy appetite. It didn't matter what she ate, Rebecca was entranced. After he cleared away the dishes, he rubbed her feet until she was purring with delight as he found the exact place in her misshapen instep that cured all her pains.

He talked to her about the houses he had demolished, and then rebuilt, his eyes lively as he walked her through the process. She listened, and fell head over heels in love with this very special man.

In her heart, she'd always kept Christmas in a place far away from the rest of things. It was her talisman and her strength, but it wasn't Christmas in her heart anymore. It was him. So rough and hard at times, so tender and awkward at others. They made love that night in front of the fire, and she watched him with selfish eyes, keeping him close and near.

She watched over him while he slept, uncurled his fists when the nightmares came. He woke her in the morning, early, before dawn, and slid inside her, warmer than the sun.

Monday continued as the day before. They made a snowman in the morning, made love in the afternoon. She fell asleep listening to Christmas carols. When she woke up early in the evening, Cory was waiting with a box.

No wrapping paper, no bow. Plain and unadorned.

"Got something," he said, pushing it across the bed.

She lifted the lid and dug through the tissue paper, only to find...

A pair of wool socks with a neatly stitched pattern of snowflakes.

Rebecca began to cry.

Her mascara was running, she knew her mascara was running, and she couldn't stop the silly tears from flowing down her cheeks, ruining the natural finish to her blush. Oh, heck.

"Don't cry, Bec," he said, which made her laugh in her tears, because Cory wasn't a "Bec" guy. He didn't use nicknames, didn't use endearments, anything that would personalize anything.

Except for snowflake-patterned socks.

Which started her bawling all over again.

He pulled her into his arms, hardened, tough arms with work-roughened hands, and slowly he rocked her, like a child. It was done with a slow, hesitant movement, a man so unused to this. Unused to touch, unused to love.

She cried for him, cried for the scars on his palms, cried for the nights he'd lost, and she cried for all the things that would never be righted.

"You're strong, Rebecca. Stronger than you'll ever know," he murmured against her hair, her face, covering her tears with his lips. He thought it was her pain that was killing her, but it was his.

She wanted to lash out at the people who hadn't cared about him when he was younger. Stupid people. People who didn't know him, know what was buried inside. So deeply buried. She cried for a long time, and she knew he was worried and confused, but she couldn't stop. At some point the kisses changed. No comfort anymore. There was an edge of desperation there, she tasted it in him, and she took shameless advantage. She wanted to feel him next to her, bare and raw, and soon he was. She used her mouth to love him, to taste the salty heat of his skin.

He cried out when she took his sex in her mouth, his muscles straining, but she stroked him with her hands, with her mouth, soothing him, pleasuring him, loving him.

It was so easy to love him, but he wouldn't let her finish. He pulled her up, and then rose above her, so careful not to hurt her, but she was having none of that. She scored her fingers into his back, wringing a shudder from him.

Then he thrust inside her, and she met his eyes, met his lips. Outside the snow began to fall again, the sounds of sleigh bells and laughter. Inside, it was quiet. So quiet she could hear her silent whispers.

Later, when the sounds were gone, he touched her cheek, kissed her mouth, traced her eyes. His eyes were so worried, and she stroked his face. It should have been forever, but this wasn't, and she knew it. It was there in his face.

Cory was saying goodbye.

8

Tuesday, December 24

THE TRAIN RIDE from Lake Placid to her parents' home in Connecticut was longer than she imagined. Fourteen hours of sitting, with nothing to do but think. Now she had a new regret weighing heavy on her. Cory Bell.

He'd left while she was asleep. She knew that would be his way. Odd to have been strangers before Friday. Four days later and she had seen his soul.

There were so many things that she should have told him. But he hadn't said a word, and she hadn't said a word. And so they had a solitary, magical moment in time.

Ha. She rubbed her heart because the pain was strong. Did love come that fast? Would it fade so quickly? She knew it wouldn't. She had confided in him and he'd stayed by her.

Outside the window, snow was falling, and she watched it, writing a name on the fogged glass like a schoolgirl. As the compartment heated, the name faded, but the memories would stay with her for a long, long time.

CORY WAS DRIVING in the shadow of the Laurentian Mountains when the snow started to fly in huge, blinding flakes. The road was nearly invisible. He turned on the radio to drown out the yelling in his head, but there was nothing but Christmas music.

Damn.

He'd never heard yelling in his head before, never felt this pain screaming inside him, but he wished it would go away. He wanted the numbness back.

He shoved the wiper switch to high, but it didn't matter. He couldn't see jack, so he pulled off the road. Cory slammed his hands against the steering wheel because damn it, her suitcase weighed a ton and she'd have to change stations four times to get from the lodge to her parents' place in Stafford Hill.

He hadn't meant to ask anything this morning, only wanted to disappear at dawn, but when he'd seen Mrs. Krause at the desk, he'd asked. Like he had a right to know.

The old woman had sent him off with a ham sandwich, home-made chocolate-chip cookies, and a piece of paper with a Connecticut address on it. At the Canadian border, he'd stopped and looked at the paper. When he got to Montreal, he pulled into an electronics store and checked her route on a computer. Now here he was, nearly at his destination in the mountains, when the name-calling started.

Idiot. Moron. Jerk. He deserved it. There was never a woman he wanted more than Rebecca. Why was he running away from the best, the purest woman he'd ever known, touched or loved?

No, that was it. Cory Bell was done running. He was driving to Connecticut—in a blizzard.

Six hours later, he had made it to New York. Barely. He stopped, got more coffee and bought a Connecticut map. The clerk was a teenager with a name tag that said Happy To Serve You.

"Merry Christmas," Cory said, slapping some change on the counter.

The kid frowned, glanced at him as if he was a nut job. "Merry Christmas to you, too."

It was three hundred and ten miles and some five hours later before he reached the tiny town where he'd find her. He should have been bone-tired, but after all the caffeine and something that felt suspiciously like hope in his heart, Cory was more alive than he'd ever been.

The streets were decorated with lights that glimmered in the darkness, and he found the Neumann house easily—it was the one with thirty-seven cars lined down the block. In the window, the Christmas tree shined and beckoned. Just like her.

Inside the security of his truck, his palms were sweating, and he rubbed them on his jeans. For a long time he stared at the house, waiting for the familiar need to run. The clock on the dashboard said it was seven o'clock, five hours to midnight, and Christmas Day.

Ten minutes later, then twenty minutes. Two hours later, with the moon high in the sky, he realized the panic inside him was gone. He had other needs now. Rebecca. He walked up the snow-covered sidewalk and rang the bell.

An older woman answered, a light-up reindeer pin clipped to her sweater. "Mrs. Neumann?" he asked.

"Yes?"

"I'm here to see Rebecca."

"Certainly. Come in."

"I'll wait outside, thanks," he told her.

She frowned, but nodded and went to find her daughter.

The noises coming from inside the house were loud. Laughing, singing, a million voices were talking at once. Those sounds alone terrified him. This was new and strange. But he would do this. He could do this.

Rebecca came to the door, and when she saw him she smiled at him, her eyes full of excitement and hope. He looked at her, looked at the sprig of mistletoe hanging over the door, and smiled back.

Then he kissed her. Full on the lips.

"Merry Christmas," she whispered against his mouth.

"I'm late. I had to go to Canada, but I'm back. For good."

"I told you the French language was overrated."

"Yeah," was about all that he could say, because he had to kiss her again.

Dear Santa,

I just want you to know up-front that Rebecca is making me write this letter to thank you. She's convinced you're real. Me? It'll take a while to convince. I'm not so big on the whole Christmas experience, and Santa, and "peace, love and joy," but I'm starting to understand, especially the love part. That I'm getting down. So, thank you.

Sincerely,
Cory Bell

Epilogue

"WHAT IS IT ABOUT the snow that makes people fall in love?"

Roland heard his wife's question as he burrowed in the refrigerator looking for the ingredients for his wife's favorite cocktail. He knew some of the younger guys tried to sway their dates with expensive champagne, but Roland had learned long ago that hot chocolate was his wife's aphrodisiac of choice.

And Roland had learned never to argue with anything that made his wife sigh with happiness.

"Well, it's pretty." He poured milk in a pan and turned it on just high enough that he wouldn't scorch it while Helen kept her eyes trained on a spot out on the lake.

Their home was a stone's throw away from the inn. Close enough for them to run over in an emergency, but far enough away to let them feel as though they could get away from it all on the hard days.

"Roland Krause." She turned from the window to frown at him, clearly displeased. "Is that the best you can do? Your wife asks you a thoughtful question about the nature of love and what inspires something so profound and you suggest that snow is *pretty?*"

He hid a grin as he stirred the cocoa into the pan, and attempted to give her question more serious thought. Because no matter how effective chocolate had been at lighting his wife's fire in the past, he knew from long experience that the best aphrodisiac for a woman—for his woman—was a sense of mental connection.

It had taken him ten years of marriage to come up with that, but it was a notion he'd put to good use since then. Who said you couldn't teach an old guy new tricks?

"You're right." He took his time thinking, waiting for his wife's good humor to come around, the drink to warm and inspiration to strike. "I think it's the freshness of the snow that does it."

He poured some cocoa for him and poured hers into her favorite pewter mug, the one they'd bought on a honeymoon trip up to Montreal. He still smiled to remember that.

"What do you mean?" Helen drew closer, her eyes all for him now.

He handed her the drink and kissed her on the forehead.

"I think snow brings to mind fresh starts and new beginnings. It's clean and it's pretty, it makes the world around us quiet, and it forces us to stay home and look inward instead of racing around the countryside looking for happiness under any old rock."

He settled across the kitchen table from his wife in her blue bathrobe and fuzzy slippers, her hair pinned high on her head after her nightly bath. She smelled good. Looked better.

And, ah yes, her eyes took on that soft glow of approval that told him he'd done something right.

"And people think *I'm* the matchmaker in this house." Her voice was full of chiding. "If only they knew what a romantic I'm married to."

"Me?" He straightened. "Helen Krause, it wasn't me who called the cab company and tracked down the car on its way here all in the name of matchmaking. One of these days, a guest won't appreciate that kind of thing, you mark my words."

"Did you see how happy they were, though?" Unrepentant, she grinned at him over her mug, the slightest hint of whipped cream on the corner of her mouth.

He brushed it off with his thumb and tugged her chair closer.

"No happier than we are."

"Isn't it nice to share a little Christmas magic with our guests, Roland?" Her eyes sparkled even in the dim kitchen and he knew she wanted him to admit she'd chosen good targets for her gentle interference. "For the rest of my life I'll be able to say 'I married that handsome Eric Breslin.'"

Roland laughed. "I suppose that comes with the territory of you being an ordained minister. But you might want to finish that sentence to include you 'married Eric Breslin to Jessica Hayden.'"

"Yes, I did," Helen said with a satisfied smile. "And I'm sure they're enjoying their honeymoon here at the lodge. Especially now that their families have gone home and left them alone. And don't forget our success with Cory and Rebecca."

"*Our* success?"

"You did help with the battery cables," she reminded him gently. "Currently they're happily on their way back to Manhattan. Together. She should have found him ten years ago…" Her voice trailed off for a minute. "These things take time. And then, of course, there's Heather and Jared…"

"No one could ever accuse you of not having the Christmas spirit, my love." He stepped around that one diplomatically, or at least he thought he'd done so successfully judging by the way she smiled contentedly enough.

Of course, her smile might have more to do with the effects of the cocoa kicking in. Making his move, he covered her hand with his.

"Now, how about sharing a little Christmas magic with me?"

Her eyes took on a wicked gleam, but she didn't follow his cue to go upstairs to bed. Instead she raised her mug in a toast.

"First, let's drink to new beginnings. The Timberline Lodge—and the freshness of new snow—inspired some wonderful new beginnings this year." She took a sip, dreamy-eyed at all the love sprouting up around the business they'd built together.

"To new beginnings…and happy endings." Roland grinned and clinked her mug with his. When he finished his drink he rose, offering her his hand.

She smiled back, giving up her drink and letting him pull her into his arms. He'd never get enough of the happiness that came with knowing she was his for a lifetime, for every Christmas ever after.

"Happy endings." She kissed his cheek and tucked closer to him. "Now how can I say no to that?"

* * * * *

Turn the page for a sneak preview
of the first book in the new miniseries
DIAMONDS DOWN UNDER
from Silhouette Desire®
VOWS & A VENGEFUL GROOM
by Bronwyn Jameson

Available January 2008
(SD #1843)

Silhouette Desire®
Always Powerful, Passionate and Provocative

Kimberley Blackstone didn't notice the waiting horde of media until it was too late. Flashbulbs exploded around her like a New Year's light show. She skidded to a halt, so abruptly her trailing suitcase all but overtook her.

This had to be a case of mistaken identity. Surely. Kimberley hadn't been on the paparazzi hit list for close to a decade, not since she'd estranged herself from her billionaire father and his headline-hungry diamond business.

But no, it was *her* name they called. *Her* face was the focus of a swarm of lenses that circled her like avid hornets. Her heart started to pound with fear-fueled adrenaline.

What did they want?

What was going on?

With a rising sense of bewilderment she scanned the crowd for a clue, and her gaze fastened on a tall, leonine figure forcing his way to the front. A tall, familiar figure. Her head came up in stunned recognition, and their gazes collided across the sea of heads before the cameras erupted with another barrage of flashes, this time right in her exposed face.

Blinded by the flashbulbs—and by the shock of that momentary eye-meet—Kimberley didn't realize his intent until he'd forged his way to her side, possibly by the sheer strength of his personality. She felt his arm wrap around her shoulder, pulling her into the protective shelter of his body, allowing her no time to object. No chance to lift her hands to ward him off.

In the space of a hastily drawn breath, she found herself plastered knee-to-nose against six feet two inches of hard-bodied male.

Ric Perrini.

Her lover for ten torrid weeks, her husband for ten tumultuous days.

Her ex for ten tranquil years.

After all this time, he should not have felt so familiar but, oh dear, he did. She knew the scent of that body and its lean, muscular strength. She knew its heat and its slick power and every response it could draw from hers.

She also recognized the ease with which he'd taken control of the moment and the decisiveness of his deep voice when it rumbled close to her ear. "I have a car waiting outside. Is this your only luggage?"

Kimberley nodded. "I assume you will tell me," she said tightly, "what this welcome party is all about."

"Not while the welcome party is within earshot. No."

Barking a request for the cameramen to stand aside, Perrini took her hand and pulled her into step with his ground-eating stride. Kimberley let him, because he was right, damn his arrogant, Italian-suited hide. Despite the speed with which he whisked her across the airport terminal, she could almost feel the hot breath of the pursuing media on her back.

This was neither the time nor the place for explanations. Inside his car, however, she would get answers.

Now that the initial shock had been blown away—by the haste of their retreat, by the heat of her gathering indignation, by the rush of adrenaline fired by Perrini's presence and the looming verbal battle—her brain was starting to tick over. This had to be her father's doing. And if it was a Howard Blackstone publicity ploy, then it had to be about Blackstone Diamonds, the company that ruled his life.

The knowledge made her chest tighten with a familiar ache of disillusionment.

She'd known her father would be flying in from Sydney for today's opening of the newest in his chain of exclusive, high-end jewelry boutiques. The opulent shopfront sat adjacent to the rival business where Kimberley worked. No coincidence, she thought bitterly, just as it was no coincidence that Ric Perrini was here in Auckland ushering her to his car.

Perrini was Howard Blackstone's right-hand man, second in command at Blackstone Diamonds, a legacy of his short-lived marriage to the boss's daughter. No doubt her father had sent him to fetch her; the question was *why?*

* * * * *

Get swept away down under with the glitz and glamour of the Blackstone empire as Kimberley tries to determine the real reason behind her "reunion" with Ric….

Look for
VOWS & A VENGEFUL GROOM
By Bronwyn Jameson
In stores January 2008

When Kimberley Blackstone's father is
presumed dead, Kimberley is required to take
over the helm of Blackstone Diamonds. She
has to work closely with her ex, Ric Perrini, to
battle not only the press, but also the fierce
attraction still sizzling between them. Does Ric
feel the same...or is it the power her share of
Blackstone Diamonds will provide him as he
battles for boardroom supremacy.

Look for

VOWS &
A VENGEFUL GROOM

by

BRONWYN
JAMESON

Available January wherever you buy books

nocturne™

Jachin Black always knew he was an outcast.
Not only was he a vampire, he was a vampire
banished from the Sanguinas society. Jachin, forced
to survive among mortals, is determined to buy
his way back into the clan one day.

Ariel Swanson, debut author of a vampire novel, could
be the ticket he needs to get revenge and take his
rightful place among the Sanguinas again. However,
the unsuspecting mortal woman has no idea of the
dark and sensual path she will be forced to travel.

Look for

RESURRECTION: THE BEGINNING

by

PATRICE MICHELLE

Available January 2008 wherever you buy books.

REQUEST YOUR FREE BOOKS!

2 FREE NOVELS PLUS 2 FREE GIFTS!

HARLEQUIN®

Blaze®

Red-hot reads!

YES! Please send me 2 FREE Harlequin® Blaze® novels and my 2 FREE gifts. After receiving them, if I don't wish to receive any more books, I can return the shipping statement marked "cancel." If I don't cancel, I will receive 6 brand-new novels every month and be billed just $3.99 per book in the U.S., or $4.47 per book in Canada, plus 25¢ shipping and handling per book and applicable taxes, if any*. That's a savings of at least 15% off the cover price! I understand that accepting the 2 free books and gifts places me under no obligation to buy anything. I can always return a shipment and cancel at any time. Even if I never buy another book from Harlequin, the two free books and gifts are mine to keep forever.

151 HDN EF3W   351 HDN EF3X

Name _____ (PLEASE PRINT)

Address _____ Apt. _____

City _____ State/Prov. _____ Zip/Postal Code _____

Signature (if under 18, a parent or guardian must sign)

Mail to the **Harlequin Reader Service®**:
IN U.S.A.: P.O. Box 1867, Buffalo, NY 14240-1867
IN CANADA: P.O. Box 609, Fort Erie, Ontario L2A 5X3

Not valid to current Harlequin Blaze subscribers.

Want to try two free books from another line?
Call 1-800-873-8635 or visit www.morefreebooks.com.

* Terms and prices subject to change without notice. NY residents add applicable sales tax. Canadian residents will be charged applicable provincial taxes and GST. This offer is limited to one order per household. All orders subject to approval. Credit or debit balances in a customer's account(s) may be offset by any other outstanding balance owed by or to the customer. Please allow 4 to 6 weeks for delivery.

Your Privacy: Harlequin is committed to protecting your privacy. Our Privacy Policy is available online at www.eHarlequin.com or upon request from the Reader Service. From time to time we make our lists of customers available to reputable firms who may have a product or service of interest to you. If you would prefer we not share your name and address, please check here. ☐

HB07

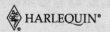

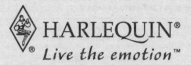

HARLEQUIN®

Blaze™

COMING NEXT MONTH

#369 ONE WILD WEDDING NIGHT Leslie Kelly
Blaze Encounters—One blazing book, five sizzling stories
Girls just want to have fun.... And for five bridesmaids, their friend's wedding night
is the perfect time for the rest of them to let loose. After all, love is in the air. And so,
they soon discover, is great sex…

#370 MY GUILTY PLEASURE Jamie Denton
The Martini Dares, Bk. 3
The trial is supposed to come first for the legal-eagle duo of Josephine Winfield and
Sebastian Stanhope. But the long hours—and sizzling attraction—are taking their
toll. Is it a simple case of lust in the first degree? Or dare she think there's more?

#371 BARE NECESSITIES Marie Donovan
A sexy striptease ignites an intense affair between longtime friends Adam Hale, a
play-by-the-rules financial trader, and Bridget Weiss, a break-all-the-rules lingerie
designer. But what will happen to their friendship now that their secret lust for each
other is no longer a secret?

#372 DOES SHE DARE? Tawny Weber
Blush
When no-nonsense Isabel Santos decides to make a "man plan," she never dreams
she'll have a chance to try it out with the guy who inspired it—her high school
crush, hottie Dante Luciano. He's still everything she's ever wanted. And she'll make
sure she's everything he'll *never* forget….

#373 AT YOUR COMMAND Julie Miller
Marry in haste? Eighteen months ago Captain Zachariah Clark loved, married,
then left Becky Clark. Now Zach's back home, and he's suddenly realized he knows
nothing about his wife except her erogenous zones. Then again, great sex isn't such
a bad place to start….

#374 THE TAO OF SEX Jade Lee
Extreme
Landlord Tracy Williams wants to sell her building, almost as much as she wants
her tenant, sexy Nathan Gao. But when Nathan puts a sale at risk by giving Tantric
classes, Tracy has to bring a stop to them. That is, until he offers her some private
hands-on instruction…

www.eHarlequin.com

HBCNM1207